One Day *in* Apple Grove

C.H. ADMIRAND

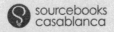

Published by Sourcebooks Casablanca, an imprint of Sourcebooks, Inc.
P.O. Box 4410, Naperville, Illinois 60567-4410
(630) 961-3900
FAX: (630) 961-2168
www.sourcebooks.com

Printed and bound in Canada
WC 10 9 8 7 6 5 4 3 2 1

This book is dedicated to my personal handyman: my darling husband, Dave. In the thirty years since we've lived in our home, we've done most of the work ourselves, with the help of our families before we had kids…and our kids once they were big enough.

I already knew how to paint, put up wallpaper, and garden—and knew the difference between a Phillips-head screwdriver and a flat-head screwdriver—but since I've been married to Dave, I've learned how to mix concrete, put up sheetrock, and even install a wood laminate floor in our kitchen this past fall. But more importantly, I learned NOT to take photos in the middle of a project that was not going according to plan. I still have this image in my head of the frame for the shower plumbing flying out of the bathroom and hurtling down the cellar stairs. Yep, now I take pics before the project…when he goes outside for more materials…and when it's done. :)

When we were dating, he needed me to remove the alternator from his Fiat 124 Spider—smaller hands were needed for that tight fit—then there was the time he taught me how to change the oil filter in my first car, but that's another story for another day…

And to the real Jameson, a.k.a. Jamie, who healed our hearts after losing our faithful shepherd/rottweiler Ginger, with his exuberance, lavish puppy kisses, and his little black lips and underbite.

Buttermilk Pie

Makes two pies

This recipe has become a favorite of my guys, discriminating pie experts. Pie—it's what's for breakfast! ~C.H.

> *1 tablespoon butter*
> *4 tablespoons Heckers unbleached flour*
> *3 egg yolks, beaten*
> *1 cup sugar*
> *2 cups buttermilk*
> *1 teaspoon concentrated lemon juice*
> *Your favorite piecrust—or mine, if you email me!*

Blend the butter and flour and add egg yolks and sugar, stirring until smooth. Slowly add the buttermilk and lemon extract until thoroughly mixed.

Line two eight- or nine-inch pie plates with piecrust and pour in filling, dividing equally. Bake in a 425 degree oven for ten minutes. Lower temperature to 350 degrees for twenty to twenty-five minutes, or until set.*

*Remove and cover with meringue (recipe on next page), baking for an additional ten to twelve minutes, or until the meringue is lightly browned.
**Alternative topping: freshly whipped cream and raspberries—easier and just as delicious!

Meringue Topping for Two Pies

3 egg whites
3 tablespoons white sugar
¼ to 1 teaspoon concentrated lemon juice

Beat the egg whites until soft peaks form; slowly add the sugar and lemon juice and continue beating until stiff. Spread over the tops of both pies, forming tiny peaks if you're feeling creative; if you're pressed for time, like me, just spread it out flat. Bake in a 350 degree oven for ten to twelve minutes.

Apple Grove, Ohio:
Population 597

Apple Grove has always boasted that it's a small town with big-town amenities. Some of the local hot spots are:

Honey's Hair Salon—Owned by Honey B. Harrington, who has weekly specials from cuts to coloring and likes to advertise the weekly special by changing her hair color every week. (She's been trying to snag Sheriff Wallace's attention for the last fifteen years, but he's firmly holding on to his bachelorhood.)

The Apple Grove Diner—Owned by Peggy and Katie McCormack, featuring Peggy's Pastries.

Bob's Gas and Gears—Owned by Robert Stuart, former stock car driver who doubles as the mechanic.

Murphy's Market—Owned by the lovely widow Mary Murphy (who has her eye on Joseph Mulcahy—and he has his on her), where you can buy anything from soup to nuts—the metal kind—but it's her free-range chickens that lay the best eggs in Licking County and have people driving for miles to buy them.

Trudi's Garden Center—Owned by eighty-year-old Trudi Philo who likes to wear khaki jodhpurs and

Wellingtons everywhere; she specializes in perennials and heirloom vegetables and flowers, and has been planting and caring for the flowers in the town square since she was in grade school, taking the job over from her grandmother Phoebe Philo, when she passed the business on to her fifty years ago.

The Apple Grove Public Library—Run by Beatrice Wallace, the sheriff's sister—open three days a week!

The Knitting Room—A thriving Internet business run by Apple Grove resident Melanie Culpepper, who had to close up her shop when she became pregnant with twins.

Slater's Mill—Built circa 1850, this converted mill and historic site is a favorite among locals both young and old. Famous for its charcoal-broiled burgers and crispy fries served in the first-floor family restaurant, it's also been a favorite place for the younger set to congregate at the mile-long bar on the second floor.

Chapter 1

DR. JACK GANNON CLOSED THE DOOR TO HIS OFFICE, looked down Main Street, and smiled. Spring in his hometown meant green and growing—nothing like the Middle East desert peppered with hiding places where insurgents had lain in wait. He shoved those thoughts, and his years as a navy corpsman, back into the tiny box he'd visualized so many times while lying helpless in that hospital bed.

After all the stories he'd heard from this father, Jack had been the first one in the navy recruiter's line all those years ago. But none of the places he'd traveled as a hospital corpsman held a candle to the town he called home—Apple Grove.

A soft breeze caressed his face, a loving touch and gentle reminder that he had so much to be grateful for. The marine he'd been struggling to save when they'd been hit filled his mind. Struggling to bury the memory, and the guilt, deep, he focused on one of the lessons he'd learned early in life: There is a time and purpose for everything. He remembered floundering when he'd woken up strapped to a gurney as he was rushed into surgery. A year and a half later, he'd been able to stand, to walk and was alive—applying his experience in the navy toward college credits and then med school—he had a life…choices…unlike the marine he'd tried to save but couldn't.

Growing up in a town where farming was a way of life for most, he'd come to appreciate that spring was the season for growth. Sinking his shriveled roots back into the warm, rich, life-giving soil of his hometown just might satisfy his need for personal growth. No one in town knew the depth of his pain or the extent of his injuries. To them, he was simply old Doc Gannon's son coming home to pick up where his father left off, taking care of the people in this tight-knit community. If he could continue to keep a lid on the roiling pot of guilt, pain, and uncertainty, no one would ever have to know the truth—that he should have been the one to die.

The wind shifted, clearing his head of the thoughts haunting him. He caught the fleeting, teasing scent of fresh-baked pies wafting toward him from the open door of the Apple Grove Diner. Glad to redirect his thoughts, he wondered if the diner was still gossip central. It had been for as far back as he could remember—the latest news, good and bad, served up with a man-sized slice of pie, a hot cup of coffee, and a smile. "God, I really missed this place."

As a teenager, he couldn't wait to leave; now he took the time to admire Miss Trudi's flowers, a riot of color circling the gazebo in the town square, the focal point of countless Founder's Day Picnic speeches. One of Apple Grove's more outspoken octogenarians, Miss Trudi was a marvel. How she managed to do so much at her age amazed him. He'd have to stop by and check up on her this afternoon…without letting her know what he was up to, or else she'd never let him hear the end of it. A more capable woman over the age of eighty simply didn't exist.

The breeze rustled the broad green leaves of the sugar maples lining Main Street. The trees graced the sidewalk and shaded his steps from the front door of his office clear down to the sheriff's at the other end of the street. He'd make a point to see Mitch, Sheriff Wallace, today as well. His day was rapidly filling up with people he needed to see, not all of them for medical reasons. He had to start that list—which was the main thing he intended to discuss with Mitch—of some of the older people in town and schedule routine check-ins—even if they were likely to be crabby about it. But in Apple Grove, people always wanted to help.

The tantalizing scent of baked goods was stronger as he drew closer to the diner. Stepping through the open door to the diner, he paused at the threshold, drawing in another deep breath. Freshly brewed coffee and the scent of just-baked sweetness beckoned to him. Jack smiled, knowing it would be a McCormack who would greet him.

"How was your flight back?" Peggy McCormack asked. "You flew right through that rainstorm."

"Uneventful," he said, smiling at the older of the two sisters. "Just the way I like it."

"How many broken hearts did you leave behind, Doc?" Peggy's sister Kate asked. When he just shook his head, she added, "There are plenty of women in town who'd be more than happy to take the edge off…if you know what I mean."

"Don't scare him off when he's only just arrived," Peggy told her. "We haven't gotten any news from him yet." Making a shooing motion toward the coffeepot, she smiled at Jack and told her sister, "Grab some coffee for Doc."

Jack hesitated, wondering if he should leave now, before they picked his brain clean, or if he should stick around for a slice of heaven on a plate.

"What?" Kate frowned, reaching for the coffeepot and turning back around. "How many women have you heard make that offer while waiting for our hometown hero to return?"

Jack raised his eyes to the ceiling and fought his embarrassment. He should come back later, when it was busy and he could be ignored.

Peggy's question interrupted that thought. "How 'bout a piece of our grandma's buttermilk pie to go with your coffee?"

Kate motioned for him to sit down while Peggy sliced a piece of pie for him. A stronger man than him could forgo the flaky confection calling his name. Where pie was concerned, especially from the Apple Grove Diner, he had no choice. He gave in, had to have that pie.

"Thanks." Taking a seat at the counter, he shifted on the vinyl stool until he was comfortable—his leg ached—they'd be getting rain by nightfall. Doing his best to ignore the pain, he looked up when a fragrant cup of coffee and a megaslice of pie appeared like magic.

"Did you know one of the hardest parts of leaving town was missing Grandma McCormack's pies? You can't get service or baked goods like this where I've been." He took a bite and sighed in pleasure.

"It's been a while in between your visits home," Kate said while he ate. "Peggy and I were trying to remember how long but can't."

With his mouth filled with the decadent combination of lemony-flavored custard and delectable meringue topping, he couldn't answer right away, so he chewed, swallowed, and said, "A while."

Forking up another bite, he gave in and let himself enjoy the flavors dancing on his tongue. It had been quiet for a few minutes before he realized the sisters were watching him closely. He lifted a forkful of pie and said, "Delicious."

"Thanks," Peggy said. "So, how many years were you in the navy?"

Blowing across the surface to cool his coffee, he paused and glanced up. "Almost ten."

"And then you went to school," Peggy added.

He took a sip of his coffee and said, "I had earned plenty of college credits, so finishing up and going to med school didn't take as long as I'd thought it would."

"Do you miss it?" Kate asked.

"The navy or med school?" he asked.

"The navy," Kate said.

"Why couldn't you spend the last two years doing rehab here?" Peggy wanted to know. "Couldn't your dad have taken care of you?"

Jack nearly snorted up that last mouthful of fragrant brew. Had he really thought they wouldn't touch on the parts of his military career he hadn't wanted to discuss? This was one aspect he hadn't missed—being grilled so that the midmorning crowd coming into the diner would have fresh fodder to pass along.

He didn't want to talk about it, but maybe if he told them something no one had heard before, the sisters would be satisfied for the next little bit.

Jack met Peggy's gaze and said, "They didn't think I'd survive the plane ride home." While the reality of his comment hit home, he looked at Kate and hoped to distract her by saying, "My mom and dad wanted me to say hello for them and to ask how your parents and grandmother are doing."

Peggy was the first to recover from the gossip-worthy bomb he'd dropped. She grasped his hand and squeezed it tight before letting it go. Her nod told him that she'd let the subject drop. "Are your parents really going to buy that house in Florida?" Peggy asked. "Wouldn't it be better to keep renting? They might change their mind during another wicked hurricane season."

"Mornin', Miss Kate. Mornin', Miss Peggy." Deputy Jones walked into the diner and smiled at the sisters before turning to look at Jack. "Morning, Doc. Heard you're meeting with the sheriff later today. It's a good thing you're doing for Apple Grove."

Jack shrugged. "When Mitch was filling me in on the latest emergencies at the office, we got to talking about how to avoid some of them. We think it'll work."

Deputy Jones was fighting not to smile when he added, "We may catch some grief from the people on that list."

Jack agreed. "Most of them won't mind, but there are a few independent curmudgeons who will."

"What have you two cooked up?" Kate asked.

"You have been busy," Peggy said, at the same time, handing a paper bag and two coffees to go to the sheriff's right-hand man.

"Duty calls. Thank you, ladies," Deputy Jones said with a wave and was gone.

Kate sighed as she watched him leave, while Peggy waited for Jack to answer.

Jack finished his pie and the rest of his coffee. "My dad planted the idea. Mitch called me right after I hung up with my dad, and between the two of us, we figured out a way to implement it."

He reached into his pocket, but before he could take his wallet—or his hand—out of his pocket, Peggy patted his arm and said, "It's on the house."

"You won't make any money if you keep giving away what people will pay good money for," he warned her.

Peggy and Kate smiled, and he knew there was one more reason why people in town flocked to the diner— the friendly smiles and caring that lay beneath the sisters' need to spread the news.

"Now you sound just like him," Peggy said.

He tilted his head to one side and asked, "Who?"

They laughed, drawing the attention of a few early morning regulars. "Old Doc Gannon," Kate told him.

He smiled. "So what does that make me?"

Kate grinned. "Young Doc Gannon."

"Hey, wait!" Peggy said, as Jack got up. "Aren't you going to tell us who is on that list?"

He shrugged. "I thought I gave you enough to talk about this morning."

"Hot roast turkey sandwich platters are the lunch special today," Peggy said.

He paused in the doorway. "With cranberry sauce? Corn bread stuffing?"

Peggy nodded.

He'd missed home cooking most of all. "I'll be back after my noon appointment. Save me some."

"Doc?" Kate called out.

He paused and glanced over his shoulder. "Yeah?"

"Apple Grove has really missed having your dad taking care of what ails us."

His dad had told him of his search and finally finding a replacement. Had Doc known the physician wouldn't stay, leaving the job waiting for Jack when he was ready for it? Knowing his father, he probably had.

"None of us was surprised when his replacement moved on to a hospital in Columbus."

"It was touch and go there for a while when he first left," Peggy admitted.

"The hardest part for some of our older residents was trying to find a way to get to the clinic over in Newark," Kate told him. "Waiting for you to get back, we had ourselves a meeting and were hoping you'd continue one of your dad's habits," Kate said.

"Which one?"

"Making house calls for folks like Mr. Weatherbee, Mrs. Winter, and our grandma," Peggy answered. "It would be a godsend if you could."

Drawn by the worry in Peggy's voice, he turned back around. "I plan to add house calls to my weekly schedule."

She sniffed and nodded. "Thanks, Doc."

"Welcome home," Kate called out, as he walked through the door.

"Good to be back." And he meant it. He had a practice with patients anxious for him to get started, a plan he and the sheriff wanted to implement to minimize emergencies, and had had his first taste of home-cooked heaven. Maybe it wouldn't take as long to find the balance that had been missing in his life during the long road to recovery. Thinking about the scheduled appointments for the day, he didn't hear Peggy follow him out the door.

He had just passed the Mulcahys' shop when he heard her say, "We're trying our hand at beignets tomorrow."

He turned and waved. "I love beignets."

Thinking about the lightly fried doughy goodness sprinkled with powdered sugar, he crossed Dog Hollow Road. When he walked by the *Apple Grove Gazette*, Rhonda was waving at him from behind the antique printing press. He waved back. It felt good to be in a place where people knew him…he had done the right thing coming back to stay when his dad had retired.

He hoped the folks in town would be able to trust the younger Doc Gannon the same way they'd trusted his dad. Walking up the flagstone steps to his office, he was ready to greet the day. Having gone over his father's most active patient files the night before, he was confident he'd be ready for whatever medical troubles were in store for him.

"Morning, Doc," Mrs. Sweeney, his receptionist, called out.

"Morning, Mrs. Sweeney. How's your cousin doing?"

"Holding his own, Doc." She sighed. "If only he wasn't so stubborn and one of his boys would move back home."

Jack had already added her cousin to the list of those who were on the Apple Grove Health Watch. "We'll keep doing what we can to make sure he's taken care of."

"You're just what this town needed—just like your dad."

He smiled. "Thank you."

The sound of someone clearing his throat caught Jack's attention. Joseph Mulcahy sat reading a magazine in the tiny waiting room.

Jack looked at his watch and then at Joe. "Am I late?"

Joe shook his head. "Nope, I'm early."

Jack knew that the success of his father's practice had been because it was based on mutual trust between doctor and patient. Jack planned to work hard to establish a similar trust with the townsfolk. He'd start with his high school lab partner's father.

"What kind of pie did you have?" Joe asked.

Jack laughed. "Buttermilk. I haven't had any since the last time I was home on leave." Jack ushered Joe into one of the examining rooms. "Have a seat while I pull up your chart." He turned on his computer, donned his white lab coat, and placed his stethoscope around his neck—he didn't miss the flak jacket.

Jack slipped the blood pressure cuff on Joe's arm and waited for the digital numbers to register.

Joe chuckled. "There was a time when your father used to pump up the cuff and use his stethoscope to check my pressure. Times sure have changed."

Jack nodded. "But one thing remains the same: my dad and I care deeply about—and enjoy caring for—the good people of Apple Grove." While he made notes to Joe's chart, he asked, "Speaking of good people, how is Meg feeling?"

If Joe's smile was any indication, she was doing just fine. "She's gone from grim and green to glowing."

Jack and Meg had been friends—treating each other like siblings—since they toddled together at their first Founder's Day Picnic.

He smiled and said, "I've heard from my parents that she's an amazing mom and that those twins of hers are keeping her busy. If you need me to butt heads with Meg about going back to her regular work schedule, you just let me know."

Joe frowned. "She's exhausted. But Dan's keeping an eye on her, especially now that those little scamps of theirs are running her ragged and getting into everything." He waited a moment or so before adding, "Dan Eagan's a good man." Joe paused and said, "If you want to keep up with your PT, Dan usually jogs every morning. I go with him a few times a week. Give him a call."

Jack chuckled. "Hmmm, the patient giving the doctor advice, but I could use a jogging partner." He cleared his throat and added, "My dad had good things to say about him and how easily he seemed to fit in from the moment he arrived. Mom couldn't say enough about the way he rescued Charlie Doyle and Tommy Hawkins off the railroad trestle bridge."

Joe looked up at Jack and asked, "Do you believe in fate?"

"With our Irish heritage, you need to ask?" Joe was still laughing when Jack said, "My dad wanted me to make sure you are getting in your daily walks and following the diet he gave you." Joe's heart attack scare a few years ago had Jack wishing he could have gone home to see for himself that his childhood friend's father was recovering, but he was in the middle of his internship at the time.

The older man hesitated. "Not a big fan of green things."

Jack tried to keep a straight face. He could take the green stuff or leave it, but he was at least twenty years younger and thirty pounds lighter than Joe.

"Start small and add dressing if it's salad or a little bit of peanut butter if it's celery." When Joe frowned,

Jack added, "I could insist on a stricter diet, higher in vegetables and fish—"

"I'll give it another try, but I'm not promising anything."

"Do it for yourself and your daughters, Joe," Jack said quietly. "By the way, how are Cait and Grace doing?" He hadn't seen either of Meg's younger sisters in years. Cait had been eleven and Grace ten when he'd joined the navy, so if he had seen either one of them when he'd been on leave, he didn't remember.

Joe snorted with laughter, a man's man through and through. A former coast guardsman, he still ran a few times a week and wore his graying hair in military fashion: high and tight. "Driving me nuts, trying to keep me from my threat of running our handyman business again."

"Mom said that you'd retired and turned everything over to your girls." Jack pointed the tongue depressor at Joe. "Say ah."

Joe did and Jack nodded. "Looks normal. I can have a talk with your daughters, but I might not recognize them if they walked past me on the sidewalk."

Joe chuckled. "They're hard to miss. Almost half a foot taller than Meg—close to five feet eight—and both strawberry blonde, like their mother, with green eyes."

Jack sat down on his rolling stool and used his feet to push off so he was back in front of his laptop. He finished entering data and turned back around. "Any more weddings on the horizon?"

Joe sighed. "I had high hopes for one young man Cait had been dating, but she's been so busy picking up the slack, what with Meg's morning sickness, that she hasn't had the time or energy to date. Grace hasn't brought anyone around to meet me, but I know she's seeing someone from out of town."

Jack noticed Joe's worry lines when he was talking about his daughters and wanted to do something to erase them. As a physician, he would always treat his patients to the best of his ability, but here in Apple Grove, there was much more to be considered. With Joe Mulcahy, it was the link to his childhood friend and the need to help her father. "If I learned anything during my years in the navy, I learned that life and insurgents come at you with both barrels—" He buried the ever-present turmoil just bubbling below the surface to a controllable level and finished what he'd wanted to say. "Life is too short."

He thought of the marine that bled out while he had worked in earnest to stitch the young man back together under fire. If he didn't close the lid to the box where he kept those memories, he'd be up all night, positive he could hear the whistling sound of the explosive before it hit, feel the white-hot agonizing pain of having his leg shatter while bits of shrapnel imbedded into his flesh.

"Doc, are you all right?"

Jack snapped back to attention in time to see the look of concern on the older man's face. "Yeah…um…yes. Yes, I'm fine."

"War is hell," Joe stated flatly, sensing the direction of Jack's thoughts.

Jack couldn't agree more.

Chapter 2

CAITLIN MULCAHY WAS RUNNING LATE. SHE HAD promised her favorite customer, Mr. Weatherbee, that she'd get an early start, but she'd spent hours after work out in the shed by the Mulcahys' barn—her woodworking shop—where she dreamed big and built furniture for family and friends. She'd finally closed the door to her shed on the half-finished rocking chair and nearly finished set of shelves just past midnight. All the shelves needed were a light sanding and a coat of varnish to finish them. But the rocking chair needed the rockers and a good sanding before it'd be ready for a clear coat.

She hoped to surprise her sister Meg and the new niece or nephew that would add to her older sister's growing family with the shelves and the rocking chair. Being behind schedule would only add to her day and the ever-growing list of people to see and things to fix. It was hard trying to squeeze in the work of another person.

She missed Meg working in their family handyman business—and missed her sister taking care of the jobs she used to handle. "I really hate plumbing." She sighed and turned around, heading back to the shop to pick up the pipe dope, adhesive to seal the ends of the pipe, and the length of PVC pipe she'd forgotten.

It was because of her sister that they were behind on jobs and one man—make that woman—short. Not that she could really blame Meg for getting pregnant…again.

On top of chasing around her two-year-old twins, Danny and Joey, she couldn't be expected to jump right in and work the same hours she had been, even part-time.

Meg marrying Dan, the town's new phys ed teacher, had been the best thing that had ever happened to her. The ladies in town still talked about the day he stalked into Honey's Hair Salon and declared his love for Meg in front of everyone. Then again, they were also still talking about the way the sheriff stormed in and hauled salon owner Honey B. over his shoulder. Both couples had been happily married for three years…boy, how time flew by.

Love must change people, she mused. She'd never seen her sister or Honey B. so happy. Even her dad's fledgling romance with the widowed Mary Murphy had him whistling some days. "Guess with the right person, it will be worth it."

Too bad she hadn't found that right person herself, even though she'd dated the few eligible men in town who had interested her. She'd never admit it to Gracie, but her younger sister was right: there was a downside to living in a small town—there were only so many eligible bachelors.

Cait set those thoughts aside; it wouldn't do her any good to dwell on what-ifs. Concentrating on the list of parts in her hand, she gathered what she'd need for the day from the family's shop on Main Street. Toolbox in hand, she walked back outside and was distracted by the sunny glare off her grandfather's legacy—his 1950 Ford F1 pickup. The symbol of the Mulcahys' dependability, generations of Apple Grove residents sighed with relief when they saw that the Mulcahys were on their way to solve whatever problems needed fixing.

"The best part of Meggie not being here is that I get to drive the pickup." Eyes gleaming, she opened the passenger door and carefully stowed her tools and supplies.

Sliding behind the wheel, she sighed. Tonight she'd talk to her dad about hiring a part-timer to ease the heavy workload. She started the truck and put it in gear, giving a quick glance to the diner across the street. She wished she had time to stop in and catch up with her friends, Peggy and Kate. But she was already running a little late. Maybe if she pulled a U-turn instead of driving around the block, she could get to Mr. Weatherbee's faster.

Checking her mirrors, she goosed the gas pedal and cranked the wheel hard, but the pickup's turning radius wasn't as tight as she was used to. To her horror, the truck bounced up onto the sidewalk, grazing the bark on the sugar maple across from the Knitting Room—the one on the corner—right next to Mulcahys' shop! It was early and the Internet café was closed, but what if it was loud enough for her sister to hear? Grace was probably on the phone with their dad right now.

She eased the truck back onto Main Street, shaking like a leaf. When she got out of the cab, she braced herself to see the worst. "Crap!" A trio of nasty-looking scratches on the passenger-side door had gouged the paint all the way down to the metal.

Peggy called her name, and Cait looked up from the evidence that she'd done the unthinkable. "Pop's gonna kill me."

Her friend leaned close, then straightened. "Maybe it's not as bad as it looks. Can you ask Dan to take a look at it? He's always working on cars or trucks with your dad."

Cait's gaze met hers. "Those two are thick as thieves. If I asked him to help, but swore him to secrecy, he'd probably go all Boy Scout on me and tell my dad. He wouldn't want to take the chance that Pop won't let him work on the Model A if he found out Dan was covering for me—they're almost finished with the restoration."

Peggy gave her a hug as Grace rushed out the front door. "I heard a—" She stopped midsentence and stared. "Whoa. What happened?"

"Door's scratched."

Grace shook her head as she looked at the damage Cait pointed to. Grace met her gaze. "I wouldn't wait to tell him."

Cait wished she could start the whole day all over again. "I know, I know. This never would've happened if I hadn't stayed up so late out in my woodshop, which I wouldn't have had to do if you didn't keeping squeezing in so many jobs into my schedule. I would've been up on time and already at Mr. Weatherbee's."

"You're going to blame your crappy driving on me?" Grace yelled. "If it weren't for me—"

"Girls," Peggy broke in. "You're drawing a crowd. If you don't want someone to take a picture and post it online, Cait, you'd better get moving."

Caitlin scrubbed her face with her hands and sighed. "Thanks, Peggy."

Grace glared at her. "Don't forget to tell Pop."

"I'll tell him tonight."

As Cait turned onto Dog Hollow Road, her phone was ringing, but she ignored it, praying that when she got to Bob's Gas and Gears, he wouldn't already know about the damage to the truck—because if he knew, her dad would know. And Cait wanted the chance to tell him in person.

Bob Stewart's face showed instant concern when she pulled into his shop. "What happened? Did you get the guy's license plate?"

Cait's hands were shaking. She didn't want to lie, so she stalled. "It all happened so fast."

"Lucky for you, they built these trucks to last. There's no dent, but still your dad's gonna be pissed. This old truck is a part of your family, and he treats it like a baby."

She got out as Bob was gently running a hand along the door. His head shot up and he stared at her—was there any telltale bark on the door? "It was an accident," she began. Her hands were trembling, so she stuck them in her pockets. "I was pulling a U-ey on Main Street—"

"That was your first mistake—"

"I know," she told him. "I didn't realize that the truck's turning radius wasn't the same as a car."

He looked like he was going to say something but ended up shaking his head. "Was there a fire?"

Baffled, she answered, "No."

"Then where were you in such an all-fired hurry to go?" he asked.

"I was running late and forgot something at the shop—"

"So instead of driving just a little farther where you could turn around, you pull an illegal turn in the middle of town. What did you do, hit the hundred-year-old maple next to your shop?" Bob whistled. "That scratch went through three layers of paint: clear coat, color, and primer—all the way down to the metal." He looked from the door and back to Cait.

"How soon can you fix it?"

"You planning on telling your dad?"

"Later."

"If you put it off," Bob began, "he's bound to hear before you tell him. Are you sure you want to wait?"

Cait shook her head. "No. I'm not sure, but it's hard because I know how much this truck means to him."

"Means a lot to the town. People have come to associate that truck with the reputation your great-great-grandfather began and your father, and now you girls are continuing," he reminded her. "It's not just transportation."

"I know." She blinked back tears. She felt awful, but she'd make it right.

"Why don't you call your dad now?" Bob patted her on the shoulder. "I'll go look up the paint codes to see if I have to order any of them."

Cait nodded, mumbling, "He didn't let Meg drive the truck until a couple years ago. The only reason I'm driving it now is because she's been working so few hours."

"You'll feel better after you tell him."

Cait knew he was right. And as much as she wanted to tell her father in person, she also didn't want him hearing the news from someone else. Like Grace. Steeling her nerves, she dialed her father.

"Hey, Pop, it's Cait." Before he could start in with the twenty questions about how the jobs were going, she said, "I have bad news."

"You didn't get hurt on the job, did you?"

"No…I didn't—"

Before she could tell him what happened, his voice took on a frantic edge, "Is it Grace or Meg?"

"No—it's the F1…"

The silence on the other end of the line was starting to unnerve her and just when she thought she would crack, her father asked, "Is it totaled then?"

"What? No! The passenger door is badly scratched… down to the metal. I'm out at Bob's Gas and Gears and he's looking up the paint codes."

She heard him sigh and braced herself for the inquisition. "How did it happen? Where were you when you got hit?"

"If you'll give me a chance, I'll tell you."

He grumbled something she couldn't quite hear before falling silent.

"I was running late and had to pick something up at the shop. I tried to pull a U-ey on Main, but kinda ran out of road."

"Let me get this straight. You pulled an illegal turn in the middle of Main Street while driving the F1 with our name in gold letters on the side?"

Clearing her throat, she answered, "Yes."

"Didn't you realize that the turning radius on that truck isn't the same as the compact car you usually drive?" He paused, then asked, "Did you hit the tree by our shop?"

Caitlin looked over at Bob, who had stopped writing when her father's voice started to increase in volume. The older man motioned for her to continue. Knowing there was no way Bob would stop eavesdropping on her conversation, she sighed and answered her dad's questions. "I didn't exactly hit the tree…I grazed it."

"No dents?"

"Nope!" Bob answered for Caitlin.

"And you're all right?" her father asked again.

"Yes, Pop."

"We'll talk later. Put Bob on."

She handed her phone to her father's friend and walked over to the edge of the road, staring out at the field across from Bob's shop. She heard the distinctive song from the other side of the road and smiled as her love of nature distracted her while she waited for Bob to end the call. A trio of red-winged blackbirds sang as they perched on the fence by the small pond in the middle of the farmer's field. They were males; their scarlet wing bars were puffed up as they sang. "Must be trying to attract a few females."

The deep rumble of Bob's voice had her looking over her shoulder at the F1. She had made a huge mistake that could have ended badly. Desperately trying not to think of another car, another accident that ended with her mother lying in a hospital bed, she wrapped her arms around her waist, determined to focus on the trill of songbirds and the cloudless spring sky. She succeeded until Bob called her name.

She drew in a deep breath and turned around. She hoped the repair wouldn't cut too deeply into her savings, but had no idea how much it would cost to special order paint. Maybe they wouldn't have to repaint the whole door, but what she knew about removing paint would fill a thimble.

"Your dad agreed it would be best to fix it right away. Can't take a chance that the metal will rust."

Before she could ask if she was supposed to walk to Mr. Weatherbee's farm, Bob added, "Grace is coming to pick you up. Your dad said you could drop her at the shop and drive the car until the truck's finished."

"Is my dad—"

"He's in the middle of a nasty plumbing repair—his words—so he'll stop by on his way back through town." She nodded and Bob added, "Don't worry. I'll take good care of his baby and fix her right up."

"I'll let you get started." She walked over to the truck and grabbed her toolbox. "I'll start walking back to town and meet Grace halfway."

He nodded, but his attention was already focused on the pickup.

Birds swooped low in the field, keeping her company as she trudged toward town.

Grace must have left the moment their father called. Caitlin waved to get her sister's attention. Her sister slowed down and Cait got in. "Thanks for coming to get me."

Grace nodded and drove toward Bob's.

"Why aren't you going back to town?"

Grace was frowning as she pulled into the parking lot, waved to Bob, and signaled. "I am," her sister told her. "What I'm not going to do is pull a U-turn in the middle of the road. Besides, I imagine the supplies you came back to get for Mr. Weatherbee's barn are still in the truck."

"It must be tough," Caitlin grumbled.

"What?"

"Being the perfect little sister," Cait added.

Grace's hands tightened on the wheel, but she didn't say anything.

Caitlin was grateful that the ride back to town was a short one. When her sister pulled up out front and parked, Grace tossed Cait the keys without a word, slamming the driver's side door and then the front door to the shop.

Wonder how long she'll be giving me the silent treatment this time.

A few hours later, she packed up her tools, highly satisfied with the way the rebuild of Mr. Weatherbee's barn turned out. She was just finishing loading up the car when her favorite customer came walking toward her with a bit of metal and glass dangling from his hand.

"Thought you might like to hang this one with the others."

Cait's heart turned over when she saw the lovely wind chime he held out to her. "It's so beautiful." Her eyes lit up as she reached for the intricate twist of copper, silver, and green sea glass. "I love it!"

The wizened old man's face wrinkled up as he smiled, and she gave in to the urge and wrapped her arms around his neck before pressing a kiss to his cheek.

"Well now," he said, patting her back and clearing his throat. "I'd say Joe Mulcahy raised three wonderful young women who aren't afraid to work with their hands—or get dirty."

"He'd be pleased to hear it," she said, thinking about this morning.

"Don't you fret about that F1, Caitlin." Her gaze shot up to his, and from the look on his face, he knew the whole sorry story. His words confirmed it. "The hardest lessons are often the only ones we take to heart." With a nudge to her shoulders, he urged her toward her car. "I'm sure Grace has a full schedule for you. Best be getting to it."

"Thanks, Mr. Weatherbee."

"Drive safely, you hear?"

"Yes, sir." Apple Grove seemed smaller by the day.

With a sigh she drove back to town. When she stopped in to pick up more supplies, she realized that Grace had added the cold shoulder to the silent treatment. Just because Grace was without a car for the day—as if her sister couldn't walk anywhere she needed to go in town.

Little sisters could be such a pain.

Feeling a little bit better now that the F1 was in Bob's capable hands, but not quite ready to face her father—she really hated to disappoint him—she took the long way home. When an oldie came on the radio, she sang along and felt the day's problems start to unravel. The ship's mast Mr. McCormack used in place of a scarecrow came into view. Approaching the McCormack farm, she slowed down. Peggy and Kate's dad had been in the fields plowing earlier, and Cait drew in a deep breath, comforted by the scent of fresh-turned dirt.

More kids than she could remember had snuck out in the middle of the night to climb up to the crow's nest on a dare—her older sister, Meg, included. Thinking about how much trouble Meg had gotten into that time, having been rescued by the then-deputy Mitch Wallace—his first juvenile delinquent rescue, according to Mitch—made her feel just a little bit better.

Dusk lent a certain mystical quality to the air. Driving past the newly planted fields, she could just imagine faeries flitting about, waving magic wands over the earth, pond, and trees as vines, flowers, and buds burst into bloom. Letting her imagination wander, she almost didn't see the car parked at the side of the road until she was just about to pass it.

Only one car in town had a paint job like that: Doc Gannon's Jeep. Meg told her his friends had painted it in army camo as a joke to welcome him home after his first tour.

Why had he stopped? She pulled off the road in front of his vehicle, got out, and started to look for him.

"Hey, Doc—where are you?"

The silence had her gut icing over before she chastised herself that people only parked their cars and disappeared in the movies…like the one she'd watched while trying to unwind after a long night in her woodshop.

She called out again, "Do you need help?"

When he still didn't answer, she pulled out her cell phone. If anyone had gotten sick out on Eden Church Road, Peggy would have heard and would let her know. She was about to hit the speed dial when she heard a deep shout coming from across the road.

Turning toward the sound, she was knocked off balance by a small, black, fuzzy missile. Wrapping her arms around the animal so it wouldn't get hurt when she landed, her backside took the brunt of the impact—and so did her phone when it hit the pavement. Luckily, it was still in one piece.

"Hey," she said, as she looked down at the quivering puppy in her arms. "Where did you come from?"

The puppy's tiny pink tongue bathed her face, and he nipped the end of her nose. When Cait laughed, the puppy did it again. She snuggled him close and reached for her phone.

"Don't let go of him!"

His deep voice grabbed her attention. The tall, broad-shouldered man moving across the road toward her looked worried. Cait remembered how upset the whole town had been to hear of his injury. Reverend Smith had even started a prayer chain. Had Doc aggravated his wound somehow by chasing the puppy? She took in his broad shoulders and tall frame. Yes, he was limping but trying to ignore it.

She'd known Jack Gannon all her life—well, a younger version, before he enlisted—but for some reason, she didn't remember him looking so ruggedly handsome. Had she only seen what she expected to in those brief glimpses of him those few times he'd been home on leave? There was definitely more here than she remembered.

Coming to stand beside her, he stared down at her for a moment before holding his hand out to her. "Are you all right?"

She had to clear her throat to answer. "Yes, I'm fine. But what about you? What happened?"

He chuckled and it sounded rusty, as though he wasn't used to laughing. "The little rascal ran out in front of me," he explained, pulling Cait to her feet. "I had to swerve not to hit him. I've been chasing him for the last fifteen minutes. Thanks for catching him."

"All I did was show up. He's the one who decided to jump into my arms." She jiggled the puppy she held. "Hey, fella. What're you doing out here?"

Jack smiled, revealing a deep dimple.

"Wait a minute. Are you Meg's sister Caitlin?"

She felt the blood rush to her cheeks and hated that she blushed. "Yes, I am. And you're Apple Grove's hometown hero. We've been waiting for you. Welcome home, Doc."

A dark shadow crossed his features as his lips thinned and a grimace took the place of his smile, catching her off guard. What had she said that changed his mood?

"I'm no hero." He let go of her arm.

Unsure of how to continue, she looked up at the sky. "They're saying we'll have rain by midnight."

He shrugged and shoved his hands in his pockets. The silence weighed heavily between them. Wanting to get back to the friendly banter of just a few minutes ago, she asked, "So how was your first day back in town?"

He sighed. "I guess everyone in Apple Grove knows I got back last night."

She smiled. "If they didn't, Peggy and Kate wouldn't be doing their jobs down at gossip central."

He tilted his head to the side and his features softened—not quite a smile, but no longer frowning. The late afternoon sun glinted off his crew cut. She didn't remember his hair having a reddish tint. How many other things had she forgotten over the years or not paid attention to?

He cleared his throat and said, "I heard about your grandfather's truck."

"Everyone makes mistakes—" she began only to be interrupted.

"When you're in the service, you're not at liberty to make poor decisions. You need to do the right thing, at the right time—second chances aren't always an option."

The bleak look in his eyes darkened their hue to midnight blue. *Was he remembering something from his time in the navy?* "Is that why you're limping?"

Anger flashed in the depths of his gaze, warning her she'd either hit the nail on the head or was completely off the mark and had insulted him. Before she could ask, he ground out, "No."

"Sorry," she said, nuzzling her face in the soft fur of the little one she'd been neglecting. "Did you twist your ankle chasing after this little cutie?"

The dog chose that moment to lift his head and stare up at her. His head was cocked to the side, making his ears flop to the left, but it was his underbite and little black lips that had her forgetting all about Doc's flinty-eyed stare. Melting into a warm puddle, she kissed the tip of the puppy's nose.

"No."

Startled by the hard edge in his reply, she looked up in time to see a mix of anger and anguish before Doc blinked and she was left to wonder if she'd imagined it. It was time to change the subject. "What are we going to do?"

It was telling that Caitlin used "we," including him in the dilemma of what to do with the dog. "Now that he's not running wild, let's see if he has a collar."

He let the dog sniff the back of his hand before stroking the soft fur on its neck. "Good boy," he soothed. "We want to help you."

"No collar," she said. She tilted her head and looked up at him, and for a brief moment, he was lost in her pretty green eyes.

Wavy wisps of strawberry blonde hair escaped the braid hanging over her shoulder blades and curled against her cheek and neck. The sudden urge to tuck those wisps behind her ear had him reining in his wayward thoughts. Caitlin Mulcahy had grown up while he'd been away.

"We could call the sheriff and ask if there are any reports of a lost puppy."

Distracted by the fullness of her bottom lip, her words didn't register until she narrowed her eyes and reached into her pocket. *Idiot*, he told himself. *She's worried about the puppy.*

The call had already gone through before he could think of a response. "Hi Cindy," he heard her say. "It's Cait. We just found a little puppy out on Eden Church Road. Any reports of a little black dog gone missing?"

His mind raced at warp speed, trying to come up with a way to keep her with him for just a little while longer.

She disconnected and looked up at him. "No one reported a missing dog." She hesitated. "Grace is allergic to dogs…it's why we don't have one and why I can't take him home." She paused, then laid a hand on his arm. "What are we going to do? We can't just leave him here."

Now her question made perfect sense. She'd asked it of him before he realized the depth of her dilemma. "I can take him to my house," he said slowly, pleased that she still held on to his forearm, whether it was intentional or not. "But with my long hours, he'll be left alone all day. That's not a good idea with a puppy—he could get into all kinds of trouble. Maybe you could check up on him in between your repair calls."

A slight squeeze and then the warmth of her touch vanished. He missed the connection and sincerely hoped

Cait would take him up on his suggestion. Feeling oddly energized, he wondered if it was because he hadn't had a dog since before he'd left for the navy or because Caitlin would be forced to spend time with him, allowing him the luxury of exploring the confusing feelings bombarding him where the lady was concerned.

It was a win-win situation either way.

"Gracie usually gives me just enough time to get from one job to the next," she said, settling the puppy more securely in her arms. "But we've had words over the fact that I can't keep doing Meg's jobs and my own."

He nodded. "Is that why you scratched the truck?" The wave of red sweeping up her throat to her cheeks made him wonder if her temper would match her older sister's. Instead of taking a step back and dropping the subject, he added, "I don't think anyone's ever had an accident with your grandfather's truck."

"I didn't hit anyone."

He fought against the urge to smile. He didn't want her to think he was laughing at her—he was simply enjoying her display of temper. "Sorry," he said, scratching the puppy's head. "So are you going to tell me what happened?"

She started walking toward her car, puppy cuddled against her. When she was about to open the driver's side door, he called out to her, "I thought Grace was allergic to dogs?"

She paused and her shoulders slumped. He was right behind her when she grumbled, "Damn it."

The snort of laughter escaped. Before she could get her back up, he eased the puppy from her arms and walked to the passenger side of her car. Cradling the dog against his chest, he opened the door, settled the pup on the seat and locked him in. When she frowned at him, he told her, "Follow me," as he opened his driver's side door.

Unsure if she would, he made sure to drive at a snail's pace for the first couple of minutes until he saw that she had pulled out behind him and was indeed following him home. The woman Caitlin had become intrigued him.

He'd been blindsided when she'd looked up at him with the ball of black fluff in her arms. The contrast of black and strawberry blonde caught his attention—and then she'd smiled up at him. Steadier now that there was enough distance between them, he gradually picked up speed until he was cruising along Eden Church Road toward the railroad tracks.

He'd bought his parents' house from them when they'd told him their plans to retire. It was closer to the church than the center of town, but he loved the rambling old Victorian with the two-acre yard and detached garage. He'd spent his childhood exploring their yard and the trees just beyond, getting into scrapes and stumbling home with stories of the pretend battles he'd fought against imaginary foes. Little did he realize that he would relive that part of his life across the ocean in a land he could never have conjured up in his ten-year-old mind—in battles that were very, very real.

Flicking on his turn signal, he slowed down and eased his Jeep onto his street, grateful that he would have a few minutes to bury the distracting memories—both recent and childhood—before Caitlin pulled up alongside him in his driveway.

He got out and opened her door as she was reaching

across the seat to pick up the little black dog. The little ball of fuzz nibbled on her braid. She was laughing as she corrected the pup and Jack wondered if he'd gone off the deep end or just broken through the surface and was experiencing life anew.

Unsure of himself for the first time since he'd shipped out on his first tour as a corpsman attached to a marine unit, he dug deep to keep his emotions under control. *Rough water ahead, mate*, he cautioned himself. *Don't get too close to the siren on the rocks—you'll go down for sure!*

Caitlin smiled up at him as she scooted out of her car, her arms filled with the wriggling little dog, and thoughts of sea sirens and mermaids filled his tired brain, twinning with the image of Caitlin's long, wavy, strawberry-kissed hair streaming out around her. Shaking his head to clear it, he said, "Let's see if we can find something for him to sleep in tonight."

Unaware of the direction of his thoughts, the middle Mulcahy sister snuggled the puppy close to her heart and walked toward the house. "A box with an old blanket would probably work for this little guy."

"How do you know if you've never had a dog?"

Her smile seemed wistful as she answered, "The McCormacks always had a dog."

It wasn't so much what she said as how she said it that made him realize that Caitlin needed to be a part of taking care of this little dog as much as he did. Anticipating their time together and the discoveries ahead of them, Jack opened the back door and held it for her. "Come on in. I'll make us some coffee while you see if Butch here likes his temporary surroundings."

Cait chuckled, holding the dog out in front of her to look at him. "You don't look like a Butch to me. Maybe Scamp or Scooter. Something playful." While he poured cold water into the coffeemaker and hit the brew button, he kept an eye on Caitlin. She lowered herself to the floor and sat Indian-style on the worn paint-speckled linoleum floor, encouraging his new tenant to curl up in her lap. The contrast of the willow-slim woman curving herself around the little dog so that he'd settle down tugged at his heart.

Cait's slow smile had him wondering if his mom's favorite saying was true and everything did happen for a reason.

Chapter 3

HER PHONE RANG AND SHE SHIFTED TO ANSWER IT, cradling the pup in her arms. Whoever it was, she told them she was busy and would call back. After she disconnected, he asked, "Milk? Sugar?"

Her sigh sounded so forlorn, he had to stifle the urge to reach out and pat the back of her hand. They'd known one another forever, but only as acquaintances, someone you passed on the street and waved to—not someone you would open your heart to or hug close to make the sadness go away.

Odd, but that last thought wormed its way closer to his heart…and for the first time in too many years to count, he yearned for a simpler life—one without complications—where he could hold a woman in his arms and let the world go by. He couldn't change his past, but he could try to control his future. Setting those thoughts aside, he waited for her to answer.

She looked up at him, studying his face for a moment before responding. "I like milk."

He held up the sugar bowl, but she wasn't paying attention to him. When he cleared his throat, she finally looked up and laughed as he shook the sugar bowl from side to side.

"I'm sorry, I was letting my mind wander. Four sugars, please."

Jack set down the bowl and backed away from it.

"OK, as a doctor, I must caution you about the abuse of sugar. It isn't good for you."

Tucking one leg beneath her and the puppy securely in one arm, she pushed to her feet and walked over to stand beside him. "I make it a habit to ignore advice that like. Besides, my dad has been doctoring his coffee with tons of sugar for years."

"And that little warning he had a few years ago didn't show up on your radar? My mom and Miss Trudi wrote and told me about Joe's heart attack scare. It's never too soon to start paying attention to your diet and physical routine."

Her cheeks flushed a delicate pink, the color of the fairy roses his mother had planted out back by the well when Jack was in grade school. He was entranced by the woman even though he wasn't sure if she was embarrassed or angry with him. Replaying his last few words through his brain didn't help.

Handing her the dark blue enamelware cup, he warned, "Careful, the metal gets hot."

Her color quickly returned to normal as she thanked him for the coffee. "Do you have a little bowl for water?"

Taking a quick sip, he set his cup on the butcher-block counter and opened a cabinet overhead. "How's this?" He held up a small blue-and-white patterned bowl.

She winced. "Are you sure you want to use your mom's good dishes?"

He shrugged. "How can you tell that they're good?"

She shook her head at him and set her cup beside his. "My mom used to have dishes similar to this pattern. They're probably from England, aren't they?"

"I have no idea. When Mom and Dad were getting

ready to move, they didn't want to pack too much. They wanted an easier life, less unencumbered, so she left a lot of her dishes and glassware behind."

Caitlin tilted her head to the side. "Do you mind if I take a look for something less breakable?"

He waved toward the cabinets. "Not at all."

Taking the dog from her, he watched as she scanned the kitchen before lifting up on her toes and peering into the overhead cabinets. The view was subtly curved and had his mind veering off into a direction it had no business going. To distract himself, he nuzzled the dog and started talking to him.

"Your countertops are empty."

He frowned.

"No knickknacks. I like filling mason jars with wildflowers—and we still use Gram's copper cookie tin."

"I like things simple," he mumbled, not wanting to discuss his need to keep the house free of personal items.

"So are you lost?" he asked the puppy. "Where did you come from? Did someone just dump you along the side of the road, or did you run away?"

Cait's back was turned as she held up the Transformers plastic bowl he'd used every morning for ten years. "How about this?" He frowned, wincing at the thought that she'd uncovered a bit of the past he hadn't shared with anyone since before he had shipped out. Unprepared for the winsome smile on her face as she looked over her shoulder, he wondered what it was about Caitlin that got past his guard.

"Sure." He reached for the bowl and their fingers brushed against one another, sending a zing of electricity through his system.

Since her back was facing him, he could slowly exhale the breath he'd drawn in and held as he let himself react to her touch. Had she felt it too? By the time she turned around, he was smiling.

While he filled the bowl with water, Cait asked, "So did he whisper any secrets in your ear while my back was turned?"

He chuckled. "Not a word. I think he's speechless, wondering where he is and what happened to the home he knew."

"Do you really think someone just dropped him off at the side of the road?"

He reacted to the distress in her voice but, instead of answering, decided to distract her by urging her to set the bowl on the floor. When she did, he set the puppy down and watched him lap up the cool well water. "He was thirsty."

"Do you have anything to feed him?"

Jack crossed to the fridge, opened it up, and scanned the shelves. "A six-pack of beer, hot sauce, leftover turkey platter from lunch at the diner—I stopped home after lunch—and some eggs. I didn't have time to grocery shop."

"But you had time to pick up beer?"

"Beer has a lot of protein in it," he began, only to fall silent as he looked over his shoulder and watched her settle on the floor. He shut the fridge and turned around. The little dog climbed into her lap and shut his eyes, his doggy sigh of contentment echoing in the quiet.

"He likes you." Jack watched the way she slowly stroked her hand from the top of the puppy's head, down the length of the dog's spine. Mesmerized, back to thinking of mermaids and sea sirens, he couldn't look away.

"I've always wanted a dog."

He wiped his damp palms on his jeans. "I had two growing up. I still miss them."

"What happened?"

"Jake, my first dog, was a beagle," he told her. "He lived to be fourteen. I was so lonely when he died that my folks got another one right away. Sam was thirteen when she died."

"It must be like losing a member of your family," she whispered, absently rubbing the dog's ears.

Jack moved to sit beside her, sensing the direction of her thoughts. Taking a chance, he said, "You miss her."

Cait nodded. "There will be days when I wonder what my life would have been like if my mom hadn't been in that accident." She paused and the puppy squirmed until she started to pet him again. "But we had Pop and Meg."

"Your sister gave up a lot to take care of you and Grace when you were really little."

"I know."

When she remained silent, he couldn't ignore the urge to comfort her. He scooted closer and let his shoulder brush against hers. That static zing shot through him again. It wasn't just one of those things. There was something about the woman sitting on his kitchen floor that called to him on more than one level—otherwise he wouldn't be getting those shocks whenever they touched. Would he, or was he just physically drawn to her?

The knees of her jeans were nearly worn through and clung to her legs and backside like a dream, leaving little to his imagination. She was long, lean, and he couldn't help but wonder if her legs were as stellar as Meg's; although the oldest Mulcahy sister was shorter in stature, she had a first-class pair of legs. Well, he thought, the weather was getting warmer, so the chances of him seeing Caitlin's legs clad in shorts were pretty good.

It had been a really long time since he'd been obsessed with a woman's legs...longer than he cared to remember. There was more going on here than just the rescue of the little fuzzy ball of fur...had fate stepped in and decided that he needed to be rescued as well?

When Cait's pocket vibrated against his hip, he smiled. "Is that a pistol in your pocket?" he quipped.

She smiled, obviously appreciating the movie reference. "You've gotta love Mae West."

He grinned down at her. "Do you have to answer that?"

She sighed. "It's a text."

When she made no move to retrieve her phone from her pocket, he asked, "Are you going to answer it?"

"It's probably my dad, and I really don't have the energy to face him right now."

He patted her knee and then the puppy. "It won't get any easier if you put it off."

"Easy for you to say," she grumbled, shifting so the puppy could curl up in her lap again. "You didn't break the law and then scratch your dad's favorite truck—the symbol of generations of Mulcahys on the job here in Apple Grove."

"True," he agreed, "but it could have been worse."

"I know, I could have dented the door—or somebody could have been hurt."

Needing to see her smile, he offered, "I have connections if you want a paint job like mine."

When her mouth curved upward, he felt warm inside. To keep her smiling, he told her, "My knucklehead friends thought I'd get mad that they used army camo colors."

"Why didn't you?"

He grinned. "I thought it looked cool."

"So that's why you left it when you had plenty of opportunities to fix it over the years?"

He nodded and, seeing her relax, returned to the subject that was obviously troubling her. "Your father was probably worried just as much about you, but now that he knows you're fine, he has the luxury of worrying about the truck—and doing his parental duty of reminding you that you screwed up."

"I feel so much better now," she said.

A lock of hair slipped from her braid and got stuck on the tips of her eyelashes. Without thinking, he reached over and smoothed it out of her eyes. "Good." The need to pull her closer filled him, jangling his nerves. But he'd satisfied his curiosity—her hair felt soft as silk.

The silence lengthened between them until the puppy chose that moment to leap into his lap. "Oompf!" Stars swam before his eyes as a wave of nausea swept up from his toes.

"Doc, are you all right?"

The sweet sound of Caitlin's voice was like a beacon in the black of night across storm-tossed seas. He tried to focus on it as he struggled to conquer the pain and ignore the roiling in his gut. He'd learned his iron-clad control in the military; it served him well now.

"Yeah," he rasped. "Fine."

"You look a little green around the gills." Caitlin rubbed her hand on his back, an instinctive healing touch—one a mother would use on her child.

The ball of fur started nipping his chin, drawing his attention back to their little problem. "Guys are supposed to stick up for one another," he scolded. "Not maim them." As if he had told the dog how much he adored him, the puppy switched from nibbles to kisses, bathing his face with his tiny pink tongue.

"He's a rapscallion." Caitlin's soft laughter surrounded him like a hug.

"I could think of a few other names for him," Jack said quietly.

She chose to ignore his meaning, frowned at him, and said, "We should name him—and not Butch."

"I thought you had to go home."

"Not quite yet." Her eyes met his and she asked, "Unless you're kicking me out?"

"Hell no," he said, and could have kicked himself. He'd have to work harder if he were going to control his salty language now that he'd returned to Apple Grove. "Um…sorry for swearing."

Caitlin's belly laugh charmed him. "That's nothing compared to what Meg has been known to say."

He grinned. "She always had the knack for it when we were in school, but I would think she'd have had to watch what she was saying—especially now that she's a mom."

Cait agreed. "She does. It used to bug her when Grace reminded her that no swearing on the job is our company rule."

"I bet it did."

"How about Mack or Fido?" she suggested.

He laughed when the little dog tilted his head to one side and shook it. "I don't think he likes either of those names." He chucked the dog under the chin and stared into its dark brown eyes. "You look more like a Jameson…Jamie." The dog leaped up and licked Jack's face with abandon.

Caitlin reached over and began to stroke her hand along the puppy's back again. "I guess you're Jamie, then."

Jack agreed. "OK, Jamie." Holding the dog like a football in the curve of his arm, he pushed to his feet. Once he stood up, he held out his hand to Caitlin. She looked down at his hand and then up at his face before she put her hand in his and let him help her stand. When she trembled, he saw confusion mixed with want in her eyes. The same tangled emotions bubbling inside of him. He'd bide his time—but life was short. He didn't want to wait too long.

She made no move to close the distance between them, but instead thanked him and scratched the dog's face. "What are we going to feed him?"

He liked that she was still thinking in terms of them as a unit. "I've got some rice in that cabinet over there. My mom had Mrs. Murphy stock the cabinets with dry goods for me."

She walked over to where he was pointing and reached for the box as he bent to pull a small saucepan out of the cabinet by the stove.

"Nice lady, your mom—Mary Murphy too."

"Thanks," he said. "There was a note left on the counter from Mary reminding me to stop by and pick up the grocery order my mom had left with her just in case I didn't get to the store first thing this morning. I'll have to pick it up tomorrow." The dog was content to be held against Jack as he got the measuring cup and filled it with water, dumping it in the pan and flicking on the burner. "Hey, can you put a cup of rice in here?"

"Is that all you're going to feed him?"

"I was going to add some of the leftover turkey to it. I'll nuke it first though. I'll have to remember to pick up some chop meat too—not sure if it was on the list."

"You planning on making burgers?" she asked.

He shook his head. "Puppies have a tendency to eat things they shouldn't. We always had chop meat and rice on hand. It's easier for them to digest."

She scrunched her face and wrinkled her nose in obvious distaste at his suggestion. "Did you fry the meat and add the rice? It might help cover the flavor since you aren't using real rice."

"Hey, I grew up eating this kind of rice—and no, you boil the meat."

Cait sighed. "Meg was big on instant anything, but I have discovered how yummy long grain rice tastes."

Jack frowned, remembering the hard years Meg and her family lived through after their mother died. "This cooks faster."

Cait agreed.

Jack shrugged. "Besides, we don't know when he ate last and this is an old-time remedy for a puppy or dog with an upset stomach. It's not just easy to digest. The flavor encourages the dog to eat."

"You sound like you've done this before."

He chuckled and handed her the meat to unwrap and

then a plate. "Our first beagle, Jake, used to eat things he wasn't supposed to."

She placed the slice of meat and gravy in the microwave to warm up. "Like?"

"Shoes, sticks, floor tile, birdseed—"

She turned the water off and added the rice. "Your dog ate all of those things?"

"And more."

The microwave beeped and he pulled the turkey out. Jamie's little nose twitched and he licked his lips in anticipation as Jack added the warmed-up meat to the rice. "When he was going through the chewing phase, we had to make sure we put away everything that wasn't nailed down to keep Jake from chewing it." She looked as if she didn't believe him, until he added, "That's when he started on the chair rungs and table legs."

Her laughter filling his kitchen eased a hole in his life he hadn't recognized existed. It reminded him of growing up in this house; there had been a lot of laughter. Thinking of the years he'd spent away from home across the sea, when there had been no laughter, had him wondering if there could be again. His gut clenched. He hadn't even told his parents the full extent of what happened in Iraq.

"Seriously?"

When he didn't answer right away, she poked him in the shoulder.

"Hmmm…what?"

"I asked if you're serious."

"Absolutely. That dog used to drive my mom nuts with his chewing. Who knew a dog would chew the back of a chair?"

Jamie chose that moment to speak. His rough little barks, followed by Caitlin's laughter seeped into his heavily guarded soul. "I guess somebody's hungry," she observed.

"Here." He handed the dog off to her.

Mixing the meat and rice with a dash of cold water, he put a few healthy-sized scoops in the Transformers bowl, tested the temperature with his fingertip, and set it on the floor next to the water. "Chow down, buddy."

That was all of the invitation Jamie needed. He wriggled until Cait put him on the floor. He scampered over to his dinner and ate with all the gusto in his little puppy heart.

"His sides are getting bigger," Caitlin sounded worried.

Jack shook his head. "That's why you have to be so careful how much you feed a puppy. They'll just keep eating until they barf."

She wrinkled her nose and stared down at Jamie. "Did we give him too much?"

"I don't think so, but let's try to keep him calm for the next little bit to make sure his dinner stays in his stomach."

When Jack's cell phone and house line rang simultaneously, he went straight into combat-ready mode. He answered the cell first. "Gannon."

Reacting to the worry in the sheriff's dispatcher's voice, he wondered why it hadn't been the sheriff calling him instead of his dispatcher. "Don't move her, elevate her feet to get her pressure regulated, and keep her comfortable. Does Mitch know?"

"He's on his way back from Newark, had some police business over there."

"Tell him not to worry. I'm on my way."

When he disconnected, Caitlin had the dog in her arms and worry in her eyes. "Who's hurt?"

"Honey B. passed out at her shop. According to Cindy, Honey B.'s been fighting a virus...she's supposed to be my ten o'clock appointment tomorrow."

"What can I do to help?"

Her immediate offer to help resonated deep within him. He always felt the same need to pitch in wherever he could—something else they had in common.

"Could you stick around and keep an eye on Jamie while I'm gone?"

"Yes. I'll call my dad and let him know I'll be late."

"Good."

Giving in to need, he pressed a swift kiss to her brow before patting the top of Jamie's head. "I'll keep you posted."

―――――

"Well," she said, watching the screen door close. "I guess it's just you and me." Looking down into eyes the color of her favorite chocolate bar, she wondered if she knew what she was getting into. Nuzzling his face, she sighed. "I've got to call Pop."

Hitting speed dial, she braced herself when he answered. "Hey, Pop...it's me, Cait."

"I was getting ready to call Doc Gannon."

She fought to control the nervous laughter. "Funny thing about that, Pop. I'm over at his house right now."

"Doc's? Why, are you sick?"

"No...I'm puppy sitting."

"When did Doc get a dog?"

She was about to launch into the tale of how they

worked together to rescue little Jamie when the dog started to chew on her earlobe. Distracted, she shifted the puppy so he couldn't reach her ear, and told her dad, "It's a long story and the little guy is nibbling on me. Jack had an emergency call over at Honey's. I'll be here until he gets back."

"I guess you can't bring the little guy over here, what with Grace's allergies."

She paused, unsure of what to say to her father about Grandpa's truck. Finally, she decided to just tell him, "I'm really sorry, Pop."

Her shift in topic wasn't lost on her father. "I know you are, Caitlin." The disappointment coloring his words added another layer of guilt. "But the important thing is that no one was hurt."

"But Grandpa's truck—" she began.

"Is easily fixed and it's only a few days. By now the people in town know that nothing will keep a Mulcahy from fulfilling a promise to fix whatever is broken. Give a call when you're leaving Doc's."

"OK. Talk to you later."

Jameson chose that moment to squirm out of her arms and toddle to the middle of the kitchen floor and squat. "Jameson. No!"

The puppy looked up at her, and if he was human, she would have sworn he was smiling up at her…maybe it was his little underbite. But one thing was for sure: he didn't understand the word no. Either that or he chose not to listen—and peed all over the place.

Grabbing the roll of paper towels, she tore off a bunch and mopped up the puddle and was hunting up the garbage can when she heard him yipping behind her. She spun around and started laughing. Jameson had grabbed a hold of the paper towels and was running in a circle—a wide arc of white following wherever he ran.

After a few minutes, she realized he was scared of the long, flowing white trailing behind him. "It's OK, Jamie," she soothed. She scooped him up and walked to the back door. They had been here awhile and he hadn't had to do any of his doggie business. He probably had to go, especially since he peed. Petting his neck, she remembered he didn't have a collar. She had to think of something else. She didn't want to run to the risk of him running away from her in the dark.

Just the thought of that had her turning around to face the mess he'd made in the kitchen. "I guess we'd better look for some newspaper. Can't have you pooping on Jack's floor."

She found what she was looking for in the living room, a neat stack of newspaper beside the fireplace, and wondered if he rolled them up into paper logs to start a fire like her father did.

Taking the time to notice the fireplace, she wondered if it had always been a soft cream color or if the bricks had been unpainted when the house was new. She'd have to ask Miss Trudi; the town's quirky octogenarian would know.

It was getting darker by the moment, so she crossed the room and lit the floor lamp. The room was bathed in the soft glow of incandescent light, giving it an ethereal quality. She'd have to ask Jack why he wasn't replacing his light bulbs with fluorescent ones. Her dad had been all for reducing their carbon footprint—and in fact had started a mini campaign in town, doing his part to encourage those who were behind the times to step it up.

That thought had her smiling as she grabbed some newspaper and headed back to the kitchen. She set him down on the floor and spread the paper next to the back door. "OK…go ahead."

He sat down and tilted his head to the side as he looked up at her. She wondered if he understood anything she was saying. Dogs are very smart animals. "Well," she said, watching him for a sign that he had to go to the bathroom. When he didn't move, she laughed. Maybe he couldn't go because she was watching him. She turned her back and heard him on the paper. "Good dog."

Giving him a few minutes, she waited before looking over her shoulder. "Jamie!" He hadn't been going to the bathroom. He paused mid-chew and smiled an adorable little doggy smile; he was eating the paper.

She leaned down to grab it out of his mouth, and he shivered in excitement, leaning down on his front paws with his tail in the air. He was ready to play! "Open your mouth," she coaxed. He jerked his head and tugged, spreading the newspaper from the back door across to the stove.

"Jamie, no." He was making a huge mess. She would have to clean it all up before Jack got home, but as soon as she started to reach for the paper, he tossed his head from side to side as if to say no and ran for the living room, shreds of paper trailing behind him.

By the time she caught up to him, he had started to chew on the edge of the braided rug in front of the fireplace. "Oh no!" She lunged for the dog and was stepping onto the edge of the rug just as he set his teeth into the thick braid and tugged.

Caitlin had nothing to grab on to as her feet went out from underneath her and she landed on her back. Stunned, she lay there for a moment before she realized the odd noise came from her as her lungs desperately tried to drag in air. She'd knocked the wind out of herself when she'd hit the floor. She struggled to calm her racing heart and draw in that first painful breath.

She pushed herself up on one elbow as the small black juggernaut ran toward her from across the room, landing in the middle of her chest. As he licked her face from forehead to chin, she couldn't decide if she should yell at him for trying to eat the rug or for knocking her off her feet.

Deciding he wouldn't really understand why she was yelling at him, she began to stroke him from the top of his head to the tip of his tail. He lay down on top of her, putting his nose beneath her left ear and sighed a huge doggy sigh of contentment. As he started to snore, she was lost. At the tender age of twenty-six, Caitlin Cathleen Mulcahy had fallen in love—really in love—for the first time in her life, with a little black fuzzy puppy.

She couldn't bring herself to move the little guy. He must have had a tough day, either getting lost or being dumped. So she continued the soothing movement, beginning at the top of his head and stroking her hand along his spine. The weight of the dog, combined with the heat he gave off, relaxed her until she let her eyes drift closed. Contentment like she'd never experienced before filled her. With a hand to his back, she gave in to exhaustion.

—〰—

Jack fought the panic that had assailed him, arriving home to a semidark house and no one in sight. Following the trail of shredded paper towels and newspaper, he found Caitlin and Jamie asleep in the middle of the living room. The rug was all the way over by the entrance to the hallway, but that wasn't what had him kneeling down beside them. It was the soft sound of the puppy and Cait snoring.

Who knew that the middle Mulcahy sister would make such an inelegant sound when she slept? The realization that he couldn't tell anyone about this hit him like a ton of bricks. People would start to think that he and Cait hooked up and had a thing going on. Looking down at the way she had the dog curled protectively against her, he had no choice but to acknowledge the need that speared through him.

He reached out and brushed the hair out of her eyes, as was becoming a habit whenever he was around Caitlin. She shifted and moaned softly, drawing his attention to her full bottom lip and the curve of her mouth.

He was fighting the urge to press his lips to hers when Jamie woke up. His yip and accompanying wiggling woke Caitlin.

"Hey," she said, shifting the dog off of her so she could roll onto her side. "You're back. How's Honey B.?"

He grinned. "She'll be fine come fall."

Cait looked as if she had absolutely no idea what he was talking about. "What's wrong with her?"

Jack couldn't keep from smiling at her naivety. "Oh, she's not ill."

Cait sat up and rubbed at the back of her head. "That hurts."

The medic in Jack switched gears. "What hurts? What happened?" he said, reaching for her, gently letting his fingers probe the area while he watched her face for an indication of pain. Her sharply indrawn breath sounded as he found a knot at the base of her skull. "Easy, that's quite a bump. How did you fall?" She didn't answer quickly enough to suit him, so he asked another question, "Did you trip on the rug?"

She nodded and winced. "I was trying to get Jamie here to quit chewing on the rug…he had other ideas."

"Ah." Jack pushed to his feet and held out his hand to Caitlin. "Let's just take a quick look at your eyes in the kitchen. The light's better there."

"Probably because you need to get with the program and install fluorescent lights in here. It'll help reduce—"

"My carbon footprint," he finished for her. "Yes, I know. Give me a break and a little time. I just got here." He liked the feel of the calluses on her hand as he tugged gently to get her to follow along behind him. "Are you dizzy?"

"Nope." She let herself be led until they were in the middle of the mess Jamie'd made of the kitchen. "I'm really sorry about all this. I was trying to clean up the pee and then I thought maybe he'd have to do more doggy business and I—"

"It's OK, Cait," he reassured her. "I've gone through the puppy stage a couple of times over the years." He eased her onto a chair and opened the medical bag he'd left on the table when he'd come in. Using the penlight, he checked her pupils. They were the same size. "Good," he said. "They're clear." He also noted that she wasn't slurring her words. When she sighed and told him no, she wasn't nauseous or dizzy, the knot of worry between his shoulder blades eased.

"So you aren't mad at us?"

Charmed that she'd stick by the little stray, he shook his head. "Of course not. He can't help being a puppy anymore than Honey B. can help being dizzy and nauseous for the first trimester."

Cait slowly smiled. "She's going to have a baby too?"

He grinned. "After doing a more thorough exam at my office, I was able to pinpoint early November as her due date."

Caitlin's happiness radiated from deep within her, encompassing the entire room and its occupants—who at the moment happened to be himself and the little black paper shredder. "Wait until Meg hears this!"

"She was with Honey B. when she passed out and called for help."

"Can you beat that?" Cait asked. "Meg and Honey B. pregnant together again! Their kids will all grow up together just like they did." Tears filled her eyes and for a moment Jack wasn't sure what to do. Was her head bothering her, or was it a female thing?

Before he could ask, she brushed them away and grinned up at him. "It's life here in Apple Grove coming full circle."

Her words struck a chord deep within him. He had always wanted to sail anywhere the navy would take him, the seven seas beckoned to him, but now that he'd seen more than he'd imagined and less than he wanted, his gut told him that he was ready to put down roots. Right here in Apple Grove—where he'd caught his first lightning bug in a jar in the pasture behind the Mulcahy house, learned to ride a two-wheeler on the dirt road behind Ned Greely's farm, and kissed Betty Sue Seymour behind the backstop one summer night when his hormones had been raging and her sweet smile had him following along behind her like a puppy.

"Hey—are you all right?"

The grip on his arm brought him back to the present. "Yeah, sorry, I was just remembering—"

"Growing up here," she finished for him. "It's a wonderful place for kids to experience life. Family, friends, neighbors who look out for one another—even if they butt their noses in where they don't belong," she grumbled.

"Like today?" he suggested, waiting for her to look up at him again. He liked watching the myriad emotions on her face.

She blew out a breath and snorted. "Yeah."

He didn't think she crossed her arms in front of her to draw his attention to her slender curves, but while she looked down at Jamie, his gaze lingered for a moment before he found the will to look away.

Now wasn't the time to explore this sudden attraction… he had yet to get a good look at the bump on her head.

"Here," he said, motioning for her to sit. "Let me take a look at that bump."

"I've had worse," she told him.

"I am sure you have," he agreed. "Can you undo your braid? I need to see your scalp."

The man in him chomped at the bit while the physician in him waited for her to comply. Watching the waterfall of strawberry-tinted waves falling to her waist was bound to keep him up nights for the next little while.

Digging deep to shove those inappropriate thoughts aside, he warned, "This might hurt a bit, but I need to palpate the area around the bump to assess the damage."

She tensed. "Ready when you are."

He sifted through the strands until he uncovered the bump. "It didn't break the skin, which accounts for the swelling. You need to ice it."

"Are you done?"

"Just about." He checked the surrounding area, gently letting his fingers search out any other swelling or abnormalities. His fingers felt a thick ridge of skin—possibly stitches from a childhood injury—but nothing else. "Good," he said, resting a hand to her shoulder. "Just sit here while I get the ice bag."

"Don't you have any frozen peas?"

He chuckled at her request. "I'm a little old school, but I think there's still a tray of ice cubes that have small-sized cubes in the freezer. It's easier on the bump. Let me just get the ice bag."

"Don't you have a baggie?"

He looked up at the ceiling and then back at Caitlin. "Who's the doctor here?"

Her face flushed a delicate pink. Charmed by that telltale reaction, he nodded and went to the downstairs closet where his dad used to kept some of his first aid supplies: bandages, old sheets cut and folded ready to be used as a sling—or in a pinch a tourniquet—alcohol, peroxide, and among other things, the insulated ice bag his mom had used to help ease his childhood injuries. His folks must have decided to leave that for him too, knowing he'd need them more than they would.

He returned with the bag, unscrewed the lid, and

filled it with ice cubes. "Keep this on for ten minutes, off for ten. Got it?"

He raised one eyebrow when she didn't answer and waited for her to capitulate.

She frowned up at him and said, "Yeah."

"Want some aspirin?"

"No, I think I'll be fine. It was getting the wind knocked out of me that was the scariest."

He paused halfway to the coffeemaker and turned back toward her. "I should have checked for fractured ribs—"

"I think I'd know if I was hurt anywhere else," she reassured him. "I'm fine, just had the rug pulled out from under me…seriously…when Jamie tugged on it and ran." Before he could chastise the dog, she continued, "But he's just a puppy and doesn't know what he's doing—right?"

He sighed, defeated for the moment. "That's true. If you're going to be helping me watch him and checking up on him, you have to remember that he's a baby—just the fuzzy kind. They get into mischief all of the time and you have to be on your toes, ready for just about anything."

"So you have experience with babies too?"

He nodded. "My Illinois cousins on my mom's side."

"Ah," she said. "That would explain why I don't know them."

He grinned. "The Daly clan is almost as large as the Gannon clan—except for my mom and dad, my cousins all come from large families."

Caitlin's eyes danced with amusement. "Want a sister?"

He couldn't help but join in her laughter. "I think I'll pass on that right now and should remind you that you might miss her once she's gone."

Her expression changed in a heartbeat and he was left wondering if he had been the cause. "You aren't worried about Meg, are you?" The tiny shake of her head was his answer. "Good, then is it Grace?"

He wondered if she'd tell him and then wondered why he cared. He had done more soul searching and thinking in one afternoon then he had in a month of Sundays. Something about this reawakening got to him on a whole different level. He wasn't used to having his world turned upside down. Time to take back control. "Did you call your dad?"

"Yes. You were right. It was a good idea."

"Is he expecting you?"

"Are you kicking me out?"

He fought the urge to smile. "Not yet. You still need to keep the ice on your head for the next little while and I have to rig something to use as a leash for Jamie. I don't want him to run away."

"That's why I spread newspaper by the back door. I was afraid to take him outside without a leash, and I didn't want him to mess up your floor."

They both looked down at the puppy in question. He was contentedly chewing on the bottom chair rung. Jack shook his head. "Another chewer. I should have known."

"I thought all puppies chewed."

He looked at Cait and then his watch before motioning for Cait to take the ice off her head. "Some more than others. Our beagles were champion chewers."

Cait fell silent. He wondered if she was worried about her sister, the dog, Honey B., or her grandfather's truck. All of the above? "You're awfully quiet. Does your head hurt?"

"I have a bit on my mind."

Stingy, but apparently all she was willing to share with him. He liked seeing her in his kitchen, and the way she played with the puppy chipped away at the walls around his heart. He wasn't sure he wanted her to get any closer to the turmoil he kept a tight lid on, but he definitely wanted to find out what it would be like to press his lips to the pulse beat on her neck.

Should he give in to temptation? Would she think he was taking advantage of the situation and her? Way too much thinking going on here…he was normally a man of action. Time to act. "Have you ever seen someone and wondered what it would be like if you got to know them better?"

Her eyes widened for a heartbeat and then her gaze locked on his. "Are you wondering about me, Jack?"

Her softly whispered question set off a conflagration inside of him. Imagining iron bands wrapping around his inner beast to contain it helped him regain control. He drew her to her feet and slid his arms around her waist, pulling her flush against him. He could feel the rapid beat of her heart as he traced her spine with the tips of his fingers, eliciting a shiver. "Cold?"

Cait shook her head, never breaking eye contact. When she licked her lips, he had to fight to keep from moaning aloud. He wanted. No point in trying to pick apart and separate what he wanted from Caitlin. He liked to keep things simple—he wanted it all.

Textures, tastes, and long, lingering kisses that would lead to soft moans of pleasure—Jack was in serious trouble. He'd only spent a few hours with her and he was imagining them together, could see it so clearly. He never moved that fast…but then again, he'd never met anyone quite like Caitlin Mulcahy before.

Best to retreat for the moment, he thought as he let his hands fall back to his sides. He could fan the flames the next time he saw her and see where it might lead. Either way, he intended to begin a relationship with Cait— hopefully one with all of the trimmings—but he didn't want to push her into something she wasn't ready for.

God, he hoped she didn't need too much time.

"I'd better let you go." He wondered if his voice sounded as raspy to her as it did to him. Clearing his throat he added, "I've got to see about that temporary leash so he can go outside before settling down for the night."

Her eyes changed in hue from a brilliant and sparkling emerald to a pale yellow-green, the color of new grass that had been covered with a late spring snow. Had his need to keep a lid on these new feelings for Caitlin forced him to be too abrupt with her? Had he hurt her feelings in the process?

"I should be getting on home too." She bent down to rub Jamie's upturned face. "Be good for Jack."

The little dog jumped up and nipped the knee of her jeans in response. When it tore, she shrugged. "Well, they were a bit worn anyway and I needed a new pair of shorts."

"Hey, I need your number."

She smiled and gave it to him. Something warm and wonderful moved through him as their eyes met and held. The hesitation and uncertainty were gone, replaced by the laughter in her eyes. Jack had always been drawn to kindness and a giving heart.

Caitlin Mulcahy's kindness shone through when she

stopped to lend a hand, thinking he'd been stranded at the side of the road and needed help. Watching her melt before his eyes as she hesitantly reached out to pet the fuzzy black face of the pup they rescued only added to her appeal and called to him on so many different levels.

Jack could hear his mother's oft-used advice in his head: *"Keep an open mind and heart because sometimes love comes softly and blooms slowly. Best you be ready, Jackie boy."*

Chapter 4

CAITLIN THOUGHT ABOUT JACK AND JAMIE ALL THE way home. Sparks of excitement still skittered up and down her spine as she remembered the feel of his fingers sifting through her hair. Her heart conveniently forgot that he'd been in physician mode, checking the area around the bump, while his strong, capable fingers stroked the back of her head.

Had she really thought she knew all about him because Meg went to school with him, Miss Trudi used to read snippets from his letters back home, and she'd seen him whenever he was home on leave? The man who'd limped toward her worried about a fuzzy little black puppy was a complete mystery to her. But if she were honest with herself, she hoped he wouldn't be for long.

She drove the long way home, past the turn off onto Goose Pond Road, so she could go by the McCormack Farm.

Dog Hollow Road was still farther up, and right before the intersection was proof of the poor choice she'd made that morning, parked at Bob's Gas and Gears. She cringed thinking of her grandfather's truck stuck inside Bob's paint booth.

One thought led to another and soon she was dissecting her father's reaction to the news. Why wasn't he more upset? A few years ago, she'd have been grounded for life...well, she wasn't a teenager now, but she had expected more of a blast from his formidable Irish temper.

She sighed as she turned left onto Cherry Valley Road, wishing she'd taken Jack up on the silent question in his eyes. That perfect moment when he'd drawn her close against his powerful chest and bent his head…as if he were going to kiss her…but then he pulled back.

Distracted, she wondered if their first kiss would have been tentative, a mere brush of lips, or lush and full, tempting her resolve not to get lost in his heady, masculine scent or the taste of his mouth. She tingled from the top of her head to the tips of her toes.

How could she have spent the whole of her adolescent existence thinking Jack Gannon was too old for her? The memory of the deep dimple that formed when he smiled down at her caused her heart to flutter. "And that is the reason it is probably best that he didn't kiss me." It was all happening too fast and tangled up with their rescuing Jamie. She sighed as she turned right onto Peat Moss Road. Going slower than normal, she drew in one calming breath after another, hoping to cool the fire that ignited just thinking of being held in Jack's arms, imagining how his kiss would be…how his lips would mold to hers…

She gripped the steering wheel and turned into her driveway and her earlier worry of having to face her father resurfaced—her dad was waiting for her. Pulling up to the barn, she put it in park, braced herself for the onslaught, and got out.

"Hi, Pop. What are you doing out here?"

"Waiting for you."

"I thought you weren't mad."

"I'm not, but I wanted to talk to you."

The fact that she'd disappointed him had her mouth drying up and her tongue tying into a knot waiting to hear what else he wanted to tell her.

"Just one moment's distraction while driving had that driver running the red light…causing the head-on that took your mom from us."

Cait's throat tightened. She would never forget that awful time.

"I cannot lose any of my girls that way too, Cait…it would kill me."

"But, Pop, it wasn't that serious."

"It could be next time. Don't let there be a next time, all right?"

Cait sighed and walked into her father's open arms. "I promise."

He folded his arms around her and hugged her to him. "That's my girl." He pulled back and kissed her forehead. "I'm going out. Don't wait up."

From the way he hurried over to his truck, she knew he was going to Mary Murphy's. He and the widow had been keeping company since Edie and Bill's wedding three years ago. She wondered, not for the first time, if she and her sisters should interfere and push him to admit his feelings for Mary. They all liked her, but their dad was moving slower than molasses in January.

As his taillights disappeared, she couldn't help but wonder if he was afraid to commit, or if it was because of Cait and her sisters' initial reaction—or maybe it was something much deeper. No matter if he kept it quiet for a while longer or not, she was glad he had someone in

his life. Thinking of her mom, she believed in her heart
that everyone deserved to be happy…for however long
they were alive to enjoy it.

The soft glow of the light by the back door and the
one on the stovetop was a welcoming sight, proof that
he'd thought of her and didn't want her fumbling around
in the dark. Since Grace was still out, she left the stove
light on and trudged upstairs.

Her dad's words haunted her until she began to wonder how different she would be if her mom had survived
the accident. She had always felt she had missed out
when she watched her friends receive hugs and kisses
from their moms.

"It isn't Meg's fault that she wasn't mom," she grumbled, flicking on her bedroom light. "Heaven knows she
did the best she could with Gracie and me…but it just
wasn't the same as a hug from mom."

Feeling abysmally sorry for herself, she changed out
of her work clothes, grabbed her pj's, and headed for
the shower. Standing beneath the hot spray, she didn't
try to stop the tears that threatened whenever she started
to think of life without her mom. Alone with no one to
hear, she wept for the little girl who had missed out on
those hugs, kisses, and baking lessons—and then for the
adolescent who missed out on those talks about boys in
school and butterflies in her stomach.

Finally, emotionally drained, she shut off the water
and got out. Weary to the bone, she lay down but
couldn't find her sleep—something her grandmother
Mulcahy used to say when they were small. She needed
to call Meg, but knew her sister was probably asleep by
now. Cait's nephews and her sister's pregnancy were

taking a lot out of Meg. She couldn't talk to Grace because she was out on a date, and she was too tired to call Peggy, who would insist on sharing the latest gossip with her.

There wasn't anyone else she could talk to, was there?

A tall broad-shouldered man with auburn hair came to mind. "Could I call Jack?" Unsure, she hesitated with her hand on her phone. When it buzzed beneath her hand, she jolted. "Hello?"

"Hi, Cait, it's Jack."

Having a connection to someone when she'd been floundering amidst remembered grief had relief flowing through her. "Hey, everything OK?"

"I was just going to ask you that." The deep voice on the other end of the line soothed her. "I just wanted to check up on you. Are you sure you're not feeling any aftereffects from hitting your head?"

His concern wrapped around her like a hug. "Only a slight headache. It's been a long day with some really great highs…and some pretty crappy lows."

"I know what you mean. Today has been interesting."

"Do you want to tell me about it?"

It was as easy as that. She asked and Jack, hesitatingly at first, unloaded some of his burden while she listened. They talked for nearly an hour about his day, Jamie, and then her day. At last her body relaxed, the tension from the day's events slowly sliding away.

"Thank you, Jack."

"For?"

"Letting me share your day," she said quietly, wishing she were brave enough to tell him that she'd had a mini meltdown in the shower and had been close to falling apart when she first answered his call. "I needed to talk, and you're a great listener."

"I think you have it backward, Cait. You're the one who listened when I started talking about my day."

She smiled at the idea. "So we're both grateful."

"And we both needed to talk," Jack said. He hesitated, then asked, "Can you stop by tomorrow around noon to feed Jamie and let him out?"

"Absolutely...during lunch and again on my way home. Where's he sleeping tonight?"

His soft chuckle added to the unsettling effect he had on her. Then, he totally distracted her when he said, "In the middle of my bed."

Their shared laughter had her day ending far better than it would have without it. "I'll call you tomorrow after I've taken care of Jamie."

There was a slight pause before he cleared his throat and said, "I can make a late dinner for us if you wait for me. I should be home around eight o'clock."

Her heart picked up the beat as her stomach filled with butterflies at the prospect of being with Jack again. "Why don't you let me make supper for you tomorrow? You can cook dinner another time."

"I'd like that very much. Good night, Caitlin."

The sound of her name resonating through the tiny speaker in her hand had her inner child dancing a jig. "Night, Jack."

With a sigh of contentment, Caitlin turned off the light and snuggled beneath the covers. Her last thought before she closed her eyes was being held in his arms and watching Jack's dimple wink at her as his lips pressed softly against her own.

A few miles away, Jack hung up his phone and smiled, pleased with himself that he'd reached out to Caitlin. It sounded as if she'd been eager to talk to him. They'd made a connection—a solid one. It might just be the foundation they'd needed to build a relationship on.

One thing was certain, he intended to see more of Caitlin. "Hey…no bites!"

But the little ball of fur cuddled against his side wasn't listening; he was too busy lining up Jack's oblique muscle—as if to pounce on it—and Jack knew what would be next—the puppy would nip at it again.

"OK," he said, picking the pup up so they were eye level. "There are a few house rules that you're going to have to learn."

The puppy squirmed and tossed himself around until Jack had no handhold and had to let go. Jamie landed on Jack's abs and proceeded to pounce on Jack's chest before settling in to chew on his chest hair.

With a huff, he held the dog like a football and got up to grab a shirt. "Rule number one: never bite the hand that feeds you."

Jamie looked up at him, a serious expression in his big brown eyes. "OK, I'll give you that one—you weren't biting my hand, but still it's the principle of the thing." Setting the dog on the foot of the bed, he pulled his favorite PT shirt—a gray T-shirt that simply said navy on it in capital letters—over his head. "Don't chew off any body hair while I'm sleeping, got it?"

Jamie lunged at the hem of his shirt and Jack sighed. "It's gonna be a long night."

Sliding beneath the covers, he turned off the light and heard a little doggy whimper. His heart went out to the little stray. "Come here, boy."

Jamie leapt onto his chest and began to lick his face from forehead to chin. Once the dog quieted down, he settled in the curve of Jack's arm and within minutes was softly snoring.

"Night, you little devil dog." As the warmth of the little dog seeped into Jack's side, he closed his eyes and fell asleep.

—◁〜▷—

Mary Murphy was waiting on her front porch swing. "Oh, Joe, what happened? You look awful."

"Sometimes bad memories sneak up on me."

She patted the seat beside her. "Let's just rock a bit. When you're ready, we can talk about it, OK?"

Joe nodded and sat down on the swing, and Mary settled in the circle of his arms. Pushing off with one foot, he breathed a sigh of relief as the rhythmic motion started to relax him.

"Did you ever wonder what you did right in life to deserve another chance at happiness after you thought your world had come to an end?"

Mary leaned her full weight against him. "I remember lying awake at night wishing I could die…it hurt so much to be the one left behind."

Joe swallowed, but the lump in his throat remained.

"But I guess the Lord had other plans for me," she whispered.

Clearing his throat, Joe said, "I know he did. You've given me a reason to keep believing in love, Mary."

She turned in his arms, braced her hands against his chest, and stared up at him. Humbled that everything he felt for her was reflected back at him, Joe kissed her.

When he came up for air, her eyes burned with desire for him. "Come inside, Joe." Offering her hand, she waited for him to wrap his around it before leading him through the house and up the stairs.

Chapter 5

THE WARMTH OF THE SPRING SUN RADIATED THROUGH the diner's front window as Cait slid onto the red vinyl stool.

Peggy set a mug of coffee in front of her friend. "How are things this morning?"

Cait smiled. "Good."

"Your dad isn't mad?"

"He was upset, going over the what-ifs."

Peggy wiped the counter on both sides of where Cait was sitting before motioning for Cait to lift up her elbows and mug. When she did, Peggy cleaned the spot and motioned for her to set her coffee back down.

"So." Peggy's gaze locked with Cait's. "Want to hear the latest?"

Cait nodded and her friend looked to the left and then the right, satisfied that the other two patrons were too far away to hear what she was about to share with Caitlin. Leaning close, she whispered, "Honey B. is expecting again!"

Caitlin shrugged. "I know."

Peggy's mouth fell open. "How? I just found out this morning."

"I knew last night."

"And you didn't tell me?"

When Cait remained silent, Peggy relented and said, "Well, I guess you didn't really have time, what with being over at Doc's and all."

Caitlin's mind returned to the night before when Jack had called and suddenly her world had been right again. Everything had been back in perspective and the things that she'd done wrong didn't seem quite so bad.

"You OK?" Peggy asked when Cait remained silent.

"What? Yeah, just thinking." She'd never felt quite like this before. It was scary, it was exhilarating…and she just wanted to hold the feeling close to her heart for a little while longer. She'd hate to jump the gun and have been wrong about how Jack felt about her.

When she looked back up, Peggy had a speculative look in her eyes. "Must be something if you're not willing to tell me about it."

Knowing that was just what her friend intended, Cait was smiling when she said, "We aren't in high school anymore."

"We used to tell each other everything," Peggy said with a laugh. "I miss those days."

"Hey, Miss Peggy," one of the customers called. "Can I have a refill?"

"Absolutely," she answered. "Be right there." Turning back to Cait, she said, "We'll catch up later."

As Cait stood, Peggy added, "Keep me posted on that tall, good-looking doctor. OK?"

Cait smiled and her cell phone rang. "That's probably Gracie. Talk to you later, Peg."

"Bye."

She was hitting talk as she waved and walked out the door. "Hey, Sis. What's up?"

"We have a cancellation and two more jobs that just came in."

"Grace, I'm only one—"

"Woman," her sister finished for her. "Yeah, yeah. I know. Mrs. Winter canceled—she said something about waiting until Meg could come by."

Caitlin laughed as she got into the car and found her earpiece. "Hold on...switching to hands-free." There was a moment of silence and then Cait said, "OK, I'm back. Mrs. Winter loves chatting with Meg and probably woke up with the urge to bake another cherry pie."

Her sister laughed softly. "You do know our customers."

"Who else called this morning?" Putting the car in drive, she headed off to her first appointment while listening to the rhythmic tap as her sister brought up her spreadsheet for the day.

"Mr. Sweeney and Mrs. Doyle."

"How is Mr. Sweeney feeling today?"

As she drove, her sister filled her in on the health of one of their oldest customers. "His arthritis is acting up again. It's too bad his sons moved to opposite coasts, and neither one wants to move back to Apple Grove, but luckily his cousin still lives here—and his cousin's wife works for Doc Gannon."

Signaling to make the left onto Eden Church Road, Cait agreed. "I just don't understand why anyone would want to leave a beautiful little town like this."

Grace snorted, "Keyword: little."

"Before you get started, let's just agree to disagree."

Grace laughed. "By the way, I heard from Cindy Harrington over at the sheriff's office that you and Doc rescued a puppy last night and that Doc asked Mitch to put the word out."

Cait's stomach clenched. "Really?" Jack hadn't

mentioned he was going to do that this morning. *Was Jamie too much for him last night?*

"I think it's wonderful that Doc is taking the time to see if the poor little thing is a stray."

The feeling in her stomach eased. "His name is Jamie."

"Do tell, Sis. What else happened while you were helping Doc take care of the little guy?"

More than I'm ready to tell anyone. Her life had changed irrevocably yesterday…and in more ways than one. Knowing her sister would keep at her until she told her something, she told her about Jamie shredding the paper towel.

They were laughing when Grace had an incoming call and had to go. "Talk to you later."

"Bye, Gracie."

She never had a chance to ask her about Mrs. Doyle or what Mr. Sweeney needed. She'd have to ask Grace when she stopped by the shop after lunch. Guaranteed, she'd need more supplies for those two new jobs—the car just didn't have enough room for all of her tools and repair parts for a full day's worth of jobs.

Focused on a new day with new expectations, she was already looking forward to lunchtime when she'd need to swing by Jack's house to check on Jamie. She should have a few minutes then to text Grace and get her the list of parts she planned to take with her—just in case Grace was away from her desk when Cait got to the shop. Lord help her if she didn't tell Grace before she took the parts from their inventory. Thinking of the numerous trips she'd have to make back and forth from the job sites to the shop had her sighing. But she'd have to get used to tucking stuff in the trunk and backseat of the car she'd be driving for the next little while.

Crossing over the railroad tracks, she turned right onto Route 13. Mentally going over how she'd need to replace the broken window at the back of the Apple Grove United Methodist Church, she was ready when she pulled into the parking lot.

"Good morning, Caitlin!"

She looked up and smiled. "Good morning, Reverend Smith. Am I late?" He usually wasn't waiting outside for her when she arrived on the job.

"Not at all. It's a glorious day, and I was communing with nature and my boss."

She grinned at his reference, and from the way her pastor was smiling back at her, it was just the reaction he had intended. Her gaze swept the parking lot and the grouping of shade and fir trees arcing around the back of the church in a protective sweep of green. "How's Mrs. Smith feeling today?"

His smile slipped. "Better."

Relief filled her. "She's nearly finished with her chemo, isn't she?"

"One more to go, next week."

"She has everyone in town praying for her."

He reached out and patted her hand. "We're both so grateful."

"So," she said, hooking her arm through his. "Which little rascal knocked the softball through your office window this time?"

He grinned as he launched into the tale of how little eight-year-old Danny Jones had confessed his crime. "They hadn't meant to break my window."

Caitlin laughed. "He's just acting out because his dad's overseas and his mom has her hands full."

"Which is why I'm not going to go too hard on the boy," Reverend Smith said. "Besides, he has his uncle, Deputy Jones, lending a hand whenever he can so I know he'll probably have a chat with his nephew as well."

"My dad always complained about raising three girls, but I've seen what Mrs. Jones goes through with those four active, little boys." Cait shook her head. "The poor woman is always tired."

"But doesn't complain."

Cait grinned. "I probably would if I were her."

Her pastor was smiling as he opened the door to the manse—his home for as long as he was assigned to their church. "I cleaned up the glass and put up a piece of cardboard…didn't want any wildlife taking up residence in my office."

His reference to a similar repair she'd made a few months ago had the both of them chuckling. "The look on Beatrice Wallace's face whenever she tells the story about that poor little raccoon is worth the tongue-lashing that usually follows for reminding her of that awful day," Cait said.

"Why she doesn't believe any animal should live indoors is beyond my comprehension," he said, leading the way down the hallway to his office.

"Isn't it funny that Mitch loves animals and his older sister doesn't?"

"Quite a hole, isn't it?"

Cait walked over to the window and pulled down the cardboard. "Dead center. Are you sure this was an accident?"

The good reverend nodded. "Danny and I have already had a heart-to-heart about playing ball behind the manse."

"Especially when there's a ball field practically in their backyard."

"Yes," he agreed. "His mother's taken away his bicycle privileges for the next week. That boy is all over town on that thing." He was smiling when he said, "I'd better let you get to work. I'm sure you have a full schedule, what with your sister cutting her hours again."

Cait looked over her shoulder and saw him smiling. "She's feeling better and isn't that awful shade of green anymore."

"Glad to hear it. I'll be in the outdoor chapel if you need me."

"Thanks."

Envy for the time her pastor would be spending in the quiet of the fir-lined chapel was quickly dismissed as she took out her putty knife and scored the glazing that held the window in place. A short while later, she was back in the parking lot, easing the sheet of glass she had wrapped in a moving blanket from her backseat.

"Good thing it was a small window." A larger one wouldn't have fit in her car.

She was just applying the thin layer of glaze when the Reverend returned. "Ah," he said with a sigh. "Now that's more like it. Hole-free glass."

"It'll keep unwanted visitors out. If only it worked as a softball repellent too."

His smile faltered. "I don't have the money set aside for the repair—" he began.

"Don't worry about it." She'd dug deep into

her own pockets when the call first went out that Mrs. Smith had cancer and would be undergoing chemotherapy—the whole town had. The medical bills were astronomical. "Apple Grove residents take care of their own."

He nodded, a suspicious film of moisture filling his eyes. Clearing his throat, he said, "I still intend to pay you—"

"Not going to happen, Reverend," she told him. "Besides, Mrs. Jones already paid for the repair. Danny's going to be working off his debt starting this Saturday by helping my dad sweep out the shop—who knows what Deputy Jones will have to say about it or whether or not he'll add to Danny's list of chores."

Reverend Smith asked, "Didn't he break the window at the library when he was Danny's age?"

Cait shook her head. "I don't remember. You'll have to ask Miss Trudi. She has a mind like a steel trap."

"I think I will. Danny is doing enough penance for one softball. See you Sunday?"

"I'll be there."

"Good. I need to check on my wife."

"Please give her my best," Caitlin told him.

He squeezed her hand and was gone. She swept up the dried out bits of glazing that had held the old window in place and was on the road ten minutes later.

Her next stop would take her to the outskirts of town. Checking her watch, she calculated the time left and the two jobs she needed to squeeze in before taking a break. If luck held, she'd finish on time and be able to stop by Jack's house and check on Jamie as close to noon as possible.

The morning hadn't gone as smoothly as Jack had planned. Jamie had fallen asleep first last night but apparently didn't need as much sleep as Jack. And judging from the cold puddle of pee in front of the back door, the dog no longer needed to go outside.

"Damn it." Jack shook his foot and nearly lost his balance when he leaned his weight on his bad leg. Without his persistence and daily exercise routine to strengthen his leg, it might have buckled. It was usually stiff when he first woke up and beyond tired at the end of the day. Grabbing hold of the door frame, he kept himself from going down. "I guess I'll have to set my alarm a little earlier."

Armed with a new roll of paper towels, he cleaned up the mess and had the coffee filling the pot by the time he noticed Jamie whining and looking for someplace to squat.

"Hold it." He grabbed the puppy and wrenched open the door.

Jamie licked Jack's face, distracting him until he noticed the smell…his first clue that the dog hadn't been able to hold it. Looking down he laughed. "Guess you really had to go."

He set the dog on the grass and sighed. Although Jack really needed that first cup of coffee, he knew his new roommate would need to eat first to keep him distracted long enough for Jack to kick-start his day with caffeine.

Jamie was lapping up water by the time Jack had scrambled three eggs and was transferring them to a plate. The sound of water gushing out had him looking over his shoulder. Sure enough, Jamie had peed by the back door again.

Jamie tilted his head to one side as if to say, "I made it to the door again!"

"Too bad the door was closed." He'd have to rig something up if Jamie was going to be living with him; the possibility that someone was looking for the little dog wasn't something he wanted to consider and hoped he'd never have to worry about.

"OK," he said, picking the puppy up. "You're coming with me while I take a shower."

Anticipating how the hot water would ease the dull ache and stiffness in his leg, he closed his bedroom door and told the dog to sit. Mistakenly thinking the dog would obey, he left him there to get cleaned up. The muffled thud and yelp that followed had him shutting off the water, reaching for the towel, and yanking the door open.

"What's going…" His words trailed off as his gaze swept the disaster that used to be his bedroom. The comforter was on the floor and one side had a huge tear in it. The bedside table was on its side and the bowl he kept his change in was in pieces amidst quarters, dimes, nickels, and pennies.

Where was Jamie? The door was still closed so the dog had to be somewhere in the room. "Here, boy," he called, tucking the towel around his waist and stepping over the mangled comforter and around the change.

The closet door was still closed, so the dog had to be under the bed. Getting down on his hands and knees, he peered beneath the mahogany four-poster that had been in the family for a generation. Spotting the little guy, he made a point to keep his tone quiet and even. "Hey, come on out."

The dog was shaking. "I bet the table hitting the floor scared you." Lying on his stomach, he reached a hand toward Jamie. "It's OK, boy," he soothed.

Jamie licked his hand and let Jack coax him out from under the bed. "We'd better go over those rules again, boy."

But the dog wasn't paying any attention; he was too busy licking and nibbling Jack's chin. "I can probably barricade you in the kitchen for today and pick up a few baby gates on my way home."

By the time he cleaned up what was left of the bowl and collected the change, Jamie was ready to play. "I've got to get dressed first," he told the dog. His firm tone must have registered, because the pup sat down and waited patiently while Jack smoothed the comforter on the bed and got dressed.

"Hey!" he chuckled. "Give me back my shoe!" And as quickly as that, the chase was on. By the time he caught the dog, the dog had mangled one of his good shoes, leaving Jack no option but to wear his work boots.

"Serves me right for not thinking I'd need more than one pair of good shoes."

Stepping into the boots, he tied them and stood. Despite the puppy's antics, his left leg felt pretty good. The work boots were far more comfortable than his dress shoes. "Maybe I should thank that little force of destruction for ripping up my shoes so I had to wear these."

Jamie trailed after him until he saw the card table come out of the hall closet and slide in front of the doorway. As if he sensed his play area had just been downsized, the dog hung his head and waited for Jack to finish.

"Now," he said, going down on his good knee. "It's

like this, boy. I have to go to work. I have patients to see." Jamie licked the back of Jack's hand. "You be good," Jack told him, "and before you know it, Caitlin will be here to feed you and let you out."

He hated leaving the dog alone but had no other option today. His appointment book was full, and he wouldn't have time to keep an eye on Jamie.

A glance at the clock told him he would be on time if he left right then. "I'll see you tonight, boy. Kiss Caitlin for me." As soon as he said the words, warmth slid through his system.

He shook his head as he closed the front door.

Jack thought about Caitlin...all the way to town.

By the time he was halfway through his morning, he had five minutes to down a cup of lukewarm coffee before the next of a half-dozen patients arrived.

"Well now," he said, squatting down so he was eye-level with the youngest of the Doyle children. "Your mommy said that you have a rash on your belly."

Six-year-old Christina Doyle nodded.

He deliberately kept his voice soothing and his eyes on the little girl's face while he asked, "Can you show it to me?"

She lifted her pink T-shirt. "See?"

He studied the rash and asked, "Does your throat hurt?"

"Not that much."

He looked up at Mrs. Doyle. "Has she had a fever?"

"Just one night, but then she's been fine. What do you think the rash is from?"

"Let's do a strep test and rule that out." When he'd taken the swab, he said, "Now I have some special stickers. Would you like fairies or kittens?"

"Fairies," Christina said solemnly.

"If you and your mommy will just have a seat in the waiting room by Mrs. Sweeney, I will let you know the results in a few moments. The rapid test only takes ten to fifteen minutes. I will still have the sample sent out for a follow-up culture, just to be on the safe side."

"Come on, Christina," her mother said. "Let's read the book we brought."

Settled on the sofa in his waiting room, Mrs. Doyle's raven head bent toward her daughter's. The gentle way she stroked her daughter's back and brushed a lock of hair from her child's eyes filled Jack's heart with warmth. He remembered the times his mother had rubbed her hand up and down his back when he'd been ill as a child. It spoke of tender feelings…it spoke of a mother's love.

"Doc Gannon?"

He turned toward the deep voice. "Ahh, Mr. Turner," he said, greeting the older gentleman. "How is Rudy?"

At the mention of his son's name, the man smiled. "He's doing well, back home on leave. He's decided the navy is the life for him."

Jack's gut clenched remembering the reasons he hadn't extended his tour. There were times when he had absolutely loved the camaraderie of the navy and still missed it—but then he'd wake up during the middle of a violent thunderstorm reliving the horror of those moments the last time they'd been under fire.

Before his mind could replay the events of that day, he pushed those thoughts aside and focused on his friend's father. "So what brings you here today?"

"Did something to my ankle."

"Let's have a look." The older man's ankle was swollen and tender to the touch. "Can you move it at all?"

From the look on Mr. Turner's face when he tried to rotate his ankle, Jack suspected it was more than a bad sprain. He sat down on the stool with wheels on it. "Now," he said, rolling over to his terminal. "You need to have that ankle X-rayed to make certain there is no fracture." Writing the prescription for an X-ray, he handed it to the man. "One of these days, I'll have an X-ray machine, but until I do, it's only about a forty-five-minute ride to Newark. Do you have someone who can drive you?"

"As soon as my wife gets home from work, she can drive me."

"Good," Jack told him, handing him the prescription. "Until then, don't put your full weight on it. I'm going to wrap it for you. I have a pair of crutches you can borrow until you're healed."

Once Mr. Turner left, he checked the rapid test for little Christina.

"Just as I suspected." The test read positive.

"Mrs. Doyle," he said, walking into the waiting room. "The test is positive. I've already called in a prescription for Christina for amoxicillin at Weir's Drug Store. They're taking care of it for you right now."

"Thank you, Doc," she said, taking his hand in hers. "Come on, Christina. Time to go."

The little girl held up her fairy stickers and waved at Jack. "Thank you, Doc."

He grinned. "Be sure to take all of your medicine, Christina."

"Yes, sir."

He felt older than the pines surrounding his parent's home, and they'd been there long before Jack had been born. In spite of that, he was smiling as the ladies left.

"She's such a dear," Mrs. Sweeney said.

His office quiet for the moment, Jack had time to enter information into the charts of the patients he'd seen during the day. He still had a few hours to go before he was finished for the day, and he hoped that Jamie had behaved for Caitlin.

As soon as the thought of her popped into his mind, he couldn't concentrate. It was a good thing his day was almost over. Struggling to keep his mind on the job at hand, he decided that a call to see how things had been at his home when Cait stopped to check on Jamie was not out of the ordinary.

"Caitlin," he said quietly, when she answered his call. "How's little Jameson?"

"How attached were you to that card table?"

He noticed the laughter in her voice. "What happened?"

Giggles turned to chuckles, and chuckles to belly laughs before she finally started to wind down again enough to answer him. "The vinyl top is shredded and two of the legs have been gnawed on past recognition. Maybe you should have faced the vinyl top side out."

He didn't know what to say. Cait must have taken his silence for a bad thing because she was quick to add, "He peed on the newspapers by the back door, and did his other doggy business outside as soon as I let him out after feeding him. He's really smart."

Clearing his throat he managed, "I wasn't thinking about him chewing it at all...just as a way to block the doorway so he wouldn't get loose. By the way, I checked with Mitch, and no one in town has called about a missing dog. He even posted a notice on the town's website, but no hits yet."

"Then maybe he's not lost."

The hope in her voice was music to his ears, because if he was going to keep this puppy, he needed all the help he could get caring for him while he was at work. Depending on how busy schedules got, he might have to ask one more person to help, but he'd think about that later. They were OK for now. "So, did he actually eat any of the tabletop?"

"When I cleaned up the shredded mess, it seemed like most of it was there. If he did eat some, it wasn't much...besides, I don't think it tasted as good as the busy bone I left him with."

"You bought him dog treats?"

"I figured he needed a treat for staying home alone and probably being scared. Murphy's Market had some...oh and I picked up some puppy chow until you've had a chance to buy some more chicken or chop meat to boil up for the dog."

"I'll pay you back—"

"Don't even think about it. We said we'd both take care of him until we found out if he was lost or a stray needing a home. I'm sure he'll need something besides the bright red collar and leash that he's very proud of."

Jack's day suddenly seemed endless. The need to be with Caitlin—and Jamie—filled him. He had been tempted to kiss her last night, and couldn't decide today if he was the smartest man in the universe or dumb as a stump. If he asked his friends, the answers would be equally divided. Half of his friends were bachelors, like himself, and the other half were happily married.

Married. Now that was a word that didn't often enter his mind unless he was about to attend the wedding of a family member, friend, or neighbor. No siree, Bob…not a word he thought of often.

"You didn't buy him a collar too, did you?" Caitlin asked.

"No," he reassured her. "And even if I had, it wouldn't have been money wasted. It's always good to have a spare. Jake chewed through a couple of collars when he was little, until we realized we had to buy one that was a perfect fit, so that there wasn't a piece that he could grab onto and chew."

"Do you remember Brutus?" Cait asked him.

He smiled. "The McCormacks' boxer? Yes, I do. He was a walking garbage disposal." The bells on the front door rang. "I'm not sure if Mrs. Sweeney is back from running errands yet. Can you hang on one sec? Be right back." He put the call on hold as his office door opened. "Mrs. Green," he greeted his next patient. "Right on time. Come on back to the examining room. I'll be right with you." After settling her in one of three examining rooms, he walked over to the reception desk and picked up line one. "Sorry to keep you waiting, Cait, but she's not back yet and my three o'clock just arrived. Are you still making dinner for us tonight?"

"I am but undecided about what to make. After walking in on the scene of the crime—your poor table, I'm thinking it should be something quick but packed with protein, so that we'll have energy."

Desire sparked and began to simmer as he thought

of what he'd like to use that energy for. Unable to help himself, he asked, "Energy to do what?"

"Tire out Jamie. What did you think I meant?"

"It'll keep," he told her. And it would until tonight, when he'd make the first move. He couldn't spend another night wondering what it would be like kissing Caitlin…he'd seen firsthand how short life could be.

"Oh," her breath sounded a bit thready. He couldn't have been more pleased with her reaction to what he had in mind. "Jamie should be fine until I get back to your house around six thirty. I want to stop home and get cleaned up. You don't want to know where my hands have been today."

He didn't bother to echo her last statement. "See you at eight."

Straightening up, he walked over and knocked on the door to room one.

"Come in."

"So, Mrs. Green," he said, closing the door behind him. "What brings you here today?"

Chapter 6

CAITLIN FELT AS IF SHE'D BEEN SITTING ON A KEG OF dynamite all day and couldn't explain why. The feeling propelled her through her day, excitement building inside her.

"For what?" Random thoughts went zinging through her brain in time with the pulse beat of something a bit more primal than her heart—and Jack Gannon was the reason.

Hurrying through her shower, she ran through the recipes stored in her head and decided on pasta primavera. "Quick, easy, and inexpensive." If she was going to be adding dog food and treats to her budget, she'd better start economizing now.

The urge to wear something pretty was vetoed by the need to wear something durable. After all, she'd probably be sitting on the floor with Jamie once she got dinner started. But just because she had to be practical didn't mean she couldn't wear her good jeans with a body-hugging top.

Rifling through her drawers, she found the one she was looking for. Pulling the butter yellow scoop-neck shirt over her head, she frowned at the super-snug fit. "I know I haven't gained any weight—oh crap. Grace did the laundry last."

Note to self: yell at Grace later and remind her to use cold water and low heat to keep from shrinking my clothes.

Fifteen minutes later, she was pulling up in front of

Murphy's Market. List in hand, she opened the door to see Mary Murphy flirting with her father by the counter. When she heard her father's soft laughter, she smiled.

"Hi, Mary," she called out. "Hi, Pop."

"Caitlin," Mary replied. "You look lovely in that color. Are you going out tonight?"

"She hasn't gone out since Meg cut back her hours at the shop," her father chimed in as he smiled down at her. "Mary's right. I like you in yellow."

"I'm helping Jack take care of Jamie—"

"He's the little puppy they found last night," her father told Mary.

Cait enjoyed watching the subtle emotions flitting across Mary's face whenever Cait's dad spoke. The Mulcahy sisters were in wholehearted agreement on the subject of Mary and their dad continuing to date—and how their dad seemed to be moving just a little too slowly. "I just need to pick up a few things. Talk to you later, Pop."

"Let me help you," Mary offered. "Be right back, Joseph."

Mary trailed her fingertips along her father's shoulder, down to his elbow. *Maybe he isn't moving as slowly as I thought.* Cait would be calling Meg the first chance she got to give her the update.

"What do you need?"

"Fresh veggies and pasta."

"Right this way."

Cait thanked Mary for her help and waved to her dad as he closed the door behind her. Something told her to look over her shoulder, and when she did, she saw her father smiling as he turned the *open* sign around to *closed* and took Mary into his arms.

As she was closing the door and firing up the engine, she saw Susie Sanders, Apple Grove's local Realtor, drive slowly past Murphy's Market. "That does it. It'll be all over town or emblazoned across the water tower by tomorrow."

She had her earpiece in and dialed Meg. "Meg! Guess who I just saw at Murphy's Market?"

"Pop," Meg answered.

"How did you know?"

"Honey B. just called."

"Well, I hope he and Mary are ready for the gossip and speculation to start."

"Because…?" Meg said.

"Susie Sanders saw them too."

The sisters shared a laugh before Meg said, "Pop deserves a second chance at happiness—with all the trimmings."

"I know. I think so too." The rest of what she wanted to say got caught behind the lump forming in her throat. "I've gotta go," she told Meg. "Can you call Gracie for me?"

Meg agreed. "I will. You know that if I wait, my little darlings will distract me and it'll be bedtime before I remember, and that'll be too late."

"My nephews are a handful, but an adorable distraction," Cait said before adding, "You know how cranky Grace gets if she has to hear the latest about one of us over at the diner."

"Have fun tonight," Meg told her.

"I'm babysitting a puppy until Jack gets home."

"Uh-huh. Jack's a good man, Sis. Give him a chance."

"Thanks. Talk to you later."

Disconnecting, she turned right onto Eden Church and drove to Jack's house on autopilot. The first thing she heard as she pulled into the driveway was the mournful howl of a lonely puppy.

"Poor little dog." Grabbing the bag of groceries, she got out and headed for the back door. She let herself in and set the bag on the counter, relieved that the dresser she'd blocked the doorway with that afternoon had kept him corralled. Jamie was jumping for joy when he realized he had someone to play with.

"Easy, sweetie. Sit," she reinforced the command with a gentle nudge to his doggie backside. When he sat, she praised him.

"All right. I'll feed you first and then put on the water for the pasta." Keeping up a dialogue with Jamie the entire time he ate as she sliced veggies and prepared a salad, she was surprised when she heard the slam of a car door.

"Jack's home!" She marveled that she felt as excited by the prospect as Jamie. Easing back, she let Jamie greet Jack first. "Are you going to yell at him for chewing the table?" she asked as he walked through the door.

"I could, but it wouldn't do much good, seeing as it was hours ago." He bent down to pet Jamie and Caitlin couldn't help but notice the way his jeans hugged his taut backside. Since he was preoccupied with the dog, she fanned herself without worrying that he might see.

He braced his hands on the floor to stand, and Cait wondered if it was because he was tired and his leg was bothering him again. She couldn't help but notice and be impressed by the amount of muscle in Jack's back and torso. Mrs. Sweeney had told Peggy that the good doctor was definitely hiding his light under a bushel wearing that white lab coat, and of course Peggy had shared that tidbit with Cait.

The timer rang and she drained the pasta. "How was your day?"

Jack opened a bottle of wine and poured two glasses. "Busy, productive. Yours?" He handed her a glass of red wine. "It's my favorite merlot. I hope you like it."

After she took a sip, she said, "It's lovely."

Jamie chose that moment to shove his way in between them and jump up on Jack. Jack corrected the dog and then began to stroke his back, sending the puppy into doggie ecstasy. "Good boy, I know you missed us." With a look of longing at his untouched glass of wine, he sighed. "How about if we go toss the ball a few times?"

"Dinner's ready," Caitlin said. "But it can wait a little bit. It'll still taste good cold."

Jack paused in the doorway, a hand braced above him as his gaze locked with hers. Heat shot through her at the desire in his eyes. But then he blinked and the look was gone, leaving her to wonder if it was wishful thinking. That almost-kiss was amping up the anticipation and driving her nuts.

"That sounds wonderful. Thanks for going to the trouble of making dinner."

"Mmm."

He held out his hand. "Come on outside and play with us."

As she took his hand, her grip must have been a bit desperate; he looked down at their clasped hands and then into her eyes. "Tough day?"

She shrugged. "Parts of it."

"Want to talk about it?"

"Not really."

He nodded. "Can you stay with Jamie for a minute? I need to find a tennis ball."

A few moments later, he emerged from the garage with his hand in the air. "OK, boy!" He wound up like an all-star pitcher and threw the ball. Jamie gave chase and Caitlin smiled at the two of them.

A half a dozen tosses later, Jamie's tongue was hanging out of the side of his mouth and he was panting. "Water break," she called out.

Both males looked at her as if she were crazy, but then Jack must have had second thoughts. "Let's go." Jamie followed him into the house.

"I just need to wash my hands."

Since he seemed to be waiting for her to agree, she nodded and turned to fix their plates and then stopped. "Just a minute," she said. "I left the bread in the car. Be right back."

He was setting the kitchen table when she walked back in and set the bag on the counter. "Fresh-baked Italian bread."

He handed her a cutting board and bread knife. The microwave dinged and he smiled. "I thought your meal deserved to be warmed up, especially since parts of your day didn't go as well as mine."

Touched because he'd taken the time to think of her, she returned his smile.

"Thanks." She set the bread on the table and watched the way he moved about the kitchen, deftly removing one plate of pasta and inserting another and then topping off her wine. "You certainly know your way around the kitchen."

"I've had lots of practice living on my own, and my mom thought I should learn to cook at an early age."

"I learned through trial and error. Meg never had the time to learn to cook. She was too busy watching us, keeping up with schoolwork—"

"And working with your dad. I remember how worried she was that she'd do or say the wrong thing and you and Gracie would end up scarred for life." The microwave interrupted what he was going to say. Once he had removed the plate and set it on the table, he held out his hand to Caitlin.

It was warm and firm with calluses—a working man's hand. Her hand tingled and she shivered at his touch.

"Cold?"

"Um…no. I was just thinking…"

"About?" he prompted.

"Hands."

"What about them?" He seemed interested.

She cleared her throat because she wasn't about to tell him that his touch set off sparks inside of her—at least not yet. "I grew up appreciating the strength in a person's hands. My dad could do anything with his: fix the basketball hoop, lower a bicycle seat, show one of us how to change a flat tire."

Jack tightened his grip on her hand and drew her a little closer. "Hands do so many other things too."

She looked up, meeting his gaze, unable to hold back the sigh of contentment that escaped. "True," she mumbled. "We both use our hands to earn a living—you use yours to fix people. I use mine to fix things."

"Common ground." He brushed his thumb across the back of her hand, a gentle caress that shouldn't have caused her belly to flutter, but it did. They were talking about hands for goodness sake!

"I grew up wanting to use my hands like my dad—the people in Apple Grove depended on him, just like I did."

Cait hadn't been looking for one, but somehow she knew instinctively that she'd managed to find a man like her dad—strong, solid, and dependable.

The warmth of Jack's hand holding hers distracted her, and for a moment, she let her imagination run wild, wondering what it would feel like to have his hands slide to the small of her back and slowly pull her closer... "Um, we'd better eat while it's still warm." Brushing a strand of hair out of her eyes with her free hand, she added, "Pasta can get sticky after you warm it up twice."

He seemed reluctant to let go. With a knuckle, he tipped her chin up so that she could look into his eyes. "You're not what I expected, Caitlin Mulcahy."

The deep timbre of his voice skittered up her spine, distracting her until all she wanted to do was give in to temptation and lay her head against his broad chest. But at the last moment, sanity returned.

"Dinner's getting cold." She gave in to the involuntary shiver his intense looks and distracting hands caused. When she tugged on her hand again, this time he let her go.

But instead of sitting down at the table, Jack, followed by his little black shadow, walked out of the kitchen. "Nice work, Mulcahy," she grumbled. "A handsome man, a quiet dinner for two, and you somehow manage to scare him off talking about hands."

Before she could launch into a diatribe, he returned with a gray sweatshirt with dark blue letters across the chest. It simply said navy. "Your arms felt chilly." He handed it to her. "It's a little battered because it's my favorite."

She slipped it over her head, thinking the warmth of the worn fabric beat out the desire to be fashionable. "I hadn't realized I was so cold."

"When I'm tired, I tend to feel the cooler temperatures faster than I normally would." He raised his glass and smiled. "To good food, a lovely dinner companion—" Jamie's bark had them both grinning. "Companions," he corrected, looking down at the pup. When the dog stopped barking, sat, and looked up at them, Cait couldn't help but laugh. They settled down to eat and the tension from moments before melted away. Conversation came easily when speaking about Jamie.

"How are you going to bring yourself to give him back if he belongs to someone else?"

Jack paused with the fork halfway to his lips. "It's already been twenty-four hours and no one has stepped forward to claim him."

"I suppose if they were desperate, they'd be searching far and wide for him." She paused and tasted the pasta, pleased that reheating it hadn't made it rubbery.

"This bread's delicious. Who made it?"

She smiled. "I have my sources."

"It didn't come from Mary's Market or from the supermarket over in Newark."

"No," she said, "and no."

"Hmm, reminds me of a few ops during my time in the service." He passed the butter to her. "Top secret," he said with a grin. "I can tell you, but then…" He made a slicing movement across his neck.

She laughed in between bites. "Got it."

"This is delicious." His blue eyes darkened to that distracting shade of sapphire again, and she wondered if she was brave enough to ask him what he was thinking about. "I normally don't like peppers, but the yellow and orange ones taste different than the green ones." He practically inhaled his pasta.

"Hungry?" she asked.

"I was."

Her eyes sparkled with humor. "Growing up in the Mulcahy house, if you didn't like what was on the table, you could either go hungry or find the peanut butter."

"That's kinder than my house. We ate what mom cooked. Period."

"I think Pop was brought up that way too, but after mom died and he was doing the cooking, he gave us an option."

Jack looked as if he was listening, really interested. The men she'd dated had been good-looking like Jack, but so far no one measured up in other areas, criteria she hadn't even realized she'd instinctively been using as a scale to rate her dates. Odd that she only just reasoned out that her biggest yardstick was her father, the first man in her life.

"Would you like more wine?"

"Um…no thank you. I still need to drive home. I had no idea that it was already after nine."

The teasing light in his eyes belied the seriousness of his tone when he asked, "Do you have a curfew?"

"See if I let you have dessert," she teased, clearing his place first and then her own.

"Just leave the dishes," he said when she started to rinse them off. "You cook. I clean."

"I could get used to that."

"Now," he said, moving to stand beside her, "what's this about dessert?"

She opened the fridge and pointed to a bowl of raspberries and a cellophane-covered pie dish.

His attention wavered from the delectable woman in his sights to the pie in his fridge. "What kind of pie?"

She giggled and reached for the dish. "It's Peggy's buttermilk pie."

"How did you wrangle one out of her? People usually wait in line for one of those pies. I remember more than one fistfight in the parking lot over the years whenever an order got misplaced."

Cait smiled at him and his heart stuttered before picking up the beat again. "She's my best friend."

"And?" Jack figured there'd be more to the story.

"I'll fix the hole in their barn roof come Saturday… for free."

"I don't know that I'm worth the price of your labor." Her scent clouded his brain. *Lilacs*. Cait smelled of lilacs.

"Anyone who'd risk breaking his neck at dusk chasing a stray puppy through the woods to make sure that he's not injured…and then opening his home to that puppy…deserves the whole pie."

While he'd been studying her delicate bone structure and the curve of her cheek, she'd grabbed another bowl from his fridge. "Whipped cream?" he asked.

"The real kind," she told him, "not the kind from a can."

"I will owe you for this but plan to take advantage of the offer and have one piece now, one piece before bed, then breakfast…"

His gaze swept up from the bowl of whipped cream in her hands to her startled, green eyes as the gut-wrenching thought of what he'd like to do with that cream short-circuited his brain.

She cleared her throat and asked, "Still hungry?"

"Mmm." *For more than food.* Did he dare tell her that? While the silent debate was raging inside of him, she sliced, scooped, and dropped pie, cream, and berries.

"There you are." When he didn't move, she said, "Dig in."

Jamie chose that moment to bump into Jack and plaster himself to Jack's leg. He groaned watching that first forkful of flaky confection fall off his fork and get snapped up between little black lips. "Why, you little devil!"

"No more for you, Jameson," Caitlin's voice was stern. "Too much sugar will give you worms."

"Actually—" Jack began only to stop when Cait glared at him.

"Meg said that's what mom always used to say."

"But if Grace is allergic to dogs, why would your mom say that?"

Cait rolled her eyes. "Because my parents grew up with dogs."

And that, thought Jack, *is that.* He'd seen that look before on Caitlin's face and knew when to drop the subject. "Think I'll make some coffee." But while he was making coffee, the image of Caitlin wrapped in his arms kept interrupting his thought process, making it hard to think straight.

"Need any help?"

He shook his head and filled two mugs with coffee,

handing one to Cait and setting the other on the table. "Dessert looks great...dinner was amazing."

"Simple," she corrected him. "Sometimes, simple is best when you've had a long day and it's late. Besides, I can't eat a big meal after eight o'clock."

"But what about the pie?"

She looked down at her pie, topped with berries and whipped cream, and slowly smiled. "There's always room for pie."

He pulled out her chair and couldn't resist testing her reaction by brushing his fingers along the nape of her neck. The shudder she tried to suppress confirmed what he'd been wondering. Caitlin Mulcahy could not help but react to his touch. It was a good feeling to realize he was not the only one affected. Besides, it was all her fault, talking about hands and having his mind wander to what else his hands could do besides heal.

Struggling to redirect his thoughts, he focused on dessert. Sampling a few bites, he had to ask, "Why don't they serve their pie like this at the diner?"

Caitlin grinned. "It's the way my great-great-grandma always served it. Molly Mulcahy was a canny woman, who knew the way to my great-great-grandpa's heart was through his stomach."

"Not all men can be bought with food."

She sipped her coffee and let her gaze linger on him. A zing of electricity ricocheted off his heart and sent sparks of awareness to every single nerve ending in his body. Digging deep, he fought for control. He didn't think she had any idea that she'd tied him up into a reef knot—one of the strongest knots a sailor could use—the more tension on it, the tighter the knot became. He wasn't about to mention it—yet.

"Can you?"

For a moment he couldn't remember what she'd just said, but then his brain took pity on him and he remembered. There was a time when he'd have given his right arm for a home-cooked meal, but he'd survived eating MREs—and he'd survived his second tour overseas. Maybe the way to his heart was through his stomach. "I'm in danger of saying yes…this pie tastes amazing with the toppings."

"I wish I'd have had the chance to get to know my great-great-grandmother…other than through some of the recipes handed down to my dad along with some of her sage advice."

"But that's how you do get to know her." Jack watched the way Caitlin slipped a bite of pie off the fork between full, soft lips and had to look away. *Do not think about those lips.*

"There's a picture of her and my great-great-grandfather on the mantelpiece in the living room."

"Family ties run strong in the Gannon family too."

"Do you miss your folks much?"

He stopped to think about it. "I do and I don't."

"Can't you decide?"

"I spent all of my life surrounded by their love and guidance, and then spent a chunk of my adult years in the navy—after I was injured, I used the college credits I'd earned during the navy and went to med school…I guess I got used to being on my own."

"I've never been away from home," Caitlin confessed to her plate.

He wondered why she sounded so sad. "Didn't you go away to school?"

Caitlin shrugged. "That was community college, and I was only away while I was attending classes."

"Not the same as living in a dorm."

She frowned into her coffee cup. "No. It's not. Gracie was the only one of us who went away to school. And she's forever griping about Apple Grove. Her list of reasons to leave gets longer by the day."

"So she's planning on leaving town?"

Sadness filled Cait to overflowing. "Yeah." The reality of Mulcahys being run by someone other than herself and her two sisters was inconceivable, but fast becoming a reality. "She's waiting to hear back from a recruiter in Columbus." She hesitated before adding, "I can't decide whether to root for her, fingers crossed that she gets the job…or pray they hire someone else."

Intentionally pitching his voice low, he asked, "Then wouldn't her dreams of making a life for herself in the big city be squashed?"

Cait didn't answer for the longest time. When she raised her gaze to meet his, he was sorry to see the moisture gathering in her grass-green eyes. "It's not that so much as thinking that I might lose her too. I've already lost Meg."

"Have you?" he asked, rising from his seat and rounding the table to stand beside her.

She looked so alone in that one moment and then she closed her eyes and sighed. "It feels that way. It's so hard, what with Pop and Mary getting serious, Meg married and going to be a mother of three by summertime. If Grace leaves, where will I be?"

"Ah," he said, taking her hand and tugging her to her feet. "Walk with me, Cait, and tell me what dream you set aside so that you wouldn't leave your family with another hole in it."

She jerked free of his hold. "I didn't say—"

"You didn't have to," he said, slipping his arm through hers and tugging her toward the back door. "Come on, Jamie boy."

With the dog at their side, Jack opened the door and let the soft spring night weave its magic around the woman he'd come to care for in such a short time. He didn't dare think about just how much he cared…not yet. There was time to mull that over later tonight after she'd gone.

"The moon's waxing." When she didn't respond, he added, "Did you ever go for a sail on a moonlit night? Just ghosting along with the evening breeze?"

This time when their eyes met, hers were dry. "No. But Peggy and I borrowed her dad's rowboat one night and lost the oars in the middle of the pond and had to jump in and drag the boat back to shore."

He fought against the need to laugh. "I'm sure Mr. McCormack wasn't too happy about that."

"He never found out."

"He liked to go fishing in that boat. Did you have enough money saved up between the two of you to buy him a new set of oars?"

She shook her head. "I made them."

"Oars?" She'd certainly surprised him. "That must have taken weeks."

"Actually only one. I learned from the best how to use my grandfather's woodworking tools. Once Peggy and I confessed to her mom what happened, she helped keep Mr. McCormack busy so that he didn't have time to go fishing until I'd finished the oars."

"And he never knew?"

"Well…we were a lot younger then and were so worried about getting caught that when he never said anything, we figured we'd dodged getting in trouble big time. I never really thought about it until a few years ago."

Her smile had him asking, "What happened?"

"Her dad stopped by our house one night and asked if I'd be willing to make another set of oars for his cousin—like the one's I'd replaced his with!"

"He wasn't mad?"

"No." Her eyes sparkled with life and laughter as she told him, "Apparently, the grips on his old oars weren't as smooth and didn't fit his hands as well as the ones I'd made." She shrugged. "Who knew?"

"Apparently everyone but you and Peggy." When she fell silent, he slipped his arm free so he could wrap it around her waist and lead her toward the woods. "How long have you wanted to be a carpenter?"

"Half my life," she said, then pulled to a stop. "You weren't supposed to ask me that."

"Because?"

"I don't want my dad to worry that I'll stop working for the family business the way Grace plans to."

"But you've thought about it."

She sighed and began walking again. "Yeah. Does that make me disloyal?"

"To want to be able to do something other than work in the family business?" He tightened his hold on her and answered, "No." Seeing the worry on her face, he reassured her, "I don't gossip like your friends down at the diner. Your secret's safe with me."

"Did you ever think about doing something besides following in your father's footsteps?"

He looked up at the stars and smiled. "Yeah…but I got to do it."

"Oh?" she asked. "What was that?"

"Do you see that star over there?"

She turned to look in the direction he pointed. "Yes… isn't that Polaris?"

"Brightest star in the northern sky. You can navigate by it."

"You really wanted to enlist in the navy?"

"I wanted to sail the seven seas, learn to navigate the way ancient mariners did."

"I thought you were just following along with the Gannon tradition of seafaring navy men."

"There was that," he admitted. "But even as a kid, I'd sneak outside with my sleeping bag and sleep out under the stars, wondering what it'd be like to use them to find my way out on the sea."

"And did you?"

"Yes, and it was everything I'd imagined and more than I'd bargained for." Before she could ask him to explain, he turned her into his embrace. Her gentle curves pressed against the hard planes of his body, setting off sparks that threatened to ignite. He didn't have the will to step back or let her go.

"Will you kiss me in the moonlight, Cait?"

Every fiber of his being urged her to say yes. He didn't know if he'd survive the night because in his imagination, he'd already sampled the honeyed sweetness of her lips.

Just when he thought she'd refuse, the stiffness left her limbs as she melted against him. "Yes."

He lowered his mouth to hers. The tentative tasting led to a deep desire for more. When she sighed, he took advantage of the moment and traced the rim of her mouth with the tip of his tongue. When her tongue tangled with his, heat shot straight to his gut, and he angled her head back to drink from her lips. Pure and potent as wild honey, Caitlin went to his head like two fingers of Irish whiskey.

Coming up for air, he tucked her head beneath his chin and worked to steady his breathing. "You pack a lethal punch," he confessed, pressing a kiss to the top of her head.

Her arms tightened around him. "I've been kissed before," she said, "but not like that."

He eased back until he could look into the depths of her emerald eyes when he asked, "And how's that?"

"Like you'd die if you didn't kiss me."

"That about sums it up." Reeling her back in, he undid her braid and speared his fingers into the mass of waves, reveling in the fact that she was warm, willing, and eager to kiss him back.

He had a gut-deep need to taste more…touch more… but it was too soon and he didn't want to scare her off. "Caitlin—" He gave in and brushed his lips over hers.

"You make it hard to say good night," she said when he eased her back. "All I want to do is keep on kissing you, but you tempt me to want more, to do more, and I don't think I'm ready to rush into anything. I want to savor every moment—"

The urge to pull her back into his arms was so strong, he had to look away and then back, asking, "So you'll be back then? I haven't scared you off?"

She laid a hand on his arm and said, "I promised to help with Jamie. Besides," she said. "I don't scare easily."

"I can be a patient man, Caitlin." He slowly smiled and added, "I'll give you a couple of days to think about whether or not you want to do more than share a few heart-stopping kisses."

She tilted her head to one side. "My heart's still beating. Maybe you should try one more time before I go."

He tugged on her arm until she fell against him. When she gasped, he poured everything he was feeling into the kiss. Mouth, lips, teeth, and tongue gave and gave before finally, finally taking pleasure for himself.

Drunk on the heady taste of her, he set her away from him, held up his hands, and backed away. "Go now, or consider yourself shanghaied."

"Aye, aye, Cap'n." She gave a mock salute, turned, and sprinted for the driveway.

"Avast, ye coward!" he called after her. Then had to laugh at the way she turned around and grinned at him, all the while running backward toward the safety of her car.

"See you tomorrow?" she asked, holding the driver's door open.

"If you wait for me to get home. I have office hours until six o'clock tomorrow."

"Do you want me to bring dinner again?"

"No," he told her. "It's my turn to cook for you."

Her smile glowed from within. "What are we having?"

"I don't know yet…but I can guarantee it will be edible."

"Sounds perfect." She waved, climbed into her car, and was gone.

Watching her back out of his driveway, Jack felt as if the night air had cooled. She'd taken all of her warmth and sweetness with her.

He scrubbed a hand over his face. He couldn't wait until she came back.

Chapter 7

"ANYTHING NEW ON THE WATER TOWER?"

Caitlin smiled at her older sister. "Nope. It's been declared off limits since the younger Smolinsky brother fell off the ladder and dislocated his knee."

Meg sighed. "I know, but I keep hoping someone will brave the sheriff's wrath and climb up the ladder and paint a heart with their initials in it, or better yet, propose marriage."

"Like Dan did for you?" Cait asked.

Her sister stared into space. "I waited a long time to see my name painted up there in John Deere green. Never thought I would."

"Well, no one new up there yet. And definitely not Dad and Mary, if that's what you're thinking."

Meg shook her head at her sister while Cait centered the bookshelf she'd built for Meg and Dan's nursery. Taking a step back, she eyeballed the piece and ran the tips of her fingers along the top of it. "It looks good, doesn't it?"

Meg slipped her arm around her younger sister and sighed. "You build beautiful things, little sister."

Cait felt her face heat at the compliment. "Coming from you, that's high praise."

"Come on downstairs. Mrs. Winter stopped by yesterday with a cherry pie."

"Hah! I knew she wouldn't be able to hold out," Cait

said. "She talked to Grace the other day but said she'd wait until you were feeling better and could stop by."

"I'm not sick, you know," Meg grumbled. "It's just hard since I didn't have morning sickness with the twins."

Cait nodded. "Maybe God gave you a break because he knew you'd need your strength to take care of those little hooligans."

Meg chuckled. "They are, aren't they?"

If her soft smile was any indication, her sister loved every minute of it. Cait walked over to her toolbox and started to clean up. "Can I take a rain check on that pie? I've got to head out. Gracie is keeping me busy these days."

"I'm hoping to be back up to speed—"

"You need to get plenty of rest and take it slowly so that the precious little Eagan growing inside of you is healthy...and so you are too. I don't envy you riding herd on three boys."

"Who said it would be another boy?"

"Is it a girl?"

Meg's expressive face had Cait sending up a silent prayer that it would be. "I want to be surprised this time."

Cait laughed. "Danny and Joey weren't a surprise?"

Meg teared up. "They're the light of my life—so is Dan."

Cait watched her sister's eyes fill. She groaned and handed Meg a tissue. Her sister wiped her tears and blew her nose. "Sorry, but lately everything seems to make me cry."

A sound from the other room caught Meg's attention. "Let me check on the boys. They never sleep for very long." Pregnancy softened Meg's attitude and her tongue, but Cait and Grace were still taking bets that this new baby's first word would be a four-letter one, just like his—or her—older brothers'.

Which reminded her of the bet going over at the diner. "Hey, Meg," she called out walking to the boys' room. "Have you talked to Peggy or Kate lately?"

"No," she said, walking out of her bedroom. "Why?" Meg picked up Danny while Cait picked up Joey and held him close and kissed his cheeks, then traded with Meg so she could kiss Danny too. "Funny thing, that you and your best friend would be expecting right around the same time—again." She wasn't ready to tell her about the bet…yet.

"What's so funny about it?"

"Never mind that, it's what's going on at the diner that you'll probably find out about if you're going to be visiting with your pal Honey B. today."

"I am and I need to change these two before we go downstairs."

"I'll help." Cait put off telling her sister until the boys were changed and running toward the top step.

"Wait for mommy!" Meg beat Cait to the stairs and scolded. "Mommy goes first." She shook her finger at her toddlers. "Now, turn around and climb down." They did as they were told and as soon as their little sneakers touched the bottom, they were laughing and running toward the kitchen.

"Juice!" Danny hollered.

"Cookies!" Joey echoed.

"Soooo," Meg said, settling her sons at the table with their snack.

Cait paused to marvel at the ease with which her

sister cared for her twins and kept them from squabbling. Finally she said, "I think it was actually old man Sweeney talking to Mr. Weatherbee who started the betting."

Cait could feel the heat of her sister's glare and the sharp edge of Meg's temper when she asked, "Betting?"

"Yep," Cait said as cheerfully as possible. "Seems he's not the only one in town who decided it would be a good thing to bet on who delivered first...you or Honey B."

Meg's mouth opened and closed twice before any sound came out. "Is he crazy?"

"No, but he sure does have an affection for you, Sis."

As the boys finished, Meg and Cait wiped their hands and faces and set them down. "Play nice," their mother warned. The boys ran to the playroom and were chatting in their own dialect—a mix of English and twin-speak. Meg watched her darlings playing. "How's the betting going?"

Caitlin followed and told her, "I haven't talked to Peggy in a few days—"

Meg laid her hand on Cait's cheek. "You don't feel feverish."

Cait chuckled. "I'm not."

"Did you and Peggy have an argument?"

"No."

"Then why haven't you talked to her yet today?" Meg asked.

"Because I've been otherwise occupied."

"Ahh," Meg said softly. "So Pop's right."

"About what?"

"Hmmm?" Meg asked. "Oh nothing."

Cait rolled her eyes. "Come on, Meg. Have a heart. What did Pop say?"

"That you were sweet on my pal, Doc Gannon."

Cait's face heated beneath her sister's perusal. "I don't know that I'd use that exact expression."

Meg folded her arms in front of her. "Just exactly how would you describe what's been going on out there for the last few nights?"

Cait didn't know where to start. "I've been helping take care of Jamie, stopping by on my way through town."

"Then you haven't been having dinner with him, alone, every night for the last three nights?"

"Is nothing sacred in this town?"

"Not when it's newsworthy. The fact that Doc is keeping company with a female, who just happens to be my sister, is definitely that."

"It's not like we're dating or anything like that."

Meg reached for Cait's hand and squeezed it before letting go. "How would you describe what it's like?"

Cait sighed. "He makes my stomach fill with butterflies. My heart beats faster when he looks at me, and his eyes change from a gorgeous lake blue to dark and desperate sapphire right before he kisses me."

Meg's eyes rounded and then promptly filled with tears. "Oh, Cait," she sniffed. "You're in love with him!"

"I'm not…at least I don't think I am. How would I know?" she demanded. "I've never felt like this before."

"What about that landscaper over in Newark?"

"Steve? He was nice, but it's not the same."

"What's different?" Meg asked softly.

"It's the way I feel when he looks at me, as if he sees right into my heart and knows what I'm thinking."

"And?" her sister prompted.

"The way he laughs…he's got a great laugh…when he's tossing a ball to Jamie. He really loves that dog… we both do, but—"

"You're so far gone over that man that you don't even know it."

"I am?"

"Yeah."

"What am I going to do?"

"What do you want to do?"

When Caitlin just stared off into space, Meg sighed. "There is that. Have you used protection?"

"Jeez, Meg, I'm twenty-six, not sixteen!"

Meg sighed. "I know, I know. Old habits die hard. I care about you, Cait."

Cait frowned. "That's fine, but how about treating me like an adult?"

"I do…most of the time."

"Unless you're preoccupied." Cait smiled at Danny and Joey as they both tugged on the blue truck, ignoring the red one.

"Sorry. I'll work on my interrogation tactics. I'm going to need them in a few years."

It was Cait's turn to laugh. "OK, but you don't have anything to worry about. We aren't that involved yet."

Meg waited a heartbeat before asking, "Why not? Doc's a handsome man with a heart of gold, but—"

"I know. When he kisses me…" She lost her train of thought remembering the feel of being held in the protective circle of his arms, leaning against the strength of his powerful chest, feeling the pounding of his heart.

"Earth to Caitlin."

"Hmmm?"

"You were saying?"

"I was?"

"You'd better stock up on supplies over at the drug store."

Cait frowned. "Maybe I already have."

"It's hard to concentrate," Meg said. "Isn't it?"

"Yeah," Cait whispered. "Sometimes, I'll be on the job and then my mind drifts off and starts thinking about something Jack said or did and I'll lose track of where I am and what I'm supposed to be doing."

"Add in the element of danger—really sharp power tools—and it gets even trickier."

"Did you feel this way about Dan from the moment you met him?"

Meg smiled. "Yes. He's the best thing that ever happened to me—even though I ended up with stitches in my hand because I was thinking about him instead of paying attention to what I was doing."

Cait nodded. "I remember, and for what it's worth, he says the same about you."

"Nice to know," Meg said, packing her diaper bag and gathering the boys. "Honey B. will have little Mitch at the shop today. If you have a minute, maybe you can stop by."

"Sounds great. I need to get a few things from the shop before I meet you at Honey B.'s. I'll go grab my toolbox—I left it upstairs." She stopped and looked over her shoulder. "Hey, do you need help getting the boys in the car?"

"No thanks. I'm a pro."

A few minutes after Cait left, Meg had the boys strapped in and was on her way to town.

Cait walked into Honey B.'s and into bedlam. Danny, Joey, and little Mitch were playing together...at least it looked like they were playing.

"Hi, Honey B. Hey, Sis. Hi, guys!"

"Cait!" All three toddlers latched on to her legs and started babbling at once.

"So did you tell Meg?"

Honey B. shook her head. "It's been a little crazy since the boys got here."

Cait helped her sister get the boys settled again. Once they were playing nicely, she said, "About that bet. Just so you know, the money's going to a good cause."

"Really? Tell me more."

Cait shook her head. "Honey B., why don't you?"

"Well, it all started when that man stormed into my salon and carted me off on his shoulder."

Meg sighed. "I still remember the flinty-eyed look and determined set of Mitch's jaw when he came in loaded for bear."

"Quaint expression, Sis," Cait mumbled.

"He was so forceful," Mrs. Doyle chimed in.

"He swept our Honey B. up like she was a sack of potatoes."

"It's true," Meg chuckled. "Dan and I wished we'd thought to take a picture...the look on her face was priceless."

"What are friends for if not to humiliate one another?" Honey B. said. "I thought Dan was more forceful than Mitch."

"Oh really?" Cait asked, looking from Meg to Honey B. and back again. "Do tell."

"That good-for-nothing Van Orden boy waltzed in

like he owned the place, grabbed Meg by the hand, and was all set to kiss her," Mrs. Hawkins said.

"When Dan stormed in and demanded that Van Orden let her go," Mrs. Jones added.

"But it was the way Dan kissed Meg that had all of us cheering for him," Mrs. Doyle said. "He was so obviously in love with you," she said to Meg. "It did our hearts good to hear him tell Van Orden that he had his chance and blew it."

"And it was right after you two declared your love for one another that handsome sheriff stormed in and all hell broke loose," Mrs. Hawkins said with a smile.

"Now the eligible men in Apple Grove will have a higher standard of proposing to live up to," Mrs. Doyle added.

Meg and Honey B. shared a smile. "Sometimes it takes some doing, but if a man's in love, he'll eventually realize it," Honey B. said.

"And do something about it," Meg added.

Tears filled Meg's eyes and Honey B.'s. Meg sniffled and hugged her friend close. "How do you feel?"

"Crappy, how about you?"

"Better," Meg admitted.

"Maybe that news will sway the betting," Mrs. Doyle said, moving to stand closer. "Everyone knows that if you feel poorly, but look great, you're going to have a boy…and if you feel great, but lose your looks, you're going to have a girl."

Meg looked at Honey B. "So, if you win, you'll split the winnings with me?"

Honey B. shook her head. "Sorry, no can do."

"Why not? I'd share with you," Meg pouted.

Caitlin put her arm her sister's shoulder and confided, "We forgot to tell you that whoever picks the
woman, the date, and the time can choose who to
donate the winnings to." Meg's eyes filled with tears
again waiting for Cait to continue. "You know how
some of our neighbors are in bad shape financially
right now."

"Does Mitch know about it?" Meg asked.

"He does," Honey B. said quietly. "And he's all for
the idea. He and Dan are the driving force spreading the
word and are one hundred percent behind the idea that
the winner donate the money to one family, possibly
two, depending on how much we collect."

"Dan didn't say anything," Meg rasped.

"He promised he'd let me tell you," Honey B. said,
but your sister already let the cat out of the bag."

"We're in this together," Meg said. "Let's see if we
can rustle up some more donations for the cause."

Honey B.'s eyes filled with tears. Cait couldn't
remember ever seeing her sister's friend cry. "What's
the matter now?" she asked, grabbing a paper towel and
handing it to Honey B.

"The gown I bought for our vow renewal ceremony
isn't going to fit," Honey B. said, changing the subject.

"Is that all?" Mrs. Hawkins asked.

"Since we didn't get to have a real ceremony the first
time, I wanted it to be perfect. I've loved Mitch for so
long that I lost my head after he scooped me up into
his arms and didn't come back to reality until morning
sickness hit me between the eyes."

Cait already knew Honey B.'s story but never got
tired of hearing it because it was proof positive that even

a cautious man could move quickly when the situation called for it.

"I thought the simple ceremony at the justice of the peace in Newark was lovely," Meg said, bending down to take the hairbrush out of one son's hand so he would stop smacking her other son. "But I understand why you'd want to have the vow renewal—it's a chance to have everyone with you, celebrating the love you and the handsome sheriff share."

Honey B. sighed. "I didn't realize how much I wanted a real wedding, so I bought a gorgeous dress online and was all set to dazzle my husband in front of all of our friends and neighbors, but that was before I realized I was expecting again." Tears filled her eyes as she added, "And I…damn it, I don't know how to sew."

"I do," Mrs. Jenkins said with a smile. "Don't you worry about those alterations, Honey B. You're going to knock Mitch Wallace's socks off when he sees you walking toward him."

"Just leave it to us," Mrs. Hawkins told her.

"Peggy and Kate are making the cake."

"You planning on having a green cake like Edie and Bill?" Cait asked.

Honey B. just smiled. "That was the craziest wedding cake I've ever seen. I don't think I'm going to tell you what the McCormack sisters are planning for our cake. Something has to be a surprise since the whole town is in on everything else."

The conversation in the room started to escalate as everyone volunteered their ideas on a how to make Honey B. and the sheriff's vow renewal perfect. "If I ever get married," Cait said suddenly, "I'm not having a big wedding, just me and the groom—like Honey B. and Mitch did over at the county courthouse."

"That's it?" her sister asked.

"And my family."

"Ten people?" Mrs. Doyle shook her head. "That's just sad. Weddings are happy times for family, friends, and neighbors to celebrate."

Cait remained firm. "Up until Meg and Dan got married, I wanted to elope, but then I'd be breaking the family tradition of tying the knot in our barn."

"Only our grandparents, Mom and Dad, and Dan and I got married in the barn," Meg reminded her. "You could have Reverend Smith bless your vows after the fact in the barn…with a party for family and friends."

"And neighbors," Mrs. Doyle put in.

The ladies were tittering and laughing, so Cait didn't think anyone would hear her when she reminded Meg, "Remember when I asked Pop if I could borrow a ladder to elope and he just laughed and said not to bother…just to take the stairs?"

Meg nodded. "You were eight years old and so serious, he couldn't help but tease you."

Everyone started laughing and Cait realized she should have known they'd be listening. Danny was tugging on Meg's leg, so she picked him up before telling her friend, "I'm hungry."

"Me too," Honey B. said, "but I have customers."

"We'll watch the boys, Meg," Mrs. Doyle offered, holding out her arms for Danny. "Why don't you go on over to the diner and pick something up for you and Honey B.?"

Meg smiled and picked up Joey, handing him to Mrs.

Jenkins. "Be good for Mrs. Doyle and Mrs. Jenkins," she told them. "Mommy will be right back."

Three little boys called out, "Bye!"

After passing out kisses, she asked her friend, "What do you want?"

"Sausage gravy and biscuits."

"That all?"

"Mmm. I'm not that hungry."

Caitlin asked, "What would you order if you were really hungry?"

"Chicken fried steak, sausage gravy, mashed potatoes, and biscuits…why?"

"No reason." Cait grinned. "Come on, Meg, let's go get that food before Honey B. faints again."

"Not funny, squirt!" Honey B. called out, using the nickname Cait hated as Cait closed the door. Once her sister's friend couldn't see her, she let go of the laughter she held.

"What's so funny?" Meg demanded as they crossed the street to the diner.

"Nothing." Cait smiled.

"Hey there, Cait, where've you been?" Kate asked as they walked through the door.

Peggy walked out of the kitchen and smiled. "I hear she's been hanging around with a certain handsome doctor."

Cait couldn't control the urge to laugh; she gave in. "Well, we've been doing a little more than hanging around."

"Wait a minute," Kate said, "let me get a pencil and piece of paper. This might be worth putting in the *Gazette*."

"Not funny, Kate," Peggy told her sister before

nudging her toward one of the customers holding up an empty cup. "You're on coffee duty. Get lost."

Cait was trying not to cringe at the thought of someone discussing the aspects of her relationship with Jack—it was still so new, she meant to keep it to herself—but she always did have a hard time holding back when it was Peggy.

"She wouldn't really tell Rhonda—" Cait began, only to have Peggy interrupt.

"Don't worry," Peggy reassured her. "Kate's a lot of talk lately, especially since she finally broke up with her loser boyfriend."

Cait was trying not to smile when she said, "I didn't really think that you would, but sometimes I do wonder about your younger sister." When the younger McCormack sister waved her hand in the air as if to say "go ahead and talk about me," Cait leaned close and whispered, "Peggy, Meg thinks I'm in love."

Peggy squeezed Cait's hand. "Why?"

"Well, it all started when Jamie ran across the road into my arms."

"Wait," Peggy said, "you're in love with a dog?"

"That's part of it…but that was the first time I saw Jack as a person and not just someone who graduated from school with Meg, joined the navy, and came home to pick up where his dad left off—looking down the throats of everyone in town and taking their pulse."

Peggy reached out to rub a hand up and down Cait's back but didn't say anything.

Encouraged, Cait confessed, "He's funny, kind, and has this great laugh—and is one hell of a kisser."

While Meg was chatting with Kate, giving her a food

order, Cait sat down on one of the stools. "I've never felt like this before, Peggy…ever," she whispered. "And it scares the ever-living daylights out of me."

Peggy leaned on the counter and whispered, "So, how good a kisser is he?"

Cait's grin turned wicked. "You remember Tommy Stackhouse?"

Peggy's eyes widened. "Seriously?"

Cait shook her head and whispered, "Better."

"Oh. My. God," Peggy said, fanning herself.

Cait started to laugh and pulled Peggy in for a quick hug. "I didn't know if I was crazy or not."

Peggy grinned at her. "Seriously? Tommy Stackhouse?"

Kate came out of the kitchen with Meg's order and asked, "So, are you going to give me the lowdown on the town's latest heartthrob?"

Meg chuckled as she thanked Kate. "That's all you," she said to Caitlin. "See you later, Sis."

Watching Meg close the door, Peggy asked Cait, "Have you told him how you feel yet?"

Cait shook her head. "I wasn't exactly sure of it myself. Besides, what if he doesn't feel the same way?"

"Are you crazy? He'd be a fool not to fall for you."

Cait's heart lightened. "Thanks, Peggy."

"No problem."

They walked through the diner and out to the sidewalk. Standing in front of the diner's picture window, Peggy asked, "So, does Meg finally know about the bet?"

"Yeah, we were just over at Honey B.'s and everybody filled her in."

"Good," Peggy said. "It's a good thing what they're doing for our town."

"It is," Cait agreed. "Sooo," she said slowly, letting her gaze meet that of her friend. "If you were me, would *you* tell him?"

Peggy paused before answering, "Maybe not quite yet. You'll know when the moment is right."

Chapter 8

As promised, Mr. Johnson was waiting for Caitlin the following morning when she pulled into his driveway. After doing the walk-through, she knew this would be a job she'd love—expanding his barn to include a few more stalls.

"Caitlin," Mr. Johnson called out, walking toward her car. "Where's the truck?"

"It's in the shop."

Before she could elaborate, he was nodding. "Heard about the whole business, just thought it would be repainted by now." She fell silent and followed him over to the long, low building he wanted to add on to. "Now," the older man said, pointing to the left side of the building. "Here's where I think you should build the stalls I need. How you do it'll be up to you, as long as it looks like what's already there."

"Understood," she told him. "If I call in the order to the lumberyard over in Newark, I can probably have all of the materials ready for pick up this afternoon. If I pour the slab now, I can start framing first thing in the morning."

"You'll squeeze me in your schedule?" he asked. "I know it's busy since Megan started working part time." He waited a beat before asking, "She feeling all right?"

Cait smiled. "She's great and feeling better every day."

"Good. Young women were meant to be mothers. It's natural—"

"If that's the case, then who would be building your horse stalls right now?"

He slapped his knee and chuckled. "Joe Mulcahy never did suffer a fool…didn't raise any either," he said with a nod. "You'll give me a fair price?"

"Always, but I thought you and Pop already agreed on time and materials?"

"I talked to your dad about that, but the job is labor intensive…and the thing is, I just don't have a whole lot of extra right now. I need to put money back into caring for the horses. I've got a lot of paralyzed and paraplegic kids coming to learn how to ride, and I need to find another instructor to work with them."

"Pop says you already have the next two months booked solid, with a waiting list." She looked over at the horses quietly munching on hay over in the corral. "You're doing this community, and our county, a great service by starting up this riding program. How could we say no? We have to help you help these kids."

"I'm grateful that your dad raised you three girls right…even if not one of you can cook!"

"Don't believe everything you read in the *Apple Grove Gazette*. Besides, that was years ago, when I was in high school. Maybe I've learned to cook."

He shook his head and pointed at the barn. "Work up your material list, get me the price, and place the order. Pour your slab," he said. "The sooner we get things going, the sooner we'll be up and running."

"When's the next session start?"

"Two weeks."

Cait stared at the building for a moment before coming up with a new plan. "Mr. Johnson?"

He stopped halfway to the corral. "Yeah?"

"If I get my dad to help me, we can have this baby framed out with the roof on in a day or so."

"That fast?"

"We're pouring some concrete slab, not digging foundations, and adding on to an existing structure…it's not like the rebuild I did over at Mr. Weatherbee's barn."

"Thought you'd never finish it up and get to my barn."

"How about it, want me to bring my dad in on it?"

"Think he'd do it?"

Caitlin grinned. "In a heartbeat. Retirement's not as much fun as he thought it'd be. About all he has to do is work on the Model A pickup when Dan's free. Those two are thick as thieves."

"Family should stick together. I'll leave a tarp by the side of the barn. You can use it to cover the wood you drop off later. Tell your dad I said thanks." With that, he left her so she could call her father and get the lumber list together.

Her father taught her to be prepared, and she would have been if she were driving the F1. She went back to the car and pulled out the bags of concrete she'd stowed in the trunk that morning. She had the hoe she needed to work the water slowly into the concrete mix. What she didn't have was a wheelbarrow. She'd have to call her dad, because she didn't want to take a chance and ruin one of Mr. Johnson's wheelbarrows if she didn't get all the concrete washed out before it dried.

"Hey, Pop," she said when he answered. "I'm gonna get started on Mr. Johnson's slab and don't want to wreck his wheelbarrow mixing the cement. Can you bring one by?"

"Have you staked out the area and measured the depths you need?"

"I will."

"Do you have any scrap lumber pieces to create the form?"

"Yep."

"Good."

"Um…Pop?"

"Yes?"

"Mr. Johnson was hoping I could start right away, but was worried about not having enough money for time and materials, and working by myself—"

"Just ask."

"Will you help me?"

"I can be there in about fifteen minutes. While you're waiting, do the measurements, and run a chalk line to the stakes. And one more thing," he warned. "Double-check the slab in the other stalls—it would be a good idea to match it."

"Thanks, Pop," she said. "I owe you."

"That's all right," he told her. "I know where you live."

An hour later, she was breaking open the bag of concrete with a hoe and removing the paper. Her father manned the hose and added water while they both watched the consistency.

"Nice and slow," he warned as she folded the water into the mix, watching to make sure it wasn't dry and crumbly or too wet. "Good. I think you've done it."

"I know how to mix concrete, Pop."

"I know, but Meg was the one who spent more time learning how to mix up a batch than you."

She grinned. "I learn things faster than Meg," she

said, flexing her elbows as she picked up the wheelbarrow and rolled it up the makeshift ramp her dad had put together after they'd built the form for the slab.

"Is it too heavy?"

"No," she said. "I've got it." Shifting the wheelbarrow left and right to empty all of the mix into the form, she backed it up.

"Now," he said, nodding at the pile, "smooth it out—"

"I know—into an even layer while you get the next bag going," she called out over her shoulder.

Her father chuckled and did just that.

By the time they'd repeated the process enough times to complete the job, she was ready for a break. "I'm beat."

"It's tough work but looks great." He beamed. "I brought some plastic to lay overtop of the forms so nothing gets into the cement before it dries. Are you going to break for lunch?" he asked. "It's after one o'clock."

"Oh no! I have to let Jamie out."

"OK," her father said, looking at his watch. "Why don't you meet me at the shop after you take care of Jamie. I'll have a sandwich waiting for you."

She leaned up on her toes and kissed his cheek. "You're the best."

He chuckled. "It's my cross to bear."

She was laughing as she turned around and drove to Jack's house to check on Jamie. The mournful howling had her heart breaking for the little dog. He must have heard her footsteps on the deck because he was jumping up, looking out the back door window.

"Hey there, Jameson," she called out as she let herself in the back door.

He didn't make a sound as he launched himself at

her. She braced for impact, rubbed his sides until he stopped trying to climb into her arms, then got down on his level. "You've got some bad habits we'll have to work on, dog."

But Jamie wasn't listening as he bathed her face with kisses. When he settled down and sat on her lap, she pulled him close and rested her face on his soft puppy fur. "You're such a lover. I wish Gracie wasn't allergic to dogs. You'd love it at our house. We've got the field in the back and the barn and…" *No use thinking about what can't be.* "Maybe Jack can drive you on over to run in the field with us, or maybe if I ask Peggy nicely, she'll ask her dad if you can visit the McCormack farm—as long as you promise not to chase their chickens."

Speaking of Jack, Cait wondered if she should just come out and say how she felt. She sensed that he returned part of what she was feeling—the heat was there in his eyes—and she was pretty sure he was beyond interested in the kissing stage.

She was getting hot and bothered just thinking about the last time he'd pulled her into his arms.

As if aware of her inner turmoil, Jamie sat quietly while she talked to him and stroked his head and back. "Mr. Johnson's riding clinic for kids with disabilities is going to be great." Jamie seemed to be listening. "Pop's helping me add on a couple of horse stalls. It feels good to be a part of something important like this."

Jamie started to squirm, so she let him go outside and do his doggy business. With that done, she gave him fresh water and some kibble to eat. "You're a good dog," she told him before asking, "How's Jack today?"

At the sound of his temporary master's name, he

barked joyfully. "I know," she confided, pressing her lips to the top of the puppy's head. "I feel the same way about him. I'm busy tonight and can't have dinner with you guys, but maybe tomorrow."

She settled Jamie in his bed and reminded him to be a good boy until Jack got home. His eyes were sad, but he didn't follow her to the door. He was smart and knew the routine, that Jack would be back in a couple of hours.

Texting Jack to let him know that Jamie was all right and reminding him that she would be working late over at Johnson's, she got back in her car and drove to town.

She was starving by the time she pulled around the back of Mulcahys, and she was pleased to see her father gathering supplies in the back of the shop. "Hi, Pop!"

Her father looked up and grinned. "My favorite carpenter."

"You're only saying that because you'll be working with me on the Johnson project."

"I saw the bookshelves you built for Meg and Dan, and the curio cabinet you built for Miss Trudi's birthday. She's going to love it." He paused and told her, "You've a gift, Caitlin."

She cleared her throat. "Thanks." She hadn't expected him to say something like that, although he usually told them if he thought they did a good job with something. This was different—this was her dream. "It means a lot that you think so."

He grinned and held out a sub sandwich.

"You are the seriously the best! I'm starved."

While she ate, they talked about the Johnson job and the order in which they'd be doing the construction.

When they'd gone over everything, he asked, "So, does the lumberyard have our order ready for pick up?"

"Yes, but that's the problem," she said, finishing up the sub. "I'm still driving the car and don't have a lot of room."

"I guess you didn't look out front," he told her.

"No. I came around back. Why?"

"Follow me."

When they walked through the shop, Gracie looked up from her terminal, but from the glazed look in her eyes, she was either setting up tomorrow's schedule or doing their quarterly reports for taxes.

Cait knew better than to interrupt now; she could talk to her sister later.

When her father opened the front door and held it, she stepped past him and felt her mouth drop open. "It's finished?" She walked over to the F1, examining the passenger door up close. "It's great…you can't tell that it was scratched or anything."

"Bob does good work."

Her eyes filled as she spun around to face him. "I'm so sorry—"

"I know you are." He took her hand and turned it so her palm was facing up, placed the keys in her hand, and gently closed her fingers around them. "Take care of our legacy."

Clearing her throat, she promised, "I won't let you down again."

"That's my girl. Let's tell Grace where we're headed."

The lumberyard was busy, but Joe and Cait had been there countless times before, and knew their way around. They pulled up in front of one of the buildings in the back and were greeted by one of the owners. "Glad you two are still speaking to one another," he said, eyeing the gleaming black F1. "Bob Stewart does good work."

Cait silently cursed and waited until they'd loaded up the truck bed and paid for the lumber before saying anything. "Did you have to tell him about the truck?"

Joe stared out the front window as she drove. "Didn't have to."

"But this isn't Apple Grove."

"Close enough that news travels fast—good and bad."

"Maybe I get why Grace doesn't want to stay in town. Everybody knows everyone else's business and talks about it over coffee at the diner…or at the lumberyard a few towns over."

Her dad frowned. "She's been wanting to go back to the city ever since she graduated. I keep expecting her to tell me she's leaving any day now."

"I know, but I haven't given up hope that she'd change her mind."

Her father sighed. "Mulcahys is my life, but that doesn't mean it has to be Meg's, or yours, or Grace's."

"But when you retired—"

"None of you were engaged or married, so I didn't have to hire outside the family. I hoped it would always be that way, Mulcahys working for Mulcahys, but that's my dream, and I am a realist."

He fell silent for the next few miles.

She didn't mind riding without talking because that meant that her dad would be working out a problem in his mind, but the sudden thought that she and Grace might be the problem unnerved her enough to break the silence.

"So, are you and Mary going to get married soon?"

His head whipped around so fast she wondered that he didn't get whiplash. "What makes you ask?"

"Just something about the way the two of you were communicating without words."

"When?"

"The other day at the market…when you turned the sign around and kissed her."

"You saw that?" He sounded resigned.

"Yep, thought about taking a pic and sending it to Rhonda, but then realized that you might not like being front page center news in the *Gazette*."

Her father was mumbling beneath his breath as they pulled into Johnson's driveway. "You and your sister see too much."

"Pop," Cait said as she parked the truck. "For what it's worth, we all like her and want you to be happy."

"You and your sisters have been the light of my life for so long." He shook his head as he got out of the truck. "I wasn't thinking about dating when Mary and I met for the first cup of coffee at the diner, but now…"

Cait got out and worked with her father unloading the truck bed. "She's kind, has a nice smile, and must have some other redeeming qualities, or you wouldn't be stuck on her."

His head reared up and his eyes flashed a split-second warning that his temper was on the rise. "Who said anything about being stuck?" he grumbled. "I'm not stuck."

Cait heard the panic in his voice and felt they had something more in common than just good genes and big hearts—fear of taking the next step in a relationship when it mattered. "I didn't think I was either, but you were right." Her emerald-bright gaze met his and the look of complete and utter terror faded.

"Jack's a good man, Cait."

"I know, but I'm surprised that it took me this long to realize it. Why does that happen?"

"What happen?" he asked, unloading another length of wood and adding it to the growing stack by the side of the barn.

"You pass someone on the street nearly every day of your life, you wave," she said, lifting another board. When he lifted his end, she continued, "They wave back, and you both smile. But then one day, something changes…maybe it's the Earth tilting on its axis toward springtime, maybe you've just contracted the bubonic plague…maybe he's been away and finally back home, and you see them—really see them—and you realize you don't know them at all."

Her father helped her lift the last of the boards before answering. "It was like that with Mary. We'd known one another all our lives. Her husband was a good man. We went to his wake and funeral, said whatever nonsensical words one says to comfort the bereaved while they numbly nod to you, waiting for the next person in line to do the same."

Cait brushed her hands on the seat of her jeans and tossed her braid over her shoulder. They pulled the tarp over the wood and placed a rock on it to make sure it wouldn't blow off.

"It was the week before Bill and Edie's wedding three years ago that I walked into Murphy's Market and saw Mary standing in a pool of sunlight. She had her eyes closed and a sweet smile on her face as she lifted it toward the sun." He cleared his throat as Cait turned the key in the ignition, engaged the clutch, and put it in reverse. "I hadn't seen a smile like that in fifteen years. After your mom died, I was so wrapped up in grief and trying to raise you girls that I'd forgotten how vibrant a woman looks when she smiles."

They drove for a bit without speaking until she turned onto Route 13 and asked, "How'd you like to meet Jamie?"

Her dad grinned. "Want to text Jack first and ask him?"

"He might be home by now. His last appointment for the day canceled."

"How do you know that?"

"He, uh, texted me to let me know and asked if I could stop by."

"So, you're really hoping I won't mind making a detour because you can't wait to see him?"

She signaled and pulled into Jack's driveway. "You've always been the smartest man I know, Pop."

He grinned, got out of the truck, and paused. "Any chance of the puppy running out here and jumping on the truck?"

"No, he stays in the backyard or the house. He's pretty smart for a puppy."

"Let's go then."

Cait raised her hand to knock on the back door when she heard a shout from inside. "Sounds like puppy trouble," she said with a grin and knocked.

"Get back here, you devil dog!"

Her father chuckled. "I used to have one of those as a kid."

They heard something crash on the other side of the

door, followed by a playful yip. "Maybe Jack can't hear you over that racket," her father said. "Try again."

"Hold on!" There was a muffled curse, another yip, and Jack yanked the door open, saying, "Thank God you're here, Cait. Can you help me get my boxers—"

——〜〜〜——

A dripping Jack tightened his hold on the towel he'd wrapped around his waist before chasing the dog. He looked from Cait to her father and back. "I, uh…come in."

Joe stared at him but didn't say anything, while Caitlin called Jamie and damned if the little pup didn't just trot right over to her and sit, offering his front paw and the now-mangled pair of boxers.

She tossed them to Jack who had to snag them mid-air before Jamie got another chance to grab them again. "That's the third pair this week."

"Don't you have a hamper?" Joe asked.

"Yeah, but it doesn't have a padlock on it, and as soon as I get home and grab a shower, he's in the bathroom with me, pouncing on the damned thing."

Cait cleared her throat when she realized her father was frowning. "We can wait here with Jamie while you get dressed."

He felt his face go hot and cursed the fact that, with his pale Irish skin, he was prone to flushing when angry or embarrassed. "Thanks. Be right back."

He wondered why Cait had decided to bring her father by. If she'd have warned him, he might have shown up wearing more than a towel. Then again, he had thought about ditching the towel because he was expecting Cait, thinking maybe it would help them get past the hesitation they were both feeling. Good thing he hadn't!

That had him smiling for a moment, but then he realized he'd forgotten about the mass of scars on his left leg…something that never happened before. Caitlin Mulcahy messed with his mind like no other woman. *Had she seen? Had Joe? Did it really matter?*

By the time he was dressed, he could hear playful growls coming from the kitchen. When he walked in, Joe had one end of Jamie's rope toy and the puppy had the other, tugging and growling with abandon.

"Thanks for distracting him. He'll live to see another day."

Cait walked over and poked him in the middle of his chest, a worried look on her face. "That's nothing to joke about," she told him. "If not for us, he might not be here right now."

"True," Jack said. "I was just joking. If you've never raised a puppy, you might not understand."

Joe grinned. "There was this coonhound that we had when I was really little, my dad always swore that dog was one beating away from that big hunting ground in the sky."

Too late, Jack noticed that the worry on Cait's face morphed into fear. She really didn't understand. "Your dad's joking."

"Oh." She glanced at her dad, who nodded to reassure her. "OK."

Jack looked down at Jamie, who was as low as he could go in order to brace himself and pull against Joe, and then up at Cait's dad, who had a shit-eating grin on his face. It hit him then that Joe needed a dog as badly as Cait did. Too bad Grace was allergic to dogs. With Joe being retired, Jamie could keep him company and ride shotgun all around town in Joe's truck. Because he could see it, he almost asked, but then something held him back.

Jamie must have just noticed that Jack had come back in the room. He gave a happy bark and jumped up, trying to lick Jack's face. "Kiss up," he said, ruffling the dog's fur. "Down, boy."

"We're working on manners," Cait told her dad.

"You've got a ways to go," Joe told them. "But he's young yet."

"Yeah, but he's a great dog…despite the fact that he has these bad habits of tackling people and tearing apart my laundry."

Cait's laugh had him staring at her. When their gazes met, he couldn't help but wonder if she was as distracted as he was remembering their last kiss and the power of the lure between them. If her father wasn't here, he would have taken her in his arms and feasted on that tempting mouth of hers. He sighed. He'd have to be patient.

Joe said, "I've got to head on home or Gracie will be on my case. She's cooking dinner tonight."

"Oh." Cait's smile faltered and she said to Jack, "I guess I'll see you tomorrow."

Jack tried not to let his disappointment show, but it was work.

"Tell you what," her dad said, looking from Cait to Jack and back again. "Why don't you stay here since you two obviously want to spend more time…with the puppy."

Jack gave the man extra points for saying that with a straight face. "Thanks."

"Are you sure?" Cait asked.

"See you later." He opened the back door. "I'm sure Jack won't mind giving you a ride home. Will you, Jack?"

Jack caught the look that seemed to be both a warning and a blessing. "Not at all."

Her dad pet Jamie and was gone.

Once they heard the truck start up, he told her, "Your dad's a great guy."

"He really likes you, Jack."

"Good," he said. "I like him too."

"About the other night," Jack said, watching Cait's face so he could gauge what she was thinking. "Waiting to kiss you again has been hell on Earth. Waiting to take the next step…making love to you has been keeping me up nights…and taking a lot of cold showers."

His lips hovered a breath above hers while he waited for her to make the next move. His ploy worked when she huffed out a breath, slid her hands around his neck, and pulled him in for a kiss that was just short of carnal.

Lips, teeth, and tongue tangled as the flames of desire burned inside of him, making him desperate to taste the skin at the base of her throat. He thought they were on the same page, but before he let his imagination run away with him, he needed to know that they both wanted the same thing—to spend the next few hours sharing what was inside their hearts without need for words…a press of lips here and slide of skin there. He was breathing hard when he pulled away and held her at arm's length.

"Was that your answer?"

She smiled and tilted her head to one side. "Do you need me to tell you again?" she asked as she leaned toward him.

He shook his head. "You pack a punch, Mulcahy." Taking hold of her hand, he said, "Let's continue our conversation on the couch."

Her eyes slid from where they stood just inside the kitchen doorway to the low-backed sofa that stretched out along one wall in the living room. "OK."

This time, she was the one doing the tugging. Pulling him so he fell with her to the cushions. Jamie jumped on top of Jack's back and began to tug on his jeans. "Down, boy," he said, gently pushing the dog off the couch.

Jamie hung his head, but Jack's attention was snagged elsewhere when Caitlin sat up and tugged her T-shirt up and over her head. "God, you're beautiful." He reached for her. Pulling her close, he let his mouth feast on her sumptuous skin. "You taste like heaven."

"Your turn," she said, tugging on the hem of his shirt. He didn't hesitate; he let her help him pull it off. "Why are you hiding the fact that you're totally ripped from the ladies in town?"

He laughed until he felt her hands gliding up his pecs and over his shoulders, strong but tender, in a fluid movement over and over that hypnotized him. "I love the way your hands feel on me."

Knowing he needed more time to show Cait how he felt about her, he put his hand over hers. "My turn."

Her eyes widened, but she didn't speak, choosing to communicate with a nod, moan, and the undulation of her body.

Hands splayed at the small of her back, he pulled her toward him. She gripped the back of his shoulders for balance.

"I love the way your eyes go cloudy right before I kiss

you." He bent his head and brushed his mouth across hers. "You skin is so soft, except for the hands you use to work hard for a living." When she would have jerked them off of him, he covered her hands with his and shook his head. "The strength in them turns me on." Her gaze met his and from the softening in hers, he could tell she understood. "I'm going to touch you, Cait. Will you let me?"

Her sigh of contentment echoed through the living room. Jamie started to whine, but Jack didn't pay any attention; his every thought, every movement, was concentrated on the woman vibrating beneath his touch.

His fingertips brushed along the length of her shoulders, taking the straps of her bra with them as he swept his hands down to her wrists and then back. When she moaned, he swept them from her hips to beneath her ribs and then back again, before unhooking her bra and letting it fall to the floor.

He repeated the movement again, touching her shoulders, sweeping them down to her wrists, up from her hips to her ribs...and each time he brushed closer to his goal, her delicate breasts. He wanted to feel their weight in his hands as he teased them into readiness for his lips and tongue.

She moaned out his name. "Don't make me beg— touch me!"

He filled his hands with her soft flesh, caressing and molding her breasts until her breathing became ragged, her eyes closed, and she tilted her head back. Awed by her trust, desperate not to scare her off with the need clawing inside him, he pulled her close and held her to his heart. When her breathing quieted and he was in control once again, he pressed his lips beneath her ear and then followed an invisible line along her collarbone; when he reached the hollow of her throat, he let his tongue linger.

Her soft moan of pleasure was music to his ears as she leaned back, offering herself to him.

Humbled, Jack vowed to take no more than she gave and to give all he could.

His pulse pounded as he flicked his tongue against the skin at the base of her throat and tasted her salty-sweet essence. His hands skimmed over her neck to waist, breast to belly, again and again until she began to writhe.

"Let me touch you," she whispered against his neck.

"Not yet." He stroked the underside of her left breast with his tongue.

Garbled words made a nonsensical sound as he continued his assault on her senses and she gasped for air. Finally, she uttered the word he'd been waiting to hear: "Now!"

Desperate to take, he yanked back on need a second time and took one breast and then the other into his mouth. Suckling her, he feasted, flicking, swirling, licking, and suckling again until she screamed out his name and went limp in his arms.

Caitlin couldn't move. Her heart threatened to pound out of her chest and her arms and legs felt like water. *Oh my God*. No one had ever made her spontaneously combust like that before with just his mouth on her neck and breasts.

"Jack," she rasped. When he didn't answer her, she cleared her throat and tried again to be heard. "Jack?"

"Caitlin," he whispered, letting his forehead rest against hers. "You destroy me."

Laughter caught her by surprise. Feeling loose, she gave in to it, chuckling softly. "Last time I checked, you weren't the one screaming my name while you came apart in my arms."

He raised his head and stared down at her. "True enough. Want to do something about that?"

"Oh yeah," she said as the strength surged back into her arms and legs. She pushed him until he fell onto his back on the couch and straddled his hips. "My turn." Taking her time, she trailed the tip of her tongue along the clean, strong line of his jaw, teasing the underside of it as she settled herself firmly against his growing erection. "Someone's already warmed up."

The dark and desperate desire in his eyes had her squirming, wishing she'd thought to step out of her jeans before her assault. "I think we're overdressed."

"Wait," he said, stilling her movement with a hand to her thigh, before closing his eyes.

She stared down at him as he opened his eyes and an emotion she wasn't used to filled her, threatening to drag her under.

"Don't stop touching me, Cait."

The tender way he said her name had need coursing through her again. She began to explore his torso with her lips, teeth, and tongue. Tiny flicks of her tongue were followed up by nips of her teeth, testing the strength of his pecs and the firmness of his abs. She wiggled lower, so she could twist and flick her tongue beneath the waistband of his jeans. She felt the heat of him and remembered that the dog had shredded his boxers…was he commando beneath his jeans?

She hadn't realized she asked the question out loud until she heard his raspy chuckle. "Only you would ask me that now." He pulled her back up his body and cupped her face in his hands, wordlessly urging her to stop as he lifted her away from temptation.

"I didn't get to go beneath the equator—you can't either," he told her. "Unless you don't intend to play fair."

Instead of answering him, she slid off the couch so she had a better angle to tease him from. "You're delicious," she said, blowing softly across the taut skin of his abdomen before teasing it again with the tip of her tongue.

"God, Cait…I can't wait."

She sat back on her heels and met his gaze. "Then don't."

"Are you sure?" He sat up and pushed off the couch, so he could pull her to her feet.

When she was in his arms, she shivered at the feel of his hot skin pressed against her breasts. "Thinking about what it would be like to make love with you has been making me crazy too" she confessed. "Besides, now that I've tasted you, there's no going back. You're addictive."

"You go to my head like a shot of whiskey." Easing back from her, he unsnapped his jeans and hesitated. "Cait, there's something I forgot to tell you."

"Is it important?"

"To me."

"OK," she said. "Tell me."

He drew in a breath before beginning, "I was injured over in Iraq."

"I know," Cait said. "We were so worried when we

found out you'd been hurt and broken your leg. That's why you were limping the day you chased Jamie into my arms, isn't it?"

"Yes, but that's not the extent of what happened," he rasped. Their eyes met and held. "An IED exploded, broke my leg, and filled it with shrapnel."

Tears filled her eyes as the thought of him being in so much pain speared through her. "You must have been in agony."

He brushed at the first tear that fell. "I was…it still bothers me."

"All the time, or when the weather changes?"

Before he could answer her, she added, "Mr. Weatherbee's always complaining that he can tell when a storm's coming because the wrist he broke as a kid starts to hurt."

He brushed his thumb along the curve of her cheek and then the fullness of her bottom lip. "There's something you need to know."

"Oh Lord, is there still shrapnel in your leg?"

"Legs," he corrected. "Some, not as much as there used to be. It took a couple of operations to remove the worst of it."

"But didn't I hear you and my brother-in-law talking about running together?"

"Yeah."

"How can you run if it still hurts?"

"I run early in the day when my leg is strong. After standing most of the day, it bothers me."

Looking at the way he frowned, she urged him to sit. "You should rest." Worry for him was eating her alive. "Do you need an aspirin? Glass of water?"

"Cait, please!" he said, tugging until she stopped trying to force him to sit on the couch. "I wanted to tell you about the scars before you saw them."

"Oh, OK."

He paused and then whispered, "They're hideous."

She wanted to throw her hands up in the air but knew that was too dramatic, and she didn't want him to think she was flippant when he was baring his soul to her. Finally, she shrugged, and said, "They're scars. They're not supposed to be pretty."

He opened his mouth to say something but then closed it again and shook his head.

"What?" she demanded, starting to get ticked. Was he was worried she'd bail if she saw his scars? "Did you really think I'd change my mind about making love with you once I saw your scars?"

"Others have."

"Well, I have news for you, Jackie boy," she bit out. "I'm not like anyone else."

"Amen to that," he said.

"Are you making fun of me?"

"Not on your life, babe," he said, kissing her until her toes curled and her head felt light. "I just wanted to prepare you before you saw them, but you got to my head so fast, I forgot until it was almost too late."

Taking back control, she needed to show him, without words, how she felt. She pushed out of his arms, flipped open the snap of her jeans, and shimmied them over her hips and let them fall to the floor. "I've got scars on both knees from falling on them so often as a kid. It's why I don't wear skirts too often unless they come below the knee."

He started to speak, but she held up her hand. "And here," she said, pointing to her right side, "is the scar I have from when they took out my appendix." Before he could respond, she lifted the braid off the back of her neck and turned so he could see. "And here is where I fell on a rock when I was a kid. Knocked me out cold and bled like crazy...don't remember how many stitches that took to close it up. But my dad turns green if I try to ask him, so I just let it go."

"Cait," he said quietly—twice before she answered him.

"What?"

"Shut up and kiss me."

She threw her arms around him and nearly died with pleasure feeling the brush of his crisp chest hair against her breasts, and the bulge behind his zipper, but it was the wild beat of his heart that had her asking, "So will you trust me with your scars, since I showed you mine?"

He leaned his forehead against hers, drew in a breath, eased back, and unzipped his jeans. Pausing with his hands hooked in the waistband, he was undone by the tender look on Cait's face...it encouraged him. He shoved his pants down his legs and kicked them aside.

Cait held her hand out to him, beckoning him.

Could she see the mass of scars, riddling his leg, pinching the skin where it should be smooth? He held his breath.

She stepped closer and locked gazes with him as she trailed the tips of her fingers along his shoulders, then down his torso, stopping at his hips.

Before he could guess her intention, she knelt and pressed her mouth to the middle of his thigh and the tangled web of scar tissue.

His breath whooshed out and his head felt light as her tongue traced the meandering path, the sunburst pattern—the reminder of the agonizing day he tried to put behind him.

He thought she'd stop there and wasn't prepared when her tongue detoured to his hipbone across to his navel, where she dipped her tongue in before retreating back to his scarred leg.

"Cait." Her name was a prayer, a benediction. The tender way she included his scars in their lovemaking made him feel almost normal—almost.

He bent down and urged her to stand. Heart to heart, he nestled between her legs and let her feel what her mouth did to him. Tipping her head back, she lifted her lips and was rewarded by a toe-tingling, mind-bending, air-stealing kiss that rocked her world.

When he shifted his handhold to beneath her back-side, she lifted her legs and wrapped them around his waist. "Am I too heavy?"

"No. Kiss me, Cait."

She tangled her tongue with his before remembering her earlier worry. "Do you have any condoms?"

"I'm a doctor, Cait. I have everything we need." He slid his hand between them and brought her to peak with his clever fingers.

Her head dropped back and he kissed her before easing her onto the sofa. "Don't move," he told her.

She was about to argue with him, when he pointed a finger at her until she agreed. While she watched, he bent down and pulled a foil packet out of the back pocket of his jeans, stood, and covered himself. When he was fully sheathed, he knelt above her on the sofa and slowly lowered himself, teasing her with the tip of his erection.

"Jack," she moaned. "Please, don't tease me."

He took her at her word and slowly slid into her. When they were joined, heart pressed to heart, he closed his eyes and let his body take over. She met him thrust for thrust, marveling at his stamina.

"Jack, I can't—"

"I think you can," he ground out.

She closed her eyes as the orgasm stole her breath. When she had gathered her strength, she lifted her hips and pistoned them against him, lifting up off the couch, hanging on to his taut backside with both hands. "Your turn, Jack."

When he slowed his movements, she pressed her lips to the side of his neck and kissed him before biting the tender skin there. Her love bite had him moaning in pleasure, so she moved to another spot and kissed, then nipped twice more. She could feel the change coming over him as he stiffened and moaned out her name.

But instead of going with the moment as she'd thought he would, he bent to take her breast in his mouth, whipping her to peak so they rode the crest together, crashing on the other side.

Chapter 9

"I can't feel my legs," Caitlin whispered, but she wasn't worried. "But you're a doctor, so you can probably fix me, right?"

His laughter caught her by surprise. "What's so funny?" She trailed the tips of her fingers along the firm muscles of his back. It was hard to work up any temper when she felt so loose, so limber, so happy being in love. Meg was right—she loved Jack.

When he kept laughing and didn't answer her, she nipped his shoulder to get his attention.

He braced his hands on the couch and pushed back, his biceps taut from holding his weight off of her. The strength in his upper body reminded her of the way he'd held back so she'd find fulfillment first. *A generous lover.*

When he smiled down at her, she felt all warm and gooey inside. "You're so beautiful."

His smile turned to one that reeked of satisfied male. "Not even half as beautiful as you," he rasped, bracing his weight on one arm to smooth a strand of hair out of her eyes.

Her belly clutched and fresh need sprinted through her. "If the other ladies in town knew how talented you are—" she began, only to close her mouth at his frown.

"You planning on taking out an ad in the *Gazette*?"

She let her finger slide over his breastbone and down to his navel. "Maybe," she admitted. "But then everyone would want a turn and you'd be too tired to make love with me."

He was chuckling as he lay back down and shifted so she was on top. "I'm too heavy for you."

"You felt just right," she said, leaning down to press her lips to his chin. "And for the record, I'm not telling anyone how talented you are because I want to keep you all to myself."

"Is that a promise?"

She leaned back and made an X over her heart. "Promise."

"Works for me," he said. "Now about that talent…"

Jack woke when a cold wet nose pressed against his side. "Hey, boy." When Jamie whined, he shifted a sleeping Caitlin onto her side and got up to let the dog out.

After Jamie peed, Jack opened the door and nearly walked into Caitlin. "Whoa," he said, steadying her. "What's wrong?"

"I woke up when I got chilly." Brushing a hand over his shoulder, she smiled and his heart tumbled further toward love. "Did we scar him for life?"

He chuckled at her reference to making love in front of the dog. "I think he's impressed by my mad skills."

Her delighted laughter wrapped around his heart, tugging him the rest of the way into love. "I wish you could stay the night."

Jack pulled her against him and reveled in the feel of her whisper-soft skin slowly heating against his. "I love the way you feel in my arms. If I talk to your father, do you think he'd let you stay?"

"So his darling daughter could engage in another mind-boggling bout of heart-stopping sex?"

He chuckled even though he tried to be stern. "I thought we made love?"

Her eyes softened. "We did, and it was amazing."

He had to agree. "But we need—"

"To get going," she finished for him. "I know." She looked him in the eye and tried to frown as she said, "Someone told my dad he'd give me a ride home."

With a sigh of frustrated regret, he released her. "The last thing I want to do is give your dad a reason to doubt my word."

"Hmmm…I guess so. Hey, do you think he thinks we're playing canasta?"

Jack just shook his head. "I hate to burst your bubble, babe, but I don't think so." He looked down at Jamie and asked, "You want to go for a ride?" Jamie bounced up and down before settling down when Jack told him to sit.

"Can I go too?" Caitlin asked, brushing up against him again, skin to skin teasing him to the point of madness.

"Quit teasing me," he grumbled. "I've got to take you home, woman."

"Don't remind me."

"Come on," he urged. "Go get dressed."

She paused in the doorway. "Aren't you coming?"

He shook his head at her. "If I go with you, one of us will definitely be coming, but then we'll be late."

Her eyes darkened to forest green and he fought against the need to grab her, toss her over his shoulder, and sprint for the stairs. He wanted her in his house, in his bed…in his life. But it was too soon to tell her without her wondering if it was just great sex talking, wasn't it? They'd been drawn together because of Jamie, but the sparks and tension between them had been there from the first, tempting him.

Finally, she dragged her feet, but left the room and returned dressed.

"OK, my turn," he said, easing past her so they didn't touch. If they did, he wouldn't be able to keep from grabbing her and burying his face in her hair, then one thing would lead to another, and they'd end up where they both wanted to be—his bed.

When they were finally ready, he grabbed Jamie's leash. "Ready to go for a ride, boy?"

Once they had the dog clipped to his leash, they walked out the back door. "I don't know if I'm going to be able to sleep tonight," she confessed. "I'll be thinking of you, wishing you were there beside me."

They got in the car and his hands clenched the wheel, desperate to touch the woman who'd turned him inside out, knowing if he did, he'd yank on the wheel, pull a one-eighty, and head back to his house. Yep, he'd lock the door and keep her.

As they drove along Eden Church Road, she talked to the dog as if she expected him to answer. Much to Jack's surprise, the dog barked or whined in response to Cait's questions. He chuckled until he realized he was in way over his head. *Could she be real? Did his scars only bother him?* He needed Cait in his life, not just in his bed. All he had to do was convince her.

Cait was watching him out of the corner of her eye.

"What?" he asked.

"You have a great laugh."

When he didn't say anything, she nuzzled the top of Jamie's head. "Has Sheriff Wallace heard from anyone yet?"

"No," Jack said with a glance at Jamie. "Looks like this guy is here to stay."

"Good," Cait said.

Jack echoed that sentiment. "I'm used to having him in my life…it would too quiet without him."

She agreed. "It's become part of my routine, stopping by a few times a day to make sure he's all right. He's always ready with a happy bark and busy tongue." They fell into a comfortable silence as he turned onto Peat Moss Road. "My dad really liked him."

He grinned. "What's not to like?" He patted Jamie on the top of his head. "He's a great dog."

"Are you both going to walk me to the door?"

Jamie barked and Jack laughed. "Sorry, boy, not this time." One at a time, they slipped out so Jamie didn't escape. They walked hand in hand to the door and Jamie started to howl.

Jack's lips brushed gently against her cheek before capturing her lips in a silky-sweet kiss. "Dream of me, Caitlin."

She rested a hand on his chest as she eased out of his embrace and pushed away from him, feeling the chill after so much warmth. "I already do." She squeezed his hand and added, "Miss me, OK?"

Jamie's entire body wagged as he leaned on the top edge of the passenger door and barked. Caitlin smiled. "Keep an eye on him for me, boy."

She watched them leave and, in a moment of painful insight, knew that the ache she felt now was not even one-tenth of the ache a military wife would feel watching her man as he prepared to deploy.

Had Jack had someone all those years ago whom he hated to leave behind? Had he broken anyone's heart here in town? She didn't understand her need to find out but knew she'd be asking Meg. Her sister would know.

Letting herself in, she shut off the light on the stove. Halfway to her room, she remembered they'd be getting an early start and walked to the bathroom instead. The hot water soothed tired muscles and a few aches that had her smiling, remembering how she'd earned them. Squeaky clean, wearing her favorite sleep shirt, she slipped beneath the covers. Lying in bed, she stared at her ceiling, glad that she never painted over the fluffy clouds and rainbows her mother had painted there years before. It made her feel closer to her mom. Meg liked to go to the cemetery to talk to their mom, and Grace, hmmm…she had no idea what Grace did to remember their mom.

Shifting to her side, she wondered what Jack and Jamie were doing right then. Probably snuggling up in bed together. *Maybe next time, we can make love in his bed.*

She closed her eyes as thoughts of Jack and his tender kisses filled her heart, giving her something lovely to think about as she drifted off to sleep.

—w—

"Cait!" a deep voice called out, rousing her from a deep sleep. "Coffee's ready!"

Rubbing the sleep from her eyes, she wished for just five minutes more. "If I ask him, he'll start the water treatment."

Then again, a few more precious minutes to dream about Jack might be worth having ice-cold water flicked in her face until she woke up, but that was guaranteed to make her dad grumpy. He was doing her a huge favor helping out at Johnson's barn, so she dragged herself out of bed. She finger combed her hair, rebraided it, and got dressed.

Her dad was at the stove frying bacon. He looked over his shoulder as she walked into the kitchen. "Hungry?"

"Always."

Knowing his routine, Cait opened the fridge and got out four eggs, rye bread, and butter. "Scrambled OK?"

He nodded. "Let me drain the pan. No sense having to wash two of them."

"Amen to that." She cracked the eggs and whipped them with a fork. "Can you do the toast?"

Her dad nodded. "Got it."

They worked well together, with an economy of movement that bespoke years of doing so. Plates full, coffee poured, they sat down to eat. Joe took a sip of his coffee and said, "Heard on the weather we've got a storm heading our way this afternoon. We need to get that addition framed out and shingled. I'd rather we didn't have to toss another tarp onto the sheathing up on the roof. It'd be better if it had tar paper and shingles."

Cait finished her toast and gulped the last of her coffee as he added, "Expecting thirty mile an hour winds with this storm."

"Then we'd better hit the road, Pop." Halfway there, she asked, "Are you really worried that we won't beat the weather?"

Her father parked in Johnson's driveway and got out. "Less talking, more working, string bean."

"Jeez, Pop!" He hadn't called her that in years, but as he'd intended, it felt like a hug so she wouldn't worry about the coming storm.

They'd pulled out their toolboxes and walked over to the tarped pile of wood by the time Mr. Johnson walked down from the house. "We've got weather coming, Joe."

"Not a problem, Scott. You've got my best girl working on it and me as her helper."

With a nod in her direction, Mr. Johnson said, "I'll keep an ear out for a change in the report and let you know if I hear anything."

"Appreciate it," Joe responded. He asked Cait, "Do you have your measurements?"

"I do, but I'd like to double-check and jot the numbers down."

Her father grinned. "Measure twice, cut once—that's my girl."

By the time they broke for lunch, they had framed out the two new stalls and were ready for the sheathing.

"Hey, Joe!"

Cait and her father looked up as Mr. Johnson came jogging toward them. "They're calling for dangerous lightning and high winds by five o'clock."

"Well, Cait, it's your project. What do you think we should do?"

Cait looked up at the still-blue sky and then at the men standing side by side. "We could work through lunch, but we've been on the job since seven this morning. I'm not sure if that's a good idea. We need to refuel and hydrate so we don't make a mistake."

Her dad looked up at the sky and then over at Scott

Johnson. "Why don't I call my son-in-law and see if we can round up a few helpers? He should be getting out of school around two thirty."

Cait felt relief wash over her. She knew it would be close framing and sheathing before the storm hit; help would ensure that they'd get it shingled as well. "You can't rush perfection," she said to Mr. Johnson. "My dad's got a good plan, and it won't increase the price. Once a Mulcahy gives his word—" she began.

"He keeps it," Mr. Johnson finished for her, nodding to her first and her father second. "Go for it. I'll keep an eye on the storm and bring you updates."

While she unpacked their lunch boxes, her father shot off a text to Dan. As she was pouring hot coffee out of the thermos, her father grunted and held out his cup. "He'll be here by quarter of three with two helpers."

Cait grinned. "Let me guess, Charlie Doyle and Tommy Hawkins?"

Her father held out a cup for her to fill. "Those boys have more than made up for their stupidity, hanging out on that damned railroad bridge."

"Dan was there to save them, Pop."

"It was meant, Cait," he said quietly. "Dan Eagan was supposed to come to Apple Grove, meet your sister, fall in love, and save those two boys. Wonder what else fate has planned for him?"

Cait laughed. "A little girl just like Meg?"

Joe joined in the laughter and said, "You have an evil streak in you, Cait."

"I wonder where I get that from?"

They were both laughing as Cait cleaned up the garbage and downed the rest of her coffee.

Joe was still smiling as they measured and cut boards for the roof rafters. They were nailing them into place when they heard a car drive up.

"Hey, Joe!" Dan called out as he got out of his car. "Brought help with me."

Cait watched the way her dad pulled Dan in for a bear hug and felt tears sting her eyes. She sensed he'd be as welcoming to Jack.

"No time for lollygagging around, Caitlin," her father rumbled. "Come on down here and help me get these boys started working."

She grinned. "Coming." Climbing down the ladder, she looked up at her father. "How about if we break down into two teams?"

He nodded. "Ever shingle a roof, Dan?"

"Not yet. I figured I'd be learning how today."

"Good answer," Cait said with a smile. "How about you boys?"

Charlie grinned. "Helped Dad patch up the hole in the garage roof after uh…" His voice trailed off and he looked at his buddy.

"What did you and Tommy do to put a hole in the roof?"

Tommy grinned at her, and said, "It was the hammer throw."

Dan started laughing. "Seriously?"

"Yeah," Charlie told him. "We were in eighth grade and wanted to see if we could throw a hammer like on the track team."

"You do realize that they don't actually throw a hammer, don't you?" Dan asked.

"Not at the time," Tommy admitted.

Joe was shaking his head. "Did you use a claw hammer?"

"Nah," Tommy said. "We got one of my dad's sledge hammers."

"Brilliant." Dan laughed.

"We were pretty good," Charlie said, "until Tommy got creative with a toss and the hammer ended up going through the roof."

Caitlin was chuckling when she told them, "All right, Dan, you and Pop can work on measuring and cutting the sheathing for the roof. If we start there, the boys and I can get it shingled while you do the sheathing for the walls."

"You got it."

As they worked, she was pleased to find out that Charlie and Tommy really did know how to shingle. She set them to work, starting with the tar paper. She'd learned the hard way as a kid that you shingled from the bottom to the top. Peggy's dad had spent a lot of time muttering, watching Cait and Peggy tear the shingles off Peggy's doghouse when they'd started from the peak and worked their way down. She and Peggy had been in seventh or eighth grade at the time.

"Storm's stalled," Mr. Johnson called out above the din of two nine-pound hammers and two nail guns.

Cait wiped the back of her arm over her forehead. The day had warmed up considerably by the time they'd gotten up on the roof. "I need some water. How about you boys?"

Charlie looked at Tommy and frowned, asking, "No soda?"

She grinned at them. "If you're going to be working bent over, it's not a good idea to drink soda until you're done. How about I treat for root beer floats over at the diner when we're done?"

"Cool…Coach Eagan is going to feed us pizza."

"Ah," she said, smiling at her brother-in-law. "Mulcahys have always worked for food. Good call," she told him.

By the time the wind started picking up, Cait and her father were nailing shingles on the peak. "Just in time."

She looked up, surprised to see dark clouds boiling above them. "Wow, we'd better finish up, Pop. That sky looks mean."

"It's not green, so that's a good thing. I'm not a fan of twister weather."

"OK, boys," Caitlin called down. "Let's start putting away the tools, the storm's almost here."

The guys had started on the siding but stopped and began to clean up at her command. By the time the first raindrops fell, their tools were stowed in the cab of the truck so they wouldn't get wet, and the boys were safely tucked into Dan's car.

"I owe you guys," Cait told them.

"Yeah," Charlie yelled from the passenger side, "meet us at the diner. I'm really thirsty."

"Me too," Tommy said.

Her father smiled down at her, "Let's go tell Scott we're done for the day."

Scott met them halfway down the path with an umbrella. "It's gonna get nasty. Hey," he said, looking at the new section of stalls they'd added. "You got the roof on."

"That was the plan. Tarps can leak if there's enough wind."

"Chances are pretty good the weather will clear and we can come back tomorrow and put up the siding," Cait told him.

Her dad shook his head. "Let's wait and see. We can call you in the morning after we see what the weather's doing."

"Great job," Scott said, holding his hand for Cait and then Joe to shake.

"Talk to you tomorrow," Joe promised.

Climbing in the truck, Cait wished for a hot cup of coffee, not an ice cream float. Good thing they were headed to the Apple Grove Diner, where you could get either one from seven o'clock in the morning until eleven o'clock at night.

Backing out of the driveway, her father said, "Those boys looked hungry."

When they arrived at the diner, he looked at Cait, and said, "Time to feed the troops."

Peggy and Kate greeted them as they ducked inside the diner to get out of the rain. "Well, looks like we're doing a brisk business for dinner tonight. What'll it be?"

Cait smiled at Peggy and said, "We owe Charlie and Tommy whatever kind of ice cream sodas they want to go with their pizza." She leaned close, "Make sure I get the check."

Charlie looked over at Dan and said, "Hey, Coach, can I have two burgers instead?"

"Yeah," Tommy added. "Pizza's great, but we're really hungry."

Dan smiled. "Not a problem, guys. Dinner's on me."

Cait shook her head. "Actually, I'm buying for the three of you, so take your time and pick whatever you want off the menu."

"What's the occasion?" Kate asked, pad and pen in hand, ready to take their order.

"Dan brought Charlie and Tommy over to Johnson's to help us with a job."

"We got to shingle the addition on the barn," Tommy told Kate.

"Meg's going to be sorry she missed out on the job," Cait said.

"There's still siding to do and interior work to finish," Joe told her. "We needed to close it up before the storm. Wouldn't have happened if these three didn't pitch in and help us, though."

"Feels good," Cait said, as she sat on the stool beside Dan.

"Real good." His phoned buzzed and he grinned. "That'll be Meg checking up on me. Excuse me."

Cait realized with a jolt that she hadn't heard from Jack since she'd texted him about not being able to take care of Jamie today. Was he busy or upset that she didn't have time to take care of his puppy?

Before she could work herself up into a state of nerves, her phone rang. Relief speared through her as she recognized the number. "Hey, Jack," she said, getting up and walking to the other side of the diner so she could hear. "How's Jamie?"

"He misses you. Are you finished over at Johnson's yet?"

"Yes. We're over at the diner. We ended up calling for help and now we're feeding them."

Jack's chuckle soothed the raw edges she hadn't realized she had. *Must be from lack of sleep.* "Dan?"

"Yeah," she said. "And he brought Charlie and Tommy with him."

"A good crew and a good day's work from the sounds of things."

"It was, but I'm beat and in desperate need of a hot shower."

"Oh." His voice went quiet before he asked, "So can you still come over tonight?"

Her heart began to pound as the blood rushed through her veins. "Do you want company?"

"I want you, Cait," he told her. "Come as you are, and I'll scrub your back in the shower."

Her salivary glands were working overtime at the thought. She swallowed and said, "I was just having a cup of coffee. I can't leave the guys yet."

"I can wait." The depth of his voice did things to her insides that were probably illegal in most states.

"I could leave money with my dad—" she began.

"No," he said. "Stay with the guys, have a bite to eat. Jamie and I will be here when you're through."

"See you in a bit," she promised.

Chapter 10

JACK TOOK JAMIE OUTSIDE, BUT NEITHER ONE REALLY wanted to be standing out in the middle of the downpour. "There's times when it must suck to be a dog."

The way Jamie looked over his shoulder at Jack as he did his doggy business had him turning his back so the puppy could have some privacy. "Finished?"

Jamie ran past him into the house and skidded to a stop at the barricade in the kitchen doorway. The length of plywood was as effective as a door and hard for the dog to sink his teeth into if the scratch marks on the side that faced the kitchen were any indication.

"You're going to get dried off before I let you in the rest of the house, pal."

The dog sat by the wood and waited, and Jack wondered what was going through his mind. Did dogs have similar thoughts to people? They both had a thing for Caitlin... "Define thing," he said aloud.

The dog yipped and Jack laughed. "Yeah. That's what I thought."

After he'd dried off the dog and mopped up the mud on the floor, he moved the plywood and Jamie bounded into the living room and onto the sofa.

An hour later, Jack finally heard a knock and then the back door open.

"Anyone home?"

"It's Cait," he whispered to Jamie.

The dog may not have responded when Jack was telling him to sit and to stay, but he sure knew who Cait was. The dog knocked into Jack, pushing him onto the sofa as he raced into the kitchen with four-paw drive.

"Hey there, you little cutie," he heard her say.

"Lucky little bastard," Jack grumbled as he stood up, wishing he hadn't had such a long day. His leg ached and he was tired. Walking into the kitchen, all thoughts of rest fled as his eyes beheld the sight of the beautiful, drenched woman laughing at the dog's antics.

Jamie was trying to jump into her arms and she was trying to avoid letting him do so. She looked up and noticed Jack. "Hey, handsome."

Her smile eased the tension that had been building when the rain started. He didn't mind rain so much; it was the threat of a thunderstorm that had him on edge. The sound of thunder—not gonna go there…

"Hey, yourself." Grabbing a dry towel off the pile of laundry he'd been folding on the kitchen table, he was about to toss it to her when he remembered she wasn't one of the guys—that and the dog would probably try to tackle her for it.

"Thanks. It's really coming down out there."

"How'd it go over at Johnson's?"

She smiled and said, "Framed, sheathed, and the roof on before the storm hit."

Her gaze met his and something warm and welcoming moved through the depths of her green eyes as she stood just inside his back door, dripping onto the ancient linoleum he hadn't had the time to replace.

His brain registered that he'd answered her, but his heart was still recovering from the blow he took when her gaze met his. Searching for something to say, when all he wanted to do was grab a hold of her and drink the rainwater off her skin, he finally managed, "Good."

"Uh-huh," she agreed. "Dad and I were worried that if the wind blew as hard as predicted, a tarp wouldn't last long or protect the roof. We had to close it up."

How could she still talk when his brain had short-circuited taking in the long length of her legs?

"Jack?"

"What?" Had she asked him something?

"I said I grabbed a quick shower before coming over…oh, and I told my dad I'd see him in the morning."

His eyes widened as what she said registered.

She stopped rubbing herself down with the towel, and a part of his brain started functioning again enough for him to say, "You're probably tired."

Her eyes sparkled and her smile had his breath snagging in his lungs. "I saved some energy for you."

Her words went straight to the part of him that strained against the zipper of his jeans. If he didn't have a taste of her soon, he was going to start howling.

When he didn't move, she closed the gap between them and laid a hand on his cheek. "Are you going to make me ask?"

Her lips claimed his in a kiss that had his engine firing on all cylinders before instinct kicked in and he kissed her back. Her lips were soft, supple, and berry sweet. Wrapping his arms around her, he deepened the kiss before pulling back to whisper, "You could catch a chill if you don't take off those wet clothes."

When she shivered and leaned against him, he decided he'd waited long enough. Easing her out of his arms, he watched her eyes as he grabbed the hem of her polo shirt in his hands; when she made no move to stop him, he peeled it off.

Goose bumps covered her body from neck to belly, but that wasn't what had him digging deep for control—it was the black lace bra that cupped her breasts, lifting them up for his tasting, that nearly did him in.

But he wanted more from her…he wanted it all. He'd sample her silky-smooth skin soon; right now, he had to get her out of the rest of her clothes. From the desire simmering in her brilliant green eyes, he knew she wanted him too. He couldn't hold back the delighted laughter that rumbled up from inside of him.

His hands trembled as he opened the top button of her jeans and slowly pulled the zipper down. Her moan sent a chill chasing up his spine. He went with it and watched her eyes widen before they focused on his hands again. "You're so beautiful, Caitlin…I don't have the words to describe what I see with my eyes and feel with my heart."

She cleared her throat and rasped, "You're doing great so far."

Her mouth curved upward and his heart stuttered until he stood on the precipice, leaning toward the point of no return.

"You have a delicious laugh," she confessed, laying a hand on his shoulder as he bent to push her jeans down mile-long legs.

He paused and gave in to need and touched the tip of his tongue to the back of her knees. When they buckled, he wrapped his arm around her legs, hauled her over his shoulder, and stood.

"Jack," she laughed, "what are you doing?"

"Taking you upstairs. I've been imagining you in my bed all day."

"I can walk," she protested.

"But this is so much more fun for me," he chuckled, moving the flat of his hand to her backside, using the other to grab hold of the handrail.

She squirmed until he got to the top and let her slide down, but instead of setting her on her feet, he shifted so she was in his arms. He strode to his bedroom and turned to use his shoulder to open the door.

He held his breath, hoping he hadn't over done it, setting the scene for the seduction he'd been planning since she left last night. He set her down but kept a hand to her waist, unable to break their physical connection.

Candlelight flickered off the single red rose he'd placed in a glass—he didn't own a vase. "Oh, Jack." She scanned the room and looked up at him. "Candles?"

"You don't like 'em?"

"I do." She walked over and bent to sniff the flower. "Oh," she breathed. "Champagne too?"

"I wanted tonight to be special."

Cait looked at the bed and got distracted. "You sleep on satin sheets?"

"Mmm…" He slid his hand up her back and un-hooked the back of her bra. With the tips of his fingers, he slipped it off one shoulder and then the other. "Your skin reminds me of my sheets." He stripped her black lace panties off and she trembled beneath his touch.

"Come here," he said, tugging on her hand until she had no choice. When they stood at the side of his bed, he urged, "Now close your eyes." He took her hand, urging her to let it brush over his bed.

"Feel the silky texture?"

"Mmm," she agreed. "It's so cool."

"You're not," he rasped, pulling her back up into his arms, crushing her breasts to him. When her eyes popped open, he rasped. "You're hot...molten...like a volcano."

"Jack," she sighed. "Don't make me wait."

He scooped her up and placed her in the middle of his bed, her pale skin reminding him of fresh cream. The tumble of her reddish-blonde hair spread across his pillow had him desperate to touch her, taste her, make love to her.

Shucking off his jeans, he ripped his T-shirt over his head and knelt on the foot of the bed and slowly, watching desire fill her eyes, climbed up the bed until his skin brushed against her toes. Masculine muscle, coiled to release, rubbed against surprisingly firm feminine leg muscles, lower abs, belly, and finally, finally, apple-firm breasts.

Settling himself in the notch between her legs, her heat teased him, but he wanted to go slow...to taste...to savor. He buried his face in her hair and inhaled. "You smell good enough to eat."

She traced the tips of her fingers up the backs of his thighs, skimming over scar tissue, to his backside, and grabbed hold of him.

"I can't go slow if you keep doing that." When she licked her lips, he groaned, taking her under with a bone-tingling kiss. When he came up for air, he leaned over her to open the drawer in the bedside table. Pushing back to his knees, he covered himself and then swept his hands beneath her backside, lifting her up so he could go deep.

He knew now that she was hot, tight, and fit him like

a glove. There was no need to rush—they had all night. Taking his time, he slid in all the way to the hilt, then just as slowly pulled out, poising at the entrance to her delicious warmth.

Dragging out their pleasure just might be the death of him, but what a way to go. Blind to everything except the need to make love with Caitlin, he focused on the woman in his arms, and the sudden desire to make her scream.

———

Cait lifted her hips to take Jack deeper. Higher and higher, faster and faster, she was whipping toward peak—again. He was a devastating lover…one she was in danger of losing her heart to.

How had this happened so quickly? She'd made love before. Why did it feel as if everything hung in the balance this time?

He shifted and swiveled his hips, shattering her into a thousand pieces. Her hands lost their grip and slid bonelessly to the bed.

"Cait?"

She opened her eyes and found herself looking into the eyes of her lover, a man she never thought to have, but now that she experienced what could be between them, she wasn't going to give him up.

"Am I too heavy?"

Just as she was wondering if she'd be able to form a coherent thought, he had his hands on either side of her face, cupping it gently, looking into her eyes. "Did I hurt you?"

She shook her head.

He relaxed and pulled her close before rolling onto his side. "You get to me, Cait."

"Is that a good thing or bad thing?"

He chuckled. "Good, definitely good...I love watching you come in my arms. Penny for your thoughts," he whispered against her ear.

She snuggled her backside against him, eliciting a low rumbling moan from deep inside him. "I was thinking that I've never felt half of what you make me feel. Does that make me semifrigid...or you amazingly hot?"

He wrapped his arms across her chest and laid his cheek against the top of her head. "Does insanity run in your family?"

She snickered. "There were times when I was little when I swore Megan was nuts."

He tightened his hold and told her, "Meg's great... she had a lot of pressure going to school, taking care of you and Grace, and then working with your dad."

"You've mentioned that before."

"We were pretty good friends. She used to talk to me when she was worried that she wasn't living up to what she thought your mom would have wanted."

"I wish I'd known—"

"It wouldn't have changed anything. Meg did the best she could and would have worried no matter what."

"Yeah...it's that Irish Catholic guilt we all suffer from."

"Tell me about it."

"Guys have it too?"

"Absolutely. Some of us succumb to the guilt—and then some of us join the navy."

She was laughing when he laid his lips on hers. Brilliant colors filled her mind as he built the tension between them again. Wanting to give as much as she received, she ran her hands up over his shoulders, then down his back to the taut backside she wanted to take a bite of.

Deciding she'd waited long enough, she pushed against him hard enough that he lifted his lips and stared down at her with one brow lifted in question. She took advantage of the situation and pushed him onto his stomach, slithering onto him, touching, teasing, tasting as she made her way to the gluts she adored.

When she kissed then nipped the muscle there, he tensed. But then she licked where she bit and he relaxed beneath her, giving her his silent permission to do what she wanted with him. His open trust pushed her over the edge as she did a free fall into love.

Where did she start? Leaning her weight against him, she pressed her breasts to his back, loving the way he groaned out her name long and low. Shifting so that she could sit on his backside, she began to knead the knots out of his shoulders—impressive shoulders—until she decided to work her way down to his waist and then back up again.

She scooted down so she was straddling his ankles. Slowly and with deliberate feather-like touches, she skimmed her hands up and down his legs, pausing at the edge of his scarred flesh to press healing kisses to each pucker, every thick line of skin. Her reward was the loving look in Jack's eyes when he rolled over and wrapped her in his arms. "I think I'm falling for you, Jack Gannon."

He tightened his hold on her. The heat and warmth of him had her closing her eyes.

"I'm glad I'm not falling alone." He pulled the satin sheets up to cover them and pressed a kiss to her forehead.

The thunder woke her. She lay quivering in bed; she hated thunderstorms. Lightning flashed and a crack of thunder struck close enough to have the hair on her arms standing on end.

Jamie whined, so she called to him, patting the bed beside her. He jumped up and curled up against her. Just as she was falling back to sleep, Jack started tossing and turning, mumbling in his sleep.

The storm was directly overhead now. Lightning flashed and thunder cracked endlessly. Jack shouted in his sleep, scaring the life out of her and Jamie. She tried to wrap herself around him, since he was still asleep, but he used his arms to break the hold she had on him. Surprised, but owing his reaction to a bad dream, she attempted to soothe him again.

This time, he jumped out of bed and shouted, "IED! Take cover!" As she tried to make sense of what was happening, he threw himself on the floor and cried out, "Bastards, can't they let me finish sewing this marine back together before they blow us to kingdom come?"

Tears filled her eyes as he went through the motions of stitching an invisible marine back together while a battle raged around him. She had no idea what to do, how to handle the situation. Should she interrupt him? Would he try to tackle her to the ground, thinking she was the enemy?

"Stay, Jamie." The little dog was terrified by the closeness of the storm outside…and the one in Jack's bedroom.

When Jack sat back on his heels, she laid a hand on his shoulder and was tossed back against the bed. Such strength seemed superhuman, but what did she know about a person's actions and reactions while they slept? She wasn't the medical expert—Jack was.

"God, help me help him," she prayed. Finally the storm moved farther away and he stumbled back to bed, pulling her into his arms.

When he started to snore, she knew he was safely sleeping—and not dreaming. She slipped out of his arms and his bed and went down to the kitchen. Hands shaking, she brewed strong coffee and waited for her delayed reaction to the violence to pass.

She had no idea how to handle a situation like this.

She poured the coffee when it was finished brewing and the shot of the caffeine hit her empty stomach hard. She ignored it, needing the jolt to shake herself free from the horror Jack seemed to be suffering from.

By the time she finished the coffee, she knew one thing—she was going to help Jack Gannon whether he wanted her to or not. The tricky part would be figuring out how.

One thing was certain—she wasn't leaving. She was sticking. The sound of the stairs creaking had her looking toward the doorway, unsure of which Jack would be walking into the kitchen—the man she'd come to know or the tortured soul still serving as a navy corpsman.

Steeling herself to face the music and the man she was falling in love with, she turned and waited.

"Caitlin?" He seemed confused and uncertain, and that more than anything went right to her heart. She'd made the right decision.

"What are you doing down here?" Noticing the cup

on the table, his gaze flicked up to meet hers. "Couldn't you sleep?"

"The storm woke me up." Watching his eyes for a reaction, she dove in head first, saying, "It sounded like something exploded, maybe one of the oak trees off the deck."

He closed his eyes and he swore. She knew he understood when he asked, "Did I hurt you?"

Odd that that would be the first thing he asked and that he didn't offer an explanation for what he must know happened. "Not really."

"Damn it, Caitlin. Don't play semantics with me. Either I hurt you when I was…dreaming, or I didn't. It's a simple question and deserves a simple answer."

"Fair enough," she said, rubbing her arms to ward off the sudden chill. "I tried to help when I realized what you were experiencing and you tossed me off like I weighed nothing."

He scrubbed his hands over his face and walked slowly toward her. "Show me where you hurt," he rasped. "Let me make it better."

Her back was sore, but where she truly hurt couldn't be fixed with a Band-Aid—she ached for the terror and nightmarish demons Jack Gannon carried inside of him. She'd just only discovered the man beneath the white lab coat he wore, but there was so much more that she wanted to know, and if this was part of it, so be it. She needed to show him that she was strong and wouldn't walk away from him.

When he asked a second time, she placed her hand to her heart and tapped it lightly.

Tears filled his eyes, but he didn't blink them away.

He acknowledged her words and ignored the fact that he stood there with a tear trickling over his cheek and his hands clenched at his sides. "If I'm sleeping deeply and the thunder starts, it happens…"

"What happens?" She really wanted to know, had to know so she could help him.

"I'm there again," he whispered.

"Iraq?"

"Yes," he said, taking a hold of her hand, staring down at it. "I've been handling it—until tonight."

"Have you talked to anyone about it?"

He dropped her hand as if it burned him. *Wrong question.*

His eyes changed in a heartbeat. Cold hard blue stared down at her.

Desperate to erase that look, she held out her hand. "Don't be angry. I want to understand and to help."

He closed his eyes, drew in one deep breath and then another. When he opened his eyes, it was the Jack she knew and loved. Needing to get him to think about something else, anything, she blurted out, "I love the smell of rain." He nodded and she continued, "And the smell of fresh-turned dirt." She knew she had his attention. "I used to beg Mr. McCormack to let me have a turn riding up on the tractor with him when Peggy and I were little."

His body language told her he was listening. Relieved that the hard, angry edge was gone, she kept talking, "If you plant flowers in the yard it doesn't have the same smell. Why is that?"

"I'm not sure, but maybe it's because of what's been planted in Mr. McCormack's fields over the years."

He paused to think about it and added, "Whenever my mom roped me in to helping her in her flower gardens, it didn't smell the same either."

"Maybe you're right about what's been planted in his fields," she said, considering. "It smells different in the spring than it does in the fall. If I had to describe how spring smells to me, I'd say fresh, clean—hopeful— even the dirt."

He ran a hand through his hair. "I used to spend all winter waiting for it to be over so I could see that first green bud, that first tiny sign that no matter how hard the winter was, spring would surely follow."

Hope welled up inside of her, like a spring of cool, clear water. "And in the fall, everything smells of decay, as if the ground has used up all of its resources and needs to go to sleep through the winter, so it can begin all over again come spring."

Going with her gut, she reached for his hand. He stared at it for a moment, as if he weren't sure he should touch her, but then finally linked fingers with her and let her draw him toward her. When he was close enough to touch, she hooked their joined hands behind her back and laid her head against his chest. The steady beat of his heart reassured her—now it was her turn to reassure him. "I'm not going anywhere."

He wrapped his other arm around her and buried his face in her hair. Standing in the semidarkness of his kitchen, she knew that she would move heaven and earth if she had to. Either way, she was going to help Jack conquer the demons inside of him.

Chapter 11

HE EASED OUT OF HER ARMS AND ASKED, "IS THERE any coffee left?"

She shook her head, glad that he seemed steadier by the moment. "I didn't want to waste it, so I only made one cup. I can make more."

He walked to the back door and stared out the window at the break in the clouds in the predawn sky. The eerie feeling that he wasn't seeing what lay beyond the door into the woods bothered her, but she wouldn't bring up the subject again…tonight. She'd have to do some research first. Jack's peace of mind was far too precious to her to have her fumble and push him over the edge.

It would break him…and kill her.

Pressing the brew button on the coffeemaker, she asked, "Are you hungry?"

He shrugged but didn't turn around when he answered, "I can always eat."

"How about if I scramble up some eggs?"

"You don't have to feed me, Cait."

"In my house, if one of us was hungry and going to cook, we were taught to offer to make more."

He grunted. She thought that might be an affirmative male response, but she'd heard her father grunt when he meant no too. Busying herself gathering the eggs and margarine, she asked, "Where do you keep your pots and pans?"

Instead of telling her, he walked over and opened one of the upper cabinets and pulled out a cast-iron frying pan. "I'd never think to keep a heavy pan like that up high."

He seemed surprised. "Why?"

She smiled. "Because it's heavy." She heard the click of the coffeemaker as it shut off and got another mug out, filling it with coffee. "Why does that first cup always smell so good?"

Jamie lifted his head at that comment and thumped his tail on the floor. "I'd forgotten you'd followed me downstairs. Are you hungry, sweetie?" Looking around for his chow and not finding it, she finally had to ask, "Where do you keep the dog food?"

He grumbled something about people who talk too much in the middle of the night and went to a door she assumed went to the cellar. It was a walk-in pantry.

She walked over to get a good look. "Nice."

He didn't answer her as he scooped up chow and dumped it in the bowl he also stored in the pantry. Jamie was doing his little *feed me now dance* waiting for Jack to set the bowl on the floor.

She picked up his water dish and filled that too before going back to the cabinets and opening and closing them searching for a bowl.

"What now?" he grumbled.

She looked over her shoulder and kept her tone cheerful. "I've got it," she said, finding a cereal bowl to whisk the eggs in. Next she rummaged in the drawers until she found a fork. Heating the pan on the gas stove top, she was about to add a good-sized pat of margarine when he set his cup back down—from the sound of it, empty this time—and joined her at the stove. "As long as you're making eggs, why not fry up some bacon or sausage first?"

The warmth of his body so close to her back had a shiver working its way up her spine.

"Cold?"

She wasn't sure if telling him that every time he got close to her she had the uncontrollable urge to shiver would add to the tension still evident in the way he held his shoulders, or if it would ease it. "I just get the shivers sometimes...Pop always said it's like someone walking over your grave."

Damn. Probably the wrong thing to say too. "Got that bacon ready for me?" she asked, hoping to get him moving. He finally stepped back and walked over to the fridge. The Gannon kitchen was bigger than her family's, but it didn't feel as cozy. She'd noticed the lack of homey touches the night they'd rescued Jamie. Was it a guy thing or because he'd only recently moved back home, or was something deeper, tied to his nightmares of Iraq?

Keeping her thoughts positive, she reasoned that not everyone liked the same things. She took the package of bacon from Jack and laid thick slices of it in the pan and made a face. She hated thick-sliced meat. *Oh well...all the more for Jack.*

Once Jamie finished his bowl of chow, he started to tease Jack, poking him in the knees, nipping his bare feet until Jack got down on the floor with him. With the dog in his arms, she realized they shared more than a love of Mr. McCormack's fields in the spring—they had Jamie and were sliding toward love themselves.

"I've asked Pop for a dog every Christmas since as

far back as I can remember." Flipping the bacon, she looked over her shoulder at the two now wrestling on the floor, the auburn hair of the man a stark contrast against the black puppy fur.

"It's hard for a kid to understand what allergic means."

"And when you did?" Jack asked, pausing with the pup in a half nelson.

She laughed at the two of them and pulled out the first slices of bacon to drain on the paper towel–lined plate. "I'm sorry to say I wasn't always a nice kid. I asked him if Gracie could move in with our grandparents."

His deep chuckle was music to her ears. Feeling that they were back on track and he was acting like the man she'd come to know, she transferred more bacon to the plate, humming a song that popped into her head, one that took her back to her childhood.

Jack slowly got to his feet and she wondered if it hurt his leg to sit on the floor like that. She was about to ask when he pulled her back against him, swept the hair off her neck, and pressed his warm, firm lips against the pulse beating there.

Through a haze of desire, she heard the fork clattering to the floor. Suppressed need rushed through her. She'd wanted to wrap him in her arms from the moment he'd wakened her, shouting. If she didn't kiss him right this moment, she'd go quietly insane. "Jack," she whispered, spinning in his arms and wrapping hers around his waist.

When his gaze met hers, she knew he wanted what she wanted. Lifting up on her toes, she brushed her mouth across his. He grabbed her upper arms and held her there while he kissed her until her head spun.

This, she thought, as he crushed her to him. *This*

is what we both feel...need...want. "I'm not going to change my mind, Jack." The need to tell him she loved him filled her, but would he believe her if she told him now, or would he think she was saying it because she felt sorry for him? She should wait to tell him...tomorrow, when the terror of the night was forgotten.

———————

The overwhelming need to put his fist through the glass window of his back door left him as he took the comfort Cait offered every time she lifted her lips to him. Every subtle movement of her body as she stood at his stove, making him breakfast, tightened one of the knots he desperately needed retied to keep his past where it had to be—buried deep where no one could find it. He was afraid of what might happen if he let everything he'd felt that day resurface. The storm had lifted the lid and a part of that shattered man emerged. But he'd shoved those doubts and feelings of guilt and inadequacy back and secured that lid.

The imagery had been working since the doctor had first explained what was happening to Jack. For the last year and a half, he'd been able to function normally, without fear that the lid would blow off and all of the anger, fear, and self-recrimination would seep over the sides and spill into the life he'd planned to carve out for himself in Apple Grove.

"I don't know if I'm ready for this," he lied. He wanted Cait in his life so badly; he prayed she wouldn't leave, desperate to keep a part of her goodness in his life. But he didn't deserve happiness. How could he, when the marine he'd fought to save had died and they'd given Jack a fucking medal for his bravery under fire?

Cait pushed out of his arms and from the look on her face, her feelings had been injured. "If you don't want me here, I can go home," she told him. "But I made a promise to you and to Jamie," she bit out. "I'll still take care of him while you are at work unless and until you make other arrangements."

"Caitlin."

With her chin lifted and fire in her eyes, he knew he'd never love another woman they way he loved her. *Love? Yeah, love, you idiot.* Why else would he let her into his life when he'd pushed so many others away? She was the first woman he'd wanted in his home and in his bed—where the danger of a thunderstorm could expose who and what he truly was.

He loved her. But if he told her now, would she believe him? Needing the physical contact to soothe the emotions rocketing around inside him, he reached for her. This time, she let him pull her back into his arms. His heart shouted, "I love you," while he murmured, "Please don't go."

Some of the rigid tension left her as she reacted to his plea. Finally, she said, "I'm hungry."

He let her go, but from the jerky movements, he knew she was still upset. He hadn't meant to hurt her feelings. But if he apologized, would she want to talk about it? *Women always want to talk about it.*

"I don't." *Jesus, had he said that out loud?*

Judging from the expression on her face, he had. The tone of her voice confirmed it. "Why don't you put on more coffee while I make toast?"

Sensing that she needed time to mull things over, he did as she asked without speaking. By the time he'd poured more coffee and she had set a plate heaped with fluffy eggs, bacon, and toast in front of him, he realized she wasn't like other women. He got up and held out her chair when she placed a second plate on the table…with the same amount of food on it.

The laugh surprised them both.

"What's so funny?"

"You really are hungry."

"I told you I was," she grumbled, and sat down, letting him guide her chair closer.

They ate and sipped coffee while the remnants of the storm petered out and the tension swirling around them dissipated.

When he sat back, replete, she finally spoke. "I love the way the air smells like it's been scrubbed clean after a storm."

"It should worry me that you and I think so much alike."

She paused with her mug halfway to her lips. "Why?"

He wanted to be honest with her about everything—everything but the part of him no one was allowed to know about. "I'm not sure."

"Well now," she told him, "that thought's nearly feminine."

He snickered into his mug, appreciating her humor almost as much as her capacity to care about a broken-down former corpsman like himself.

"There are any number of men who'd have taken offense at that comparison."

His gaze met hers. "I'm not like other men."

She slowly smiled. "That's why I'm not ready to let you chase me away, Jack." She reached across the table and covered his hand with hers, giving it a quick squeeze before letting go. "If I wanted to be with some-one predictable, I would be. I want to be with someone who gets me, who understands my need to drive out past McCormack's on a soft spring night just so I can smell the field he's spent the day plowing."

"You like dogs."

Her smile broadened. "The more rascally, the better," she told him. "But I also like chickens, horses, cows, and peeper frogs."

He laughed, a full belly laugh this time. "You're quite a woman, Ms. Mulcahy," he said, rising to his feet.

"That's what my dad tells me."

"He's right." Jack held his hand out to her, palm up, waiting for her to put her trust and her hand in his. "How do you feel about turtles and snakes?"

"Box or painter turtles, yes. Snapping turtles, no— long story. It involves a gorgeous fish I'd just caught and the big old snapper that lives in the lake."

"Understandable. Snapping turtles get greedy sometimes."

"My dad still doesn't believe that I caught such a big largemouth bass, even though Peggy swears it was."

He grinned. "Ah, the one that got away with an imaginative twist."

She was laughing with him. "I see your point, but still…"

"What about snakes?"

"You were serious?" she asked. "I thought you were trying to get a rise out of me. Who the heck likes snakes?"

"I do."

She was silent for so long he thought it might be a deal breaker, until she asked, "Do you like them outside or in the house?"

Hugging her close, he told her, "Outside."

"That's all right then," she said, tilting her head back to look up at him. "Now inside"—she let her words trail off as she brushed the tips of her fingers back and forth over his bottom lip—"would have been a deal breaker for me."

"You're a keeper, Cait."

"I'm so glad you're not tossing me back."

He covered her mouth with his and savored the taste of her. "Mmm…" he said at last. "Bacon-flavored woman…my favorite."

When Jamie yipped to get their attention and be let outside, Jack kept his arm around her, steering her out the door and onto the deck. Easing her back against him, he held on to her as the clouds slowly brightened and the early birds started to sing.

"Don't give up on me, Caitlin."

"Not a chance, Jack."

Jamie ambled up onto the deck and jumped at the back door. "I guess he's finished."

"We still have an hour or so before I need to get a cleaned up. Will you come with me?"

She didn't hesitate, following him inside. "Where?"

"I need to grab a blanket."

"What for?"

"You'll see," he told her, pleased that she wanted to go with him. A few minutes later, he returned, found Jamie's leash, and clipped it on him. "If you take him," he said, "I'll carry the rest."

"Where to?"

"There's a knoll on the edge of the property that's higher than the rest. There's a break in the trees perfect for—"

"Watching the sunrise," she finished for him. "I'd love to."

The grassy rise between a wide break in the tall pines was perfect. He laid the blanket on the ground. Even though it wasn't as wet as he'd feared, it was damp enough that he was worried Cait'd be uncomfortable. He should have known better; she never complained. Sitting beside him with the dog on her lap, he figured she was just about perfect. Watching the sun paint the sky with reds and oranges that faded to yellow with Cait at his side, the remnants of fear tangled up in his gut finally dissipated.

"I'm sure my father will want to get an early start," she said, snuggling closer. "That sky doesn't bode well for a sunny day."

"You'd have made a good farmer."

"I thought I wanted to do that for a few weeks as a kid, but then my dad had this great idea that Peggy and I spend one week at our house and then one week at hers one summer vacation."

"What happened?"

"I didn't like getting up as early as Peggy had to. And even though I like chickens, they can be mean if you ruffle their feathers trying to collect eggs."

"You dad is a smart man."

"Yep."

"A good man."

She turned toward him and laid a hand over his heart. "So are you."

"There are some people who'd disagree with you."

"Then they obviously don't know the real you."

"Do you, Cait?" he asked.

"I know as much as you've shared with me, and more that you didn't intend to."

He nodded. "True. And you wouldn't have even found out that much if we hadn't had that storm last night."

"For what it's worth, Jack," she said, slowly rubbing the spot over his heart, "I'm glad."

He stiffened. "Because?"

"You've shared more with me than any other woman."

"But it's not something I intended to do."

"That's the point," she told him, watching him closely. "My parents knew each other's faults and failings and still they loved each other like crazy for the time they had together."

When she drew in a deep breath, he wondered if she would start talking about her mother, but she surprised him.

"Meg and Dan, and Honey B. and Mitch do too." She paused, staring up at the sky. "I want what they have, not because I'm selfish and want to know your deepest, darkest secrets," she told him. "I'll tell you all of mine—you're bound to hear about them down at the diner anyway," she said on a laugh. "But because I was brought up to believe that the solid foundation of any relationship begins with trust…you can't build anything on a foundation of sand."

"What if you knew as much of the truth as someone was able to share?" he asked. "Would that be enough?"

"Why not the whole truth?" she urged.

He eased her out of his arms and slowly got to his feet. "It's getting late. We should go back."

He tried to pretend that he wasn't bothered by the sadness in her eyes and the echoing ache in his heart. But he'd already been foolish enough today. Would last night end their precious beginning? Would she be his saving grace? Would the overwhelming need to have Caitlin in his life be enough to keep her there?

Unaware of the questions roiling inside him, she took Jamie's leash and waited while he picked up the damp blanket. The silence between them wasn't as companionable as it had been the day before as they walked back to the house, but there was no help for it.

He had patients to see and she had a barn to side. Sorting things out would have to wait until tonight.

He paused at the edge of the deck and asked, "Will you have time to take care of Jamie midday today?"

She unhooked the dog's leash and let him inside. "Yes. We should be in better shape today, now that the roof's on. If I hit a snag, I'll let you know."

He nodded. "Do you want the first shower?"

"Thanks. I know my dad's probably up already and pacing around the kitchen."

"He's worried about where you are?"

She shook her head. "He doesn't want any of his girls to get their hearts broken."

"Do you think I'll break your heart, Cait?"

She shrugged. "I watched Meg get her heart broken and look how happy she and Dan are right now. They're married, have two adorable boys with another baby on the way…maybe it's part of the process to know that the person you're in love with has the capacity to forgive and when pushed to the wall will do anything to make it right."

As she walked out of the kitchen her words hit him… *Did Caitlin Mulcahy love him?* "Hey, wait!" he called after her, sprinting up the stairs.

She'd already closed the bathroom door. He thought about pounding on it until she opened it, but he was pretty sure she'd heard him calling her. Maybe she hadn't meant to let him know that she loved him. But he didn't dwell on that fact; he was grinning from ear to ear, because if Caitlin Mulcahy loved him, he was the luckiest bastard on the planet.

—ᴡᴡ—

Caitlin waited until she heard Jack's footsteps retreating before she let go of the door handle. She hadn't meant to let how she felt about him slip out. But being with him muddled her brain and jump-started her heart. That wake-up call in the middle of the night brought parts of Jack's past and his demons out into the open. Would he push her away now that he knew how deeply she felt?

Starting to pull the borrowed T-shirt over her head, she remembered Jack taking her clothes off in the kitchen. "Crap." She let it fall back into place all but covering up the boxers she'd borrowed from him. Try as she might, she didn't remember tripping over her clothes in the middle of the night when she'd first gone downstairs to think.

Resolved that she'd have to go back downstairs and face Jack and his questions while she was feeling vulnerable, she was about to open the door when he knocked. "Hey, Cait?"

She waited a moment before answering, "Yeah?"

"I just pulled your clothes out of the drier. Do you want them?"

"Oh." She put a hand to her heart. "If you leave them right outside the door, I'll get them. Thanks."

"I could hand them to you now."

His deeply rumbled offer slid over her skin like a caress. "I, uh…need to go pick up my dad."

His sigh was loud and low. "I'm leaving them on the floor."

"Thanks, Jack."

She waited until she heard his footsteps hit the stairs before opening the door a crack and reaching for her clothes. A short, hot shower had her ready to face the day and the myriad of questions her father was sure to have.

As she toweled off and got dressed, she wondered who she could go to for help with Jack's trauma. Maybe she should look up his symptoms online…less chance of gossip that way. What the heck did they call it anyway? She'd never known anyone who'd suffered from battle fatigue—that's what Mr. Weatherbee called it, but he served in the army after World War II and before the Korean Conflict. She tried to focus, but her sleep-deprived brain wasn't cooperating.

She could ask her dad, but then he'd ask all kinds of questions that she wasn't ready to answer yet. If she was going to help Jack, she was going to have to respect his privacy and need to keep his demons to himself while she searched for a way to help him conquer them.

"My turn?" a deep voice called out as she was opening the door.

Standing there looking delightfully rumpled, she wished she remembered if his hair was wavy or straight. It was hard to tell cut in the military fashion, *high and tight*. She would have liked to run her hands over it again, digging into his scalp to massage it…it always did wonders for her whenever she went to Honey B.'s for a trim. The shampooing was her favorite part.

"Are you all right?"

"What? Oh, yes," she told him. "Just thinking about something."

"Hell of a something," he mumbled, slipping past her into the bathroom. He paused and asked, "Do I need to say good-bye now?"

"Yes." She turned around to face him. "I hate to be late."

"If ever anyone tempted me to be late, Caitlin, it's you." He pressed a chaste kiss to the end of her nose and shoved her out the door and closed it.

"Call my cell if you can't come by later."

"OK." Why did it feel so intimate talking to him through the bathroom door? Maybe it was a culmination of the last few hours, but whatever the reason, right now, she'd better get her head on straight. Her dad was waiting.

By the time she'd said good-bye to Jamie and shut the door behind her, her phone had buzzed. She read the text message from her father and laughed as she typed: On my way home.

Chapter 12

"Hell of a storm last night," her dad said, getting into the passenger side of the F1.

His words hit her with the force of a blow. He had no idea how hellacious it had been.

"You're awfully quiet today."

She could feel his gaze on her but didn't take her hands off the wheel or turn toward him. "I was thinking about the slab we poured. Do you think we rushed it and it didn't cure?"

"I wouldn't have let you start the framing if the slab wasn't ready. Can't build anything on a soft foundation."

"I know," she said. "You and mom taught us well."

"Your mom wasn't handy with concrete." When she shrugged, he asked, "Is there anything on your mind you want to talk about?"

"Not yet."

"I know I don't have to ask, because I know you would trust me enough to tell me, but did Jack hurt you?"

How to answer that question without having her dad hightailing it on over to Jack's office in town and dragging him outside to pound some sense into him? Wouldn't that just be a wonderful story gracing the front page of the *Apple Grove Gazette*?

"Not really."

His eyes narrowed as he turned and frowned at her. "Hell of an answer, Cait. Now how about trying the truth?"

"Not physically."

"Keep talking," he ordered as she pulled into Johnson's driveway.

"I can't yet. I have to figure it out first." When he would have badgered her to tell him, she pleaded with him, "Can you please trust my judgment enough to wait until I've got it worked out in my head and can talk about it?"

He blew out a breath and mumbled something it was probably better that she didn't hear. "Fine."

She chuckled. "Now that's a female word if I ever heard one."

He crossed his arms in front of him, a sign he was annoyed, but instead of blasting her with his temper, he threw back his head and laughed. "I raised you right, damned if I didn't," he said as he pulled out the ladder to check the roof for lifted shingles.

"Looks great from in here," she called out, knowing her dad was still on the ladder.

"Here too!" He climbed down and walked around the outside. "We'd better get this baby sided today. Weird weather pattern expected for the next few days. Great for indoor jobs—"

"Lousy for outside."

He put his arm around her shoulders. "Mulcahys do great work."

"That we do," she agreed. "Now what's next?"

"We knock out the siding, break for lunch, and check on that cute little pup while you think about how long you're going to wait before talking to me about what's going on."

"Gee," she said, looking over at her father. "Thanks for giving me more time to decide."

He grinned. "You're welcome. Now," he said, "let's get going."

———∾∾∾———

Jack was glad his appointments were scheduled back-to-back. Not having the extra time on his hands was a godsend because it kept his mind focused and busy. The last thing he needed was to overthink the fact that he could have driven Cait away permanently after last night's fiasco.

When the morning rush was over, he had a chance to ask Mrs. Sweeney if there were any messages. Nothing from Cait on his cell or the office number, so she was probably taking care of Jamie for him. She said she'd call if she couldn't, and Cait was a woman of her word, something he appreciated.

Thinking of her reminded him of last night. What triggered the relapse, aside from the thunderstorm, when he'd been doing so well for so long?

He wasn't due to see the doctor at the VA for another month. He wondered if he should call him and talk about what happened.

He was in his office when the phone rang, interrupting his thoughts. Seeing the other line lit up, he answered the incoming call, "Doc Gannon."

"Jack, I was afraid you weren't in the office today."

"I'm here every day, Mom. How are you?" he asked. "How's Dad?"

"We're both doing just fine, dear."

"You're not homesick?"

She paused and admitted, "Well, your father does miss Apple Grove…"

Jack sensed there was an and, so he asked, "And?"

"We decided to come back a little earlier than we'd planned if you don't think we'd be in the way."

Nothing like adding in the complication of your parents as you are trying to sort out a fledgling relationship. "Of course not." He crossed his fingers as he told that falsehood, hoping his mom wouldn't be able to tell he was lying through his teeth.

"Well, if you're sure…"

"Absolutely. When will you be arriving?"

"We're visiting friends on our way north. We'll be there in two weeks."

"Sure." He wished life hadn't decided to toss in the added monkey wrench of his parents coming for a visit while he was trying to get his head on straight and figure out what he was going to do about Caitlin.

He knew what he wanted to do.

"Jack!"

"Hmmm…what?"

"I said, we'll see you in two weeks."

"Sure, Mom. Say hi to Dad for me."

After she hung up, he let his head drop into his hands. He had to get his life back on track before his parents arrived, or else they'd know something was up, and he didn't think he'd be ready for that particular conversation just yet.

With his hand on the phone, he was about to pick it up and dial when it rang, startling him. "Doc Gannon."

"Hey, Jack. It's me, Cait."

He sighed and everything in the universe suddenly made sense again as he listened to the sound of her voice. "How's your day going?"

"Great. I think we might be finished up sooner than planned over at Johnson's."

"I heard over at the diner this morning that he's got a lot of students lined up to learn how to ride."

"Some have had riding lessons before, but most are newcomers to riding."

"That could be a good thing, right?" he asked.

"Absolutely," she agreed. "I think he's doing a great thing for Apple Grove and Licking County. He's been dedicated to this cause since his son was paralyzed after he took a hard hit playing football."

"My dad was at that game." He couldn't keep the emotion from his voice. "Scotty was an amazingly gifted quarterback."

"I remember everyone talking about it. It was the first time we'd ever had a serious injury on the football field," Cait added.

"Scotty went through years of therapy and never gave up. He was the one to approach his dad about setting up the riding school."

"I'm so proud to be a part of this," she said. "Even if it's just a small part."

"Don't diminish what Mulcahys is doing to make it happen."

"Thanks, Jack." After a few moments of silence, she asked, "So, how are you doing today?"

"I just had a complication fall into my lap."

"Oh?"

He wasn't sure he liked the sound of that one word. "Yeah," he said quickly before she could say anything else. "I just talked to my mom."

"How is she?"

"She sounds great. She's looking forward to visiting."

"When will they arrive?"

He cleared his throat. "Two weeks."

"Don't you want to see them?"

"I do…it's just that I'd gotten used to being on my own."

"Ah. I've never had the pleasure of living on my own. It's on my list of things to do."

"I've always wanted to have brothers or sisters," Jack told her, not even stopping to wonder why he'd shared that with her. "But while I'm used to being alone, now that I have Jamie, things are different."

Her laugh was light and airy, a happy sound that trilled across the phone line. "There were times when I'd have gladly traded Gracie for a puppy."

"Did you tell her that?"

"Oh yeah, she didn't like the idea," Cait confided. "Didn't speak to me for three whole days that time."

"Did you guys argue often?"

"Nah," she told him. "Every other day or so."

He laughed before asking, "You're kidding right?"

She snickered. "Nope. We had these off-white quilted vinyl chests that mom got for us secondhand. We used to keep our important stuff in there, and every time we argued, one of us would move our chest out into the hallway and holler at the top of our lungs that we were through and we wanted a new roommate."

"Then what happened?"

She sighed. "Meg would come in and mediate, and by the time she was through, one of us would end up apologizing to the other. I was never really sure how she managed that feat."

"I think you and Grace probably owe Meg more than you imagine."

She fell silent, leaving him to wonder if he should have kept that thought to himself, but so many years listening while Meg confided that worry wouldn't let him. Finally, she sighed and said, "You're right, and I know it. I'm trying to make things up to her now. I just finished the first set of shelves for their nursery and am working on a rocking chair for Meg. It's going to be a surprise, so don't say anything, OK?"

"Your secret's safe with me, Cait."

"Thanks, Jack. I'm really excited about the design— it's my first rocking chair."

"You're an amazing woman, Caitlin Mulcahy."

"Thanks for saying that," she said.

"I'm not just saying it," he told her. "I mean it."

"You can come see it if you want."

"You've started building it already?"

"It's in our shed—in my wood shop."

"I'd love to. You mentioned the design. Is there something different about this chair?"

"Meg's shorter than the average woman. If you've ever tried out different rocking chairs, you'd notice that they're designed for someone with longer legs."

"I can't say that I have. It sounds like a wonderful gift… a thoughtful one from your heart. Will I see you later?"

"I wasn't sure you wanted to," Cait said.

"I do," he reassured her. "I'll call you in between patients."

"OK. Bye, Jack."

"Bye, Cait."

He was just coming out of his office when the bell on

the front door jingled. Mrs. Sweeney was up and welcoming Mrs. Hawkins when the phone rang again. "I'll get it, Mrs. Sweeney. Doc Gannon."

"It's Mitch," the sheriff said. "Can I talk to you?"

"Sure, go ahead."

"When you finish up with appointments for today, stop by my office."

"Sounds serious. Can you give me a hint as to what this is about?"

"Not over the phone. See you around five-ish?"

"I'll be there."

Mrs. Sweeney was settled at her desk, going over the appointment schedule as Jack disconnected. He could tell she wanted to know what was going on, but knew she wouldn't ask; she could be patient waiting for Jack to confide in her. Sometimes he did…and sometimes he didn't.

He knocked on the examining room door and waited for Mrs. Hawkins to answer. "Now," he said, walking into the room, "what seems to be bothering you today?"

"I hurt my wrist. I'm not sure if it's sprained or strained."

"Let's take a look."

A few hours later, he'd finished for the day. He closed the door behind him and walked down Main Street. He had an appointment to speak with the sheriff. He should have asked if it was official business or personal. But Mitch would have said so, wouldn't he?

When Rhonda poked her head out of the front door to the *Apple Grove Gazette*'s office and called a hello, he returned the greeting. Enjoying the short walk down the street, he looked around him, reassured by the simple fact that Main Street hadn't changed; it still looked the same as it had as far back as he could remember. He loved the change of seasons and watching the progress. The warmer temperatures coaxed the leaf buds till they unfurled and were now wide, glossy, green leaves.

He stopped and looked both ways before crossing Dog Hollow Road. There might have been a few subtle changes, a new bit of sidewalk replacing an old, cracked section. He noticed the raw patch where Cait's truck had scraped the bark on one of the maples before letting his gaze settle on the Knitting Room across the street. He'd heard from the McCormack sisters yesterday morning that Melanie Culpepper was thinking of starting up a knitting group during the day, now that her boys were a little older. Odd to think that what he'd heard had been the town's local Internet café for the last few years would once again be used for knitting.

Mulcahys was still open; he could see Grace sitting at her desk. "Still hard at work," he mused, "keeping the family business going."

The trees lining the street shaded the way and had him thinking back to Miss Trudi's description of what it looked like right after the Second World War when each one of the trees had had yellow ribbons wrapped around them, tied up in a bow, for all of the returning GIs.

"Hi, Doc!" He looked up, surprised that he'd passed Murphy's Market and was already in front of the diner.

"Hi, Kate."

"Stopping by for dinner?"

"No, on my way to see Mitch."

"We haven't seen you for coffee lately," she told him, standing in the doorway to the diner.

"It's been hectic."

"See you tomorrow?"

"I'm not sure, depends on Jamie."

Her knowing smile had him wondering if word was out about him and Cait. Instead of coming right out and asking, she threw him for a loop, distracting him. "How is the puppy doing?"

"He's a pistol, full of energy, likes to tear apart my laundry, but he's great company."

"He's lucky you found him," she said before looking over her shoulder when someone called her name from inside the diner. "I've got to go."

Honey B.'s salon closed up early these days, so she wouldn't overdo it again. By the time Jack'd crossed Apple Grove Road, he was starting to worry about what Mitch wanted. He walked into the sheriff's office and called out, "You in the back, Mitch?"

"Yeah."

Hmm…one word response. Not out of the ordinary for Mitch, but not what he expected.

Mitch's door was open, like usual, so Jack knocked on the doorjamb. "So, what's so important that you couldn't tell me over the phone?"

"Not couldn't," Mitch said. "Wanted to tell you face-to-face."

"What?"

"Someone called about the puppy you and Caitlin found out on Eden Church Road."

Recoiling like he'd just taken a blow to the solar plexus, he couldn't get any air in or out.

"Look, I know it's been days and you thought no one would come looking for him," Mitch said, "but if this is truly his owner, then she must have been beside herself looking for him."

"Why didn't she come looking right away?"

"Not sure, not the point."

"You're right," he said, resigned to the inevitable. "When is she coming?"

"She'll be here in an hour. Can you come back with the dog?"

Give up Jamie? His new best friend, the puppy he'd rearranged his life for? *The black ball of fluff that curled up against him in the middle of the night for comfort?* "Uh…yeah, yes. I'll come back."

Now that he knew what Mitch wanted, he wished he'd told him that he had a few house calls tonight. Mitch would never know…would he? Well, he thought, it didn't matter now. Not much mattered now; he was going to have to say good-bye to his new best friend.

He dragged his feet all the way back to his office and didn't look up this time, even when he heard his name being called. Life wasn't fair. Caitlin had lived through God knows what last night because of him, and now…now…they'd have to give up Jamie too.

He had to call Cait. She'd want to be there when he returned Jamie to his rightful owner, wouldn't she?

Walking around the back of his office, he dialed her number, unsure of how to tell her the news. When she answered, he blurted it out. "Jamie's owner wants him back."

The silence hung in the air between them until he thought he'd go quietly insane. Finally he asked, "Cait, are you there?"

"Yes. Yes, I'm here. There's no mistake?"

"Mitch just told me. She'll be here in an hour." He had to pause to clear his throat. "Will you go with me when I bring him to the sheriff's office?"

"I'll meet you at your house."

"Thanks, Cait."

Chapter 13

CAITLIN PULLED UP INTO JACK'S DRIVEWAY BEHIND HIS Jeep and got out. She wouldn't let herself think about losing Jamie...about Jack losing Jamie. Were they too old to claim finders-keepers and make his former owner go home?

And how come Jamie's owner took a whole week to try to find him? She wasn't giving up on the hope that Jack could keep the puppy.

She knocked on the back door and opened it when Jack called out to her. He was sitting in the middle of the floor with Jamie in his lap. Jamie was licking Jack's face as if he hadn't seen him in days, instead of just that morning.

Not knowing what to say to Jack, she called out to the dog, "Hey, Jamie!"

He lifted his head, yipped, and leaped off Jack, bounding to the back door to say hello. When she bent to scratch his head, she heard Jack getting up, but she couldn't bear to look at him yet, knowing she'd see the aching sadness she felt reflected in his eyes.

"Thanks for coming...I didn't know what to do."

Taking her cue that she had to be the practical one and let Jack start the separation process—she could cry later—she offered, "How about if I pack up his bed, his toys, his food, and his treats?"

"What am I going to do?"

She finally looked up at him and wished she hadn't. Stark devastation stared at her from lifeless blue eyes. "Take him outside and toss the ball. He'll like that and get some of his energy out for the ride to town."

"Cait," he said, then hesitated. "I don't know if I can—"

"You can do this," she told him.

"But, Cait—"

"No buts, Gannon," she ground out. "You gave him the temporary home he needed. He won't forget you."

Jack nodded and walked to the back door, Jamie hot on his heels.

She could hear the happy barking as the dog demanded Jack throw the ball. Drawing the ache inside of her, she got down to business, packing everything up. "You are one lucky dog, Jamie," she whispered, emptying the pantry of dog food and treats. When she was finished, she looked at the clock and shrugged. They were going to be late…*too bad*, she thought. For once in her life, Cait didn't care.

"OK, guys," she called out, stepping onto the deck.

With a nod, Jack picked up the leash he'd brought outside and clipped it onto Jamie's collar.

"Red is definitely his color," Cait said. When he didn't say anything, she decided she'd drive, so Jack and Jamie could sit together.

"OK," she said, "here's the deal. I'll drive your Jeep and you and Jamie can ride shotgun."

"Thanks."

She was so going to cry buckets later; right now, she'd do what she had to and drive them to town.

They arrived at the sheriff's office all too soon. Jack and Jamie got out first and walked around to the back, so Jamie could sniff at the privet hedge that outlined the parking lot behind the building.

"Caitlin," the sheriff called out as she stood next to the Jeep waiting for Jack to come back. "Where's Jack?"

"Walking Jamie so he doesn't pee in your office."

Mitch nodded and motioned for her to come inside, but she wasn't going until he answered a question. "How do you know this person is Jamie's owner?"

He hesitated, then said, "She showed me his adoption papers. She got him from a shelter in Newark."

"But he's a black dog…maybe she's confused him with another little black dog."

He shook his head. "The timing's right and she had a photo." He paused. "Hear her out before you get your Irish up, Mulcahy."

Chastised, she realized she'd been doing just that. "Boy you do know me," she grumbled. "But if you could see how happy Jamie is at Jack's—"

"Good to hear, but not the point."

"Sheriff."

Mitch acknowledged Jack's greeting with a nod and bent to pet Jamie. "He looks like he'd be a great dog."

"He is." Jack looked at Cait and said, "Let's get this over with."

Cait agreed. It was time. She walked inside and her first thought was that the woman was too well dressed to own a dog. The woman's sharp intake of breath and beaming smile had that thought shriveling up and dying. Dogs don't care what you wear; they respond to love and this woman obviously loved Jamie.

"Crackers," she cried, rushing over to hug the puppy. Jamie backed up and hid behind Jack. The woman pulled up short and looked from Jack to Jamie and back again. "Why is he hiding from me?"

Keeping her voice as neutral as possible, Caitlin said, "Good question. Maybe he doesn't remember you. How long did you have him before he ran away?"

The woman's hand went to her throat and she toyed with her pearls. "I…uh…" The hesitation bothered Cait, and she knew without looking that it would bother Jack too.

"Not long."

"He doesn't seem to know you," Jack said at last.

"He's mine," she insisted. "I have his adoption papers with his picture on it."

Still not convinced or ready to turn the dog over, Caitlin asked, "Sheriff, could I talk to you a minute while Jamie gets reacquainted with his owner?"

Mitch nodded and motioned for her to follow him back to his office. When they got there, she asked him to close the door. "What's going on?" she demanded.

He drew in a deep breath, and for a moment, she thought he was going to lay into her. She'd never been on the wrong side of Sheriff Wallace before, but her sister Meg had. Those tales alone had her backing up a step.

"You want to rephrase that question, Caitlin?"

"Um…yes. Sorry, Mitch. But can't you see how much that dog loves Jack? And Jack…he loves that dog."

Mitch nodded. "And so do you, I get that. But the law's the law. He belongs to Ms. Blackwood, and while she's grateful that Jack has cared for Jamie, she wants him back."

"There has to be more to the story."

"If there is, I haven't been able to get to the bottom of it yet. Legally, my hands are tied."

She whirled around and had her hand pressed to the door before she realized that she wasn't helping the situation. She turned back. "I'm sorry…it's just that it seems so wrong."

"I know. Let's finish this."

He was right. "OK." She let him open the door and walked down the hall to where Jack was now down on one knee petting Jamie, encouraging him to go to Ms. Blackwell. Something just seemed off…wrong. She'd have to let it go for now, but she'd be calling Rhonda over at the *Gazette* to help her dig up all of the information they could about the diva in the designer suit and pearls.

With a plan firmly in mind, she felt better. Action instead of reaction, her dad would be proud. "Hey, Jamie," Cait said, calling attention to herself, wanting to see the redhead's reaction when Jamie listened to Cait and not the other woman.

As expected, the little puppy tugged at his leash to get to her. Jack grinned and shook his head. "We've been working on his manners, but he forgets them when he sees someone he loves."

Jack's words went straight to her heart; she knew how hard this was for him.

—◆—

Jack watched the way the woman who claimed to be Jamie's owner frowned as Jamie jumped up on Cait. "Jamie, down," he said.

The dog put his little rump on the floor and raised his

front paw. "Good boy," Cait said with a smile, shaking his paw.

"Do you mind if I see the adoption papers?" Jack knew he'd have to turn Jamie over to her, but he didn't have to make it easy for her.

When she started to protest, Mitch added his two cents. "Seems only right, since Jack here was the one who found Jamie running wild out on Eden Church Road."

"I was there that night too," Cait said. "He had to catch him first. If he hadn't Jamie wouldn't be sitting here so healthy and happy right now."

Ms. Blackwell finally acquiesced. "I adopted him from the Newark Animal Shelter."

"But that's forty-five minutes away by car," Jack said, scanning the paperwork. The picture was definitely the dog who'd been spending his nights sleeping in Jack's bed. "How do you think he got all the way over here?" he asked, handing the paperwork to Cait for her to look it over.

"I have no idea," the woman said, but there was something in her eyes that he didn't trust. She was lying; he was sure of it.

"Lucky for you, Jack was out by the McCormack farm last week," Cait told her. Jack was grateful for the interruption; he needed to think about what to do. Did he have legal recourse? Wasn't possession nine-tenths of the law? He'd have to ask Mitch.

Before he could ask, Cait did. "I thought possession was nine-tenths of the law."

Mitch frowned. "Unless there is proof otherwise."

Ms. Blackwell had obviously had enough. "I have an appointment. May I have my dog, please?"

Jack wanted to say no but knew he had to say yes. "We have all of his stuff in the Jeep."

"He didn't have anything when I...that is when he ran away."

That one slip might be all the ammunition he'd need in order to get Jamie back. With a glance at Cait, he knew she'd heard it too. Their gazes met and held; they'd let Jamie go now, in order to get him back in a few days.

"Then you don't need his bed, food, treats, and dog toys?" He watched her face go from determined to confused.

"I don't have—" she began only to stop and start again. "Since you won't be needing any of it, thank you. I'm sure it'll make him more comfortable."

"No problem." But it would be for her, because Jack intended to find out all that he could about the woman. He'd made a mental note of her address; he'd be checking up on his dog.

Jack handed her Jamie's leash, but Jamie was far less cooperative. He lay down and wouldn't budge. "Come, Crackers," she demanded.

Jamie didn't even acknowledge her command. He closed his eyes.

She tugged on the leash. "Crackers."

Jack had seen enough, unsure if the woman would raise a hand to the dog, he told her, "He answers to Jamie or Jameson."

"I named him Crackers."

Needing to prove his point to Ms. Blackwell, he walked over to stand beside her and said, "Jamie, come." The dog got up and walked over to where Jack stood and promptly sat down, waiting for his next command.

"Fine," the woman grumbled. "Jamie, come." She tugged on his leash again.

Jack's heart broke watching the way Jamie looked at him, but after the second tug, the dog must have sensed he had to go. *Smart dog*, Jack thought watching him go.

"I'll help you get his stuff," Cait said, tugging on Jack's arm.

Grateful, he nodded. They transferred the bags to the trunk of the woman's silver, four door, late model Mercedes. *Figures*, he thought.

While Ms. Blackwell tried to get Jamie into the backseat of her car, he said, "He gets motion sickness unless you keep the window open. He likes to ride shotgun."

"Shotgun?"

Cait snickered, and said, "In the passenger seat."

With a hand to her pearls, she said, "Oh."

When everything was loaded up and Jamie was in the backseat, Jack had to dig deep to keep from going over to the car, ripping the door open, and grabbing Jamie.

The hand at his back stopped him; Cait's touch centered him. With a heavy heart, he watched Jamie spin around and put his paws on the top of the back of the seat, watching them as the Benz drove away.

"Let me drive you home," Cait offered.

"I'm OK," he told her, holding the passenger door open for her. "Are you hungry?"

She hesitated before getting inside. "Not really."

"As a doctor, I should tell you that you need to eat."

"What about you?" she asked when he got in and shut his door.

"You keep me on my toes, Mulcahy."

"Jack, I'm sorry…"

"Me too." He put the car in gear and backed up. "How about a ride before we go back and make dinner?"

"Sounds like a plan."

Cait's ready agreement had him deciding to drive out past the spot they both loved. When he turned onto Eden Church, he was surprised that she was busy sending a text instead of watching where they were going.

"Who are you texting?"

"Rhonda."

"About?"

She finally finished typing and looked over at him. "I got a hinky feeling about Jamie's owner. I understand that the law is the law, but I don't trust her. She's hiding something."

He nodded and slowed down as they approached the spot where they'd found Jamie—halfway between Bob's Gas and Gears and the McCormack farm. He pulled over and parked. "Do you want to go for a walk?"

"Sure." She got out and waited for him.

Reaching for her hand, he laced his fingers with hers and started walking toward the farm. "It's funny how life doesn't always work out the way you hope."

"This was as close as I've been to having a dog," she told him, staring at the woods off to the left.

When they passed the spot where Jamie had run into Cait's arms, he felt her stiffen and then slowly relax the farther they walked. "I wasn't planning on getting a dog yet, but now that I've had one, the house is going to feel empty without him."

"Especially if he was sleeping with you instead of in his bed."

Jack agreed. "The only time he didn't sleep with me was when you were."

He stopped and pulled her into his arms. "Will you stay with me tonight, Cait?" He didn't need to tell her that he didn't want to be alone in the house.

She didn't hesitate. "Yes." When he didn't move, she squeezed him tight and said, "Are we walking to the farm?"

"Yeah," he said. "I thought you might want to see it by moonlight."

They walked in silence, stopping now and again when a bat swooped low over the road, chasing a bug. A sharp bark off to the left had them both coming to a halt. "Was that—" she asked.

"Did you hear—" he said at the same time.

When the bark came again, he relaxed. "Sounds like a fox."

She tilted her head to one side, waiting. When it came again, she agreed. When they reached the edge of the McCormack's field, he pulled her over to the stand beside the fence. "The corn's sprouted already."

They leaned on the fence together. "It's been warm."

"What does Meg think about the bet?"

Cait nodded. "She got teary at first and then agreed that it was a great way to raise money for our neighbors who are going through tough times without making them feel beholden to anyone for helping."

"It's a great idea. Those too old coots always did have the town's best interests at heart."

"I would have thought they'd be one of the ones who could use the money, but they never see it that way," she said.

"They're from a generation that is used to going without if need be. Tough times either make a man," he told her, "or break him."

"Mmm…" she said, inhaling a deep breath. "Smells great out here."

When she stared at him, he knew what she expected and drew in a breath. "I smell rain."

She laughed. "That's not what I meant, but OK, we'll go with that for now."

He chuckled and realized it was going to be all right. As long as he had Cait in his life, he could tackle anything. Awed by the epiphany, he tucked a wayward curl behind her ear. "The ground smells good out here, but not quite the same as when it's just been plowed."

Watching the bats swooping down over the field, she finally pushed back and said, "I'm hungry."

He pressed a kiss to the tip of her nose and tugged on her hand. "I've got some burgers that are begging to be grilled."

"Do you have any potato salad?"

"Are you going to find somewhere else to eat if I don't?"

"No." After a few minutes, she asked, "Do you have any potatoes?"

He paused to think about it. "I might."

"OK," she said, "if we nuke them, they're almost as good as a baked potato…as long as you have plenty of butter and sour cream."

"Then you're in luck," he said as his Jeep came into sight. "I have all of the above."

"I might let you talk me into bed after you feed me."

He opened the door for her and leaned in to kiss her. "I promise to make it worth your while."

When they pulled into his driveway, he fought to keep from wondering what Jamie was doing right then. It was hard; he'd gotten used to having the little guy there to greet him when he got home from a long day of treating patients.

"He was a good companion."

Cait tucked her arm in his and led him around to the back door. "The best. He'll be all right, Jack."

Opening the back door, he sighed. "I know, but I'm gonna miss him like crazy."

"Me too. When Meg moved out, I had to keep busy not to think about how much I missed her."

"That's not the same thing."

"Close enough," Cait said. "She used to live with us and then she didn't."

He had to give her that much. "But still—"

Cait remained firm. "Do you need me to make the hamburger patties while you light the grill?"

"Nope already done. You can nuke the potatoes, though."

The simple routine helped take his mind off missing Jamie. It would take time to get used to a new normal. He'd never forget what it was like to have that little ball of black fuzz in his life.

Cait kept up her end of the bargain by helping him make dinner and then insisting they eat on the deck. "Cold beer and burgers on a warm spring night," she said after they'd finished. "It doesn't get any better than this."

Jack was already on his feet. "You sure about that?"

She giggled when he scooped her out of her chair and carried her into the house. "I can walk."

"Me too," he said, kissing a path along the curve of her jaw, his senses assaulted by the subtle combination of fruit and flowers. "You taste like springtime."

"New face wash."

"Do you taste like that everywhere?" he asked, taking the stairs two at a time.

"I wouldn't want to spoil all of your fun," she said as he placed her in the middle of his bed.

"You look right here." He didn't want to say too much, but he wanted her there, needed her there. "Caitlin I—"

He forgot what he was going to say when she pulled her shirt over her head and tossed it on the floor. He did the same and then reached for her jeans. She beat him to it and stood on his bed—thank goodness he had high ceilings or else she'd have bumped her head.

They were both breathless when she shimmied out of her jeans. "God, you're beautiful," he rasped, reaching for her.

She shook her head. "Your turn."

But he didn't want to wait that long to touch her. He wanted her naked in his bed. "Let's try something different." Her eyes widened as he eased her down onto her back and then proceeded to nip the lace panties at her hip and tug on them until she lifted up, so he could pull them off of her.

Licking and nibbling a path from her toes to her thighs, he nudged her legs apart and settled himself between them. Sliding his arms beneath her, he eased her legs onto his shoulders. "I'm going to take my time tonight," he warned her. "I'm not stopping until I've tasted every inch of you."

Her eyes blazed a brilliant green as desire grabbed her by the throat. "Then it'll be my turn."

"Babe, once I've had my fill of you, you won't even remember your own name."

"Big talk," she said as his lips, teeth, and tongue tormented her, brushing close to the very heart of her, until she begged him to take what he so desperately wanted.

Wild honey.

His tongue dipped inside her again and he knew he'd never tasted anything that good. One taste would never satisfy the hunger building inside of him. She moaned and writhed as he took what he craved, tasted what he hungered for.

His jeans cut into his erection, but he ignored it, needing her to come first.

Her orgasm ripped through her, the aftershocks lifting her up off of the bed before she lay limp and quivering. Easing back, he slipped off the bed and stripped out of his jeans. Her eyes fluttered open as he covered himself from tip to base, and she turned slumberous as he climbed on to the bed.

He slid his body up and over hers, delighting in each and every shiver. "You're so responsive," he rasped, kissing his way to her breasts. Licking first one and then the other. When she wrapped her legs around him, he pulled her left breast into his mouth and slid home.

Suckling and sliding in and out, he was soon lost in the primal need to find completion. The need to mate with this woman threatened to take control, but he grappled with need and won, grazing his teeth over her nipple before letting go and lavishing the same attention on her other breast. He wanted her to come twice more before giving in to the overwhelming need to drive into her until he was blind to everything but the taste, scent, and feel of her.

When she cried out his name and went limp in his arms, he dug deep and found the strength to bring it home. Whispering words of love to the woman who held his heart, he urged her to come with him with each thrust, until she lifted up to meet him again and again.

With one final surge, he lifted her up and let go of his tight control. He emptied himself, wishing he could feel her velvet-soft walls pulsing around him, instead of the latex barrier that protected her.

Not yet, he thought, *but soon.*

Their heartbeats slowed as he rolled so she was on top, and he was still inside of her. Closing his eyes, he let sleep claim him.

The rumble of thunder sounded in the distance; snuggling closer to Jack, she ignored the coming storm and drifted back to sleep.

The crack of thunder directly overhead shook her from sleep. But it was the heavy weight pressing down on her that had her gasping for breath.

"Incoming," Jack's voice shouted as he pressed his body over hers, covering her, protecting her.

"Can't breathe," she protested, punching him in the shoulder to get him to ease up. Lightning flashed and another crack struck right outside the window. Jack's weight was making her light-headed. She needed air.

Shifting, she kneed him hard. The weight lifted and she drew in a breath.

"What the hell?" he gasped, cupping himself.

"You were having a nightmare."

The way he fell quiet, she knew he understood what had happened. "I'm sorry."

"You need to talk to me about it."

"No," he said, "I don't." He got out of bed and pulled on his jeans.

"But—"

She may as well have been talking to the wind because Jack never stopped; he kept right on walking.

"Damn you!" she ground out. "You're going to tell me," she vowed. "Even if you hate me for it," she whispered. "I'm going to help you face whatever demons you have locked inside of you."

Chapter 14

EVEN THOUGH SHE WAITED FOR HIM, JACK NEVER CAME back to bed. At four o'clock, she dragged herself to the bathroom, took a shower, and got dressed.

He was sitting on the deck, wrapped in a blanket, fast asleep when she walked outside. "Do you think staying away from me will protect me?" But he didn't rouse from sleep to answer her question.

Since he didn't feel he had to tell her what he was doing or where he was going, she didn't either. Keys in hand, she walked to her truck, got in, and drove home. No one was up yet when she let herself into the house, so she made coffee and sat down with her dad's laptop.

Getting on to the Internet, she started to search out different types of trauma until she found what she was looking for—PTSD, post traumatic stress disorder. Reading the symptoms again, she bookmarked the page. Now that she had a better understanding of what was happening to Jack, she needed to find a way to help him.

She was on her second cup of coffee when her father walked in. He took one look at her and summed up the situation. "You have about five minutes and then you are going to start talking," he told her. "I'll have downed my first cup of caffeine and will be able to help you get to the heart of whatever is bothering you."

She didn't bother to argue. She needed help and could trust her father not to talk about Jack's problem

until Jack was ready to. With a nod, she walked over to
the fridge, pulled out the makings for breakfast, and set
aside her worries while she fried up sausage patties and
eggs—scrambled, just the way her dad liked them.

"Smells good," he said, putting the toast down a second time. When it popped up, he slathered both pieces
with butter and carried them over to the table. "Is this
about Jack losing Jamie or just Jack?"

"A little of both, I think," she said.

"He really took to that little guy, but it's understandable. Jamie's quite a dog."

She let the tears she'd held back fall freely. Her dad
gave her time to cry it out and then handed her a wad of
paper towels to blow her nose with.

When she did, he asked, "So, now what else is
going on?"

"I think Jack's suffering from PTSD."

Her father sat back and crossed his arms in what Cait
recognized as his thinking pose. "You sure?"

"I double-checked the symptoms online."

"The Internet isn't infallible."

"I know, Pop," she said, "but it's only happened during a thunderstorm. I read where it could sound like an
explosion and trigger a reaction."

He nodded. "Have you talked to him about it?"

"I've tried, but he just shuts me out. I need to help
him face whatever he has locked inside him."

"Maybe he already has," her father told her.

"But then why is he acting like this?"

"Like what?"

She wouldn't let her embarrassment of confirming
what her dad probably guessed—that she and Jack had

been sleeping together—get in the way of the telling. "The first time it happened, the thunder woke me up, and I saw him hunched over on the floor like he was trying to shield something—or someone—with his body and he kept yelling 'IED.'"

He father waited for her to continue.

"Last night, a huge crack of thunder woke me, but I couldn't breathe. He was lying on top of me, trying to shield me, but I couldn't get him to listen—he was trapped in whatever nightmare he goes into."

"How did you get him to wake up?"

"I had to knee him."

"I see. And when he finally woke up, what happened?"

"I tried to get him to talk to me, but he wouldn't. He just walked away."

"So you just left him?"

"I kept waiting for him to come back upstairs, but after a while, I knew he wasn't going to. He was asleep on the deck, wrapped in a blanket. I didn't want to wake him…so I left."

"You think he did that so he wouldn't take the chance of hurting you?"

"Yeah," she rasped. "Pop, I love him…what am I going to do?"

"Let me think on it."

She blew her nose again and cleared the table. "What if we can't help him?"

"Jack's a smart man, Cait," he said. "He may already be in treatment. Did you think of that?"

"No." She hadn't. "Then why—"

"I had a buddy who suffered from PTSD," he told her. "He could go for months at a time without suffering and then something would set him off and he would have an episode."

"What did he do?"

"He kept seeing his doctor and tried to analyze the warning signs to keep on top of things and prevent a full-blown episode."

"And it worked?"

"Most of the time," he said. "It may take years, and it might never fully go away, but my friend learned to live with it and control it. I might have a way to help Jack come to terms with the fact that his condition is controllable to a point. Why don't you let me tell Gracie to reschedule your day?"

"I'm fine, Pop. I'll be better if I'm busy."

"That's my girl," he said, pulling her in for a bear hug.

When she'd gone for the day, Joe got on the phone. "Jerry, it's me, Joe—I need your help."

Jack woke cold and alone. Stiff from falling asleep in a chair on the deck, he stretched to loosen the knots in his spine and bad leg. "Brilliant, Gannon," he grumbled, limping inside. Wondering if Cait was still sleeping, he walked inside and listened.

"Too quiet." He missed the scrambling of puppy feet as Jamie ran into the kitchen or bounded up the stairs. He'd get used to it, but it might take some time.

"Cait?"

When she didn't answer, he called again. Unease slithered through his gut, as he took the stairs two at a time only to find his bed empty and Caitlin long gone.

He stared at the rumpled bed and a flash of the

woman he'd turned inside out and backward with their lovemaking filled his heart and his head. "You're too stupid to deserve a woman like her."

A glance at the clock told him it was time to get cleaned up for work. The hot water eased the tension from his back, but not his leg. It was going to be a long day. He couldn't decide if he should go to the office early or track Cait down at her house.

He sent her a text, but she didn't answer it. "Big surprise." He'd had his chance and he flubbed it, but he wasn't going to give up on her. She promised she'd stick. He was going to hold her to that promise.

He might have to learn to live without his best furry friend, but he'd be damned if he'd live without Caitlin. Taking a chance, he called the Mulcahys' house.

"Hello?"

"Hi, Joe. It's Jack, can I talk to Cait?"

"She's at the shop. Did you call her cell?"

"I texted her, but she didn't answer me."

"What time's your first appointment?" Joe asked.

"In about an hour. Why?"

"Stop by the house," Joe told him. "I'd like to talk to you."

How could Jack say no? "Be there in a few."

Pulling up into the driveway of the Mulcahys' house felt weird, knowing that Cait wasn't there and that he was about to have a face-to-face conversation with her father—had she talked to her dad about last night?

Shit. How did you have a conversation with the father of the woman you've been sleeping with? Cut to the chase and admit it—making love to, because what he had with Cait was way more than just physical. He wanted a lifetime with her.

Joe came out of the house as he parked his Jeep and got out.

"Glad you could stop by." Joe looked him up and down. "You look like hell."

Jack nodded. "Rough night."

"Heard about part of it."

When he didn't say anymore, Jack waited, knowing it was bound to come out.

"Scared my little girl."

"Joe…Mr. Mulcahy—"

"Joe's fine," he told Jack. "I just have one question."

Whew, Jack thought, and waited.

"Are you finished with her?"

Jack waited a heartbeat and then asked, "Excuse me?"

"Something wrong with your hearing, Gannon?"

"No."

"Then answer the question."

"No, sir."

"Is that your answer or your stance?"

Jack had to chuckle at that. "My answer, Joe. I love Caitlin."

"Hmmpfh. You've got a funny way of showing it."

"She's the one who walked out on me."

"As I hear tell it, she waited for you to come back after you scared the shit out of her by using your body to protect her from an IED."

All of the blood rushed to Jack's feet. She'd figured out what he'd been trying so hard to control. *How did it happen?*

Was it the storm?

Was it the stress of having to give Jamie back?

Joe tugged on Jack's arm to get him to walk with him. Instead of the barn, where he knew Joe spent a lot of his time, he walked toward the field out back. "I have a buddy who suffers from PTSD. He's going for help and manages to keep it under control."

Jack nodded. "I'm not due to see the doctor at the VA for another couple of months."

Relief flooded Joe's features. "I knew I was right."

"About?"

"You being smart enough to seek help. You're a doctor and know how important something like this is."

"I do," Jack agreed. "Everything was fine until that first storm."

"By storm, do you mean my second born or the weather?"

Jack stopped walking and looked into Cait's father's eyes. "Both, maybe. It hasn't happened in a while. I've been keeping on top of the weather to know when a storm is on the way, but Cait distracted me."

"She has that talent," Joe said.

"You could say that."

"What are you going to do about it, Jack?" He turned around to walk back toward the driveway. "She deserves to know what's going on so she can understand it. My girls are strong enough to handle anything."

"She said she'd stick…but she left me," Jack rasped.

"Did you give her a choice?"

Jack shrugged. "I guess not. But I thought she knew… after last night—"

"Would that be before or after the thunderstorm?"

Jack opened his mouth and then closed it tight. Joe could boil him in oil, but there were some things that should remain private…what happened between him and Cait the night before was precious and was theirs.

Joe acknowledged Jack's silence and changed the subject. "Gracie has Cait's schedule if you're thinking about catching up with her partway through the day to apologize."

"I—" Instead of words, Jack held out his hand to Joe. When the older man took it, Jack nodded. "Thanks."

Joe nodded and said, "I'm always willing to give a man a second chance…but that's all I'll give him before I come after him for hurting one of my girls."

Jack swallowed against the lump of emotion in his throat. Cait and her dad were willing to give him another chance. He was smart; he was taking it and he wasn't gonna mess it up.

"Yes, sir." With a wave, he got into his Jeep, put it in reverse, and hightailed it into town; he had to stop at Mulcahys before his first appointment was due to arrive.

Grace was sitting in front of her computer terminal, same as always, when he pushed open the door. "Hi, Grace."

She looked up at him and then back down at her keyboard. "What do you want?"

How had word spread that fast? "I was hoping you could tell me where Cait would be around noon."

Without looking up, she asked, "Why?"

He held on to what was left of his pride. "I need to talk to her…I need to apologize."

"Really?" The hopeful tone in her voice tipped him off that Cait's sister might not know what happened; she just figured out from Cait's mood that something did happen.

"Really. So how about it?"

With a few clicks, Grace was scanning the schedule. "She'll be over at Miss Trudi's this afternoon, installing a pump for her new koi pond."

"Thanks, Grace."

With a spring in his step, Jack walked back outside and drove back to his office. Three minutes later, his first appointment walked in. He was ready to face the day and was anticipating seeing Caitlin.

A few hours later, he was headed to Miss Trudi's. He had to drive so he wouldn't take the chance of being late for his afternoon appointments. Going slowly down Apple Grove Road, he pulled up behind the black F1 and parked.

"Anybody home?" he called out, walking through the maze of plants and planters that Miss Trudi Philo had displayed. He heard them before he saw them.

"Well, I'll be," he heard Miss Trudi exclaim. "It works."

"Like a charm," Cait answered. "Now all you need to do is flip this switch, but if I were you, I'd leave it on unless there's an electrical short somewhere. The fish need that water aerated."

"You're a clever one, Miss Cait."

"Thanks."

"Hello, Caitlin," he called out, catching her off guard. The longing on her face eased part of his worry.

"I'm busy, Jack."

"Caitlin, that's no way to speak to Doc Gannon." Miss Trudi shook her head. "I'm sure she's just tired. You can tell from the dark circles beneath her eyes."

My fault, he thought. "Yes. I can. Maybe she needs one of my dad's tonics."

Miss Trudi's eyes lit up and her face beamed. "I think she just might. I have some in the house. Be right back."

"You just said that so she'd leave us alone."

"And if I did?" he challenged.

She blew out a breath and threw her hands in the air. "Jack, I need to focus on the repair schedule for today."

He grabbed her hand and tugged on it. "I'm sorry I couldn't talk to you last night."

She turned in his arms and stared up at him.

"You said you would stick," he reminded her.

"I'm sorry, Jack. After you walked out, I didn't know what to do."

"You left me," he whispered.

"I had to." Tears filled her eyes. "I needed to do some research, and I needed to think." She left him in order to help him, just as he'd left her alone in his bedroom to protect her. They both wanted the same thing; it was something in common…something to hold tight to.

He brushed his lips to her forehead and laid her head against his shoulder. "I'm sorry. There are things that are hard for me to talk about. Iraq is one of them."

"I want to help."

"I go for help every few months. I was doing all right until a certain woman turned my well-ordered existence upside down with her smile."

"I did?"

"Didn't you?" When she shrugged, he went on, "Since the night we rescued Jamie, my focus hasn't been on warning signs that the PTSD was ready to break loose again…it has been on you."

"What can I do?"

"I need you to be patient with me." He lifted her hand

and pressed a kiss to the center of her palm, watching intently as she shivered.

"Will you tell me about it?"

He looked away and then back down into her up-turned face. "Not yet…but soon."

She nodded. "OK."

"Caitlin?" Miss Trudi called out.

"I don't believe it," Cait groaned. "Is that brown bottle what I think it is?"

Jack laughed. "Yep—Dad's tonic."

"Does it taste bad?"

"If it tasted good, it wouldn't work."

"Lovely." She waved at the older woman and promised Jack, "You'll pay for this one."

"Thanks, ladies," he said, walking back through the plants. "I've got a one o'clock coming. Can't be late."

"What a nice young man," Miss Trudi said. "And so good-looking too."

Caitlin stared after him without speaking. When she turned around, Miss Trudi was holding out the bottle to her. "One teaspoonful, morning and night."

"Oh, I couldn't take your tonic."

"Land sakes, child," Miss Trudi told her. "I've got a half-dozen more in the house."

Resigned, she took the bottle. "Thanks. I'll just clean up and be on my way."

Miss Trudi was smiling when she handed Cait a spoon.

Knowing when she'd been beaten, she took the spoon and the tonic. "Good grief, that tastes awful!"

"That's how you know it will work, dear."

Bending down, she nabbed the water bottle she always had on the job and drank down the rest of it. At least it cut the taste lingering in her mouth. "What's in there?"

"Herbs and things."

"Yuck."

"Oh, but you should see the fire in your eyes right now, dear. Old Doc Gannon's tonic always did work quickly."

Cait shook her head and cleaned up her tools. Saying good-bye to Miss Trudi, she loaded up the truck and headed off to the next job on her list.

It was hard realizing that she didn't have to stop off at Jack's to take care of Jamie. Wondering how the little guy was doing, she decided she'd shoot off a text to Rhonda when she stopped at the shop to pick up supplies.

Rhonda didn't have anything concrete, but she did uncover the fact that Ms. Blackwell came from a prominent Columbus family.

"Guess she didn't earn that car she drove…probably a gift from Daddy."

Gathering the tools and supplies she'd need for the afternoon, she was surprised, then pleased to see a text from Jack: Dinner at my place? I'm buying.

She sent off her acceptance and focused on the next few jobs, so she could finish up on time and head on over to the place that was rapidly beginning to feel like home. If only she could find something wrong with Ms. Blackwell, she could tell the sheriff and have him go after her, so she could bring Jamie home where he belonged.

Exhausted, dirty, and beyond hungry, Cait called Jack to tell him she'd be later than expected. When he answered, she found herself smiling. "Hey, it's me. I'm on my way home to get cleaned up…I am icky dirty."

"What's wrong with my shower?"

"I didn't want to you to think I was taking advantage—"

"Cait," he interrupted. "Don't go home, come here… I need to see you here in the middle of my stuff. I want you in my shower. I've got something to tell you when you get here. OK?"

She blew out a breath and pulled a careful K-turn on Cherry Valley so she could get back on Eden Church Road. "I just turned around. I'm headed your way."

"Good," he said softly before saying good-bye.

Lighter in heart, she pulled into Jack's driveway. She felt a hitch when she didn't see Jamie's little black fuzzy face at the window, but the welcome on Jack's face when he opened the door and pulled her into his arms more than made up for it.

He kissed her soundly and then pushed her through the kitchen. "Hurry back."

She put on the brakes. "But I just got here!"

He kissed her cheek and grinned. "You're right, you are icky dirty."

"Why you—"

"Save it for when you're clean. I plan on getting you dirty all over again."

With that promise held close to her heart, she dashed upstairs, stripped, and turned the spigot to scalding. As she scrubbed away the dirt and stress of the day, she realized there was no point in holding back what was in her heart—she had to tell him how she felt.

All problems—Jamie and PTSD aside—she needed Jack, wanted to be with Jack. *Loved Jack.* She had to tell him.

Squeaky clean, hair loose—since it was too wet to

braid—Caitlin paused in the doorway to the kitchen. Jack was standing there looking down at the dog toy in his hand. She went to him and wrapped her arms around him, holding tight.

"I miss him so much it hurts."

"I know you do," she said. "I do too."

"I didn't even know how badly I needed a dog…"

"Not just any dog," she told him. "Jamie."

"Yeah." He turned around, so that they were face to face. "I almost blew it last night and pushed you out of my life."

She nodded. "I almost let you."

"I can't lose you too, Cait. I love you."

"Thank God I'm not in this alone," she said.

His lips found hers and kissed her softly, sweetly, reverently. "Say it, Cait."

"It," she teased.

He growled—actually growled—at her.

Knowing he needed to hear the words, she gave them to him. "I love you, Jack Gannon." Letting her hands roam his shoulders and his upper back, she reveled in the strength there. Contentment filled her. As long as they could talk to one another and took the time, they could work anything out.

When he pulled back, she lifted up on her toes and pressed a swift kiss to his mouth. "Are you going to feed me soon?"

His laughter was music to her soul.

"I've got this really great recipe for marinated steak."

"You're going to cook another meal on the grill?"

He looked at her as if she'd asked him to balance the federal budget. "I'm a guy. Guys like to grill meat."

Pushing up her sleeves, she said, "I hope you have something green in your fridge."

"I think there's a bag with cheese that I should have tossed out a few weeks ago."

"Is that something else about men? They don't eat green things?"

"Not unless they're forced by their moms."

"I've seen you eat salad before," she said, frowning at him with her hands at her hips.

"Ah," he said, "but that's because I had ulterior motives. I wanted to talk you into my bed."

Her mouth fell open in shock and he laughed, snagging her again, reeling her in for a kiss. This time it was a toe-tingling, toss-me-over-your-shoulder-and-take-me-to-bed kind of kiss.

"Maybe we could eat later," she said, slipping out of his arms and tugging on his hand.

They were laughing as they ran up the stairs.

Chapter 15

JACK SAT UP IN BED AND SAID, "DID YOU HEAR THAT?"

Cait brushed the hair out of her eyes. It was still dark outside. "What?"

Jack tilted his head to one side and said, "That!"

"No. What did you hear?"

He got out of bed and told her, "Be right back."

Intrigued enough to follow him, she pulled his T-shirt over her head and walked to the top of the stairs. When she heard him calling Jamie, her heart broke. If anyone ever needed a dog, it was Dr. Jack Gannon. She vowed to get to the bottom of Ms. Blackwell's false-sounding story, so she could find a way to get Jamie back where he belonged…with Jack.

She got back into bed but kept the shirt on. She liked the feel of the soft material as it slid off her shoulder, Jack's were so much broader than hers.

"Hey," she called out to him as he walked into the room. "Did you find whatever the noise was?"

He shook his head. "Must be hearing things."

He never said a word to her about thinking it was Jamie as he climbed back into bed and pulled her close. After a few minutes, she realized that he wasn't going to—just one more thing he kept locked inside of him, making her even more determined than ever to help him heal.

Lying there while he slept, she laid out her plan for

the day: First, she was going to stop by and see Rhonda and see if she'd dug anything up about that Blackwell woman. Second, she'd catch up with Peggy at the diner and see if her friend had heard anything about the woman who claimed Jamie. Third, she was going to talk to her dad again and see what he'd come up with to help Jack.

With that busy day planned and a full schedule of handyman jobs ahead of her, Cait slipped out of bed and hit the showers. Jack was still sleeping when she was clean and dressed, so she pressed a kiss to his forehead and headed downstairs to start breakfast.

She was turning the sausage to brown up on the other side when Jack walked in, his hair still damp from his shower. Their gazes locked, reminding her of the night before and the way they'd exhausted one another before they finally drifted off to sleep in one another's arms.

The intimacy of the moment had her belly tingling. She'd never had a relationship like this one. It had taken a man like Jack to make her realize that while she'd been in relationships with other men, not one of them had ever fully engaged her heart and her mind at the same time.

But she'd never dated anyone who'd kept something so huge from her before. *When would he confide in her?*

"Do you have any idea how right it feels coming downstairs in the morning and finding you in my kitchen?"

She laughed. "If I was drinking coffee and reading the paper, instead of making you breakfast, would it still feel right?"

He grabbed her around the waist, pulled her flush against him, and kissed her breathless. Once he set her back on her feet, he grinned. "Does that answer your question, silly woman?"

"Silly?"

"Yeah," he said, grabbing a mug and filling it with fresh, hot coffee. "You here with me is essential…you cooking is definitely a bonus."

Using the tongs, she lifted the links from the pan, and asked, "Over easy?"

"That's another thing, Cait," he said quietly. "You remember little things that matter."

"In all fairness, you know that I like my coffee with milk and too much sugar."

"That's easy. It worried the physician in me," he told her.

"Not the point." She wiped out the pan and added margarine to it.

"Why don't you just cook the eggs in the sausage drippings?"

She paused and looked down at the pan. "I've never had them that way."

"But you scramble your eggs in the bacon fat."

"That's how my dad always did it."

"So your dad's not a fan of sausage?"

She laughed. "How did we get on the subject of what my dad likes for breakfast?"

He smiled and went to the fridge. "Just making conversation."

She could hear him rummaging around in the fridge. "What are you looking for?"

"Nothing."

"Then why are you?"

"Killing time until breakfast is ready."

"Here," she said, handing him a plate. "Chow down." She turned back to take her plate off the counter and heard him move closer. "I never got to thank you last night."

The depth of his voice had chills tingling up her spine and tying up her tongue. Finally she managed, "For?"

"Everything." Turning her around to face him, he pressed his lips to her forehead, cheeks, and the end of her nose. Drawing her close, he rubbed his hands up and down her back and sighed. Picking up her plate, setting it on the table next to his, he told her, "That'll have to hold me over until I see you tonight."

Since her legs had turned rubbery, she sat down. "Are you planning on eating and running?"

He chewed and swallowed the mouthful he'd just shoveled in. "Precautionary measures." His dimple winked at her and she melted. "You might decide that if I kiss you again, you'll be late, and I know how much you hate being late."

"That's too bad." She speared a piece of sausage and bit into it. When she felt his gaze on her, she fought against the urge to laugh out loud. *Gotcha!*

"Are you going to keep me in suspense or tell me?"

She sighed. "I was going to try to convince you to try a quickie on the table after we cleared it off and put the dishes in the dishwasher."

His nostrils flared, and she knew he was imagining what she had while she'd been cooking. "I like the way your mind words, Mulcahy."

"It's a gift," she said, sliding off her chair and rinsing her dishes in the sink. When she would have put them in the dishwasher, he stayed her hand and pulled her toward him. "But the table's not clear."

"We can try it out later tonight." His eyes gleamed.

"I've been wanting to lean you over the counter since I first saw you here. Let me tell you what I've been thinking."

Caught up in the moment and his wicked whispered words, she didn't hear the house line ringing until she heard the answering machine click on and start recording.

"Jack," she heard a deep voice say, "are you there?"

He groaned and refastened the top of her jeans. "Later," he promised. "I've got to see what my dad wants." He picked up the phone. "Hey, Dad, what's up?"

Cait could tell from his expression that it was something he needed to concentrate on, so she busied herself cleaning up. Satisfied that she'd left it at least as clean as she'd found it, she slipped out of the room and used the bathroom. Borrowing some of his toothpaste, she scrubbed her teeth with her finger and rinsed her mouth.

"I'll have to start carrying a toothbrush and spare clothes with me." The funny feeling inside of her had her shaking her head. "It would be easier to leave stuff here, but his parents are going to be visiting soon…not happening while they're here…way too awkward."

With a glance at the clock, she figured she could beat Grace to the shop and snag one of the clean shirts they kept there for emergencies. Walking back into the kitchen, she was surprised to see that he was still on the phone. He smiled up at her and mouthed, "See you tonight."

She blew him a kiss and watched him catch it. She was grinning as she drove to town. "Clean shirt first, then Rhonda's."

Glad to be in a fresh shirt, she walked into the *Gazette*'s office and tapped the bell Rhonda kept on the counter. "Be right there," her friend called out.

While she waited, she texted Peggy to say she'd be there in five.

"Hey, Cait," Rhonda said, coming in from the back. "I was just going to call you. You'll never guess what I found out."

"Probably not," she agreed. "So?"

"Ms. Bonita Blackwell's been in the news," Rhonda told her. "Apparently, her good works include saving the life of a little black puppy she adopted from the pound and making a huge donation."

Cait felt her stomach slowly turn. "And?"

"She announced her engagement to a certain senator after she'd recovered the puppy she lost."

"Interesting. Do you think she really lost Jamie?"

Rhonda shrugged. "Not sure, but her fiancé has been lobbying for stricter regulations regarding animal shelters across the state. He's a supporter of neutering prior to adopting, not after. There's a picture of the three of them on the Internet this morning."

When Rhonda's expectant gaze met Cait's, Cait asked, "What?"

"Did Jamie have a swollen eye when you dropped him off at the sheriff's office?"

"No." Cait's gut iced over as she rounded the counter to stand next to Rhonda as the woman flipped through a couple of screens.

Cait focused on the little dog's face. "The whole side of his face is scraped up. What the hell happened to him?"

"Don't know, but it would have been great if you had a picture of what he looked like when you turned him over to that paparazzi-loving bitch."

Cait pulled her phone out of her pocket and flipped through the screens. "I haven't looked at it since that night, but the way Jack looked hugging Jamie, I just had to take a picture."

"Let's see if we can enlarge it. You're going to need proof before you press charges of animal cruelty."

"My charger's in the car. I'll go get it, then we can upload the picture to your computer."

Jogging back to the shop, she turned to look across the street when she heard Peggy calling her name. Her friend was standing with her hands on her hips outside the diner. Cait called out, "Can you take a break?"

Peggy nodded, stuck her head back inside for a moment, and was crossing the street by the time Cait had retrieved her phone charger.

"You've got to see this." Peggy caught Cait's urgency and the two of them ran to the *Gazette*, pushing the door open. Cait said, "OK, let me just plug this into your computer."

Once they'd selected the photo, Rhonda started playing with it, enlarging it, and brightening it so Jamie's face was perfectly clear. "Not a scratch on him," Cait pointed out.

"Check this out, Peggy," Caitlin said, pointing to the picture Rhonda found on the Internet this morning.

"Oh, the poor little puppy," her friend said. "Did someone beat him?"

"We need to tell Jack." Her hands were shaking as she dialed his cell.

"Hey, babe," he answered. "You need to stop distracting me."

"You've got to stop by the *Gazette*," she told him,

unable to keep the worry out of her voice. "You're going to want to see what Rhonda found out this morning."

"I just opened up my office," he told her. "Hang on. I'll be right there."

Her hands were shaking when she disconnected. Peggy took hold of them and told her, "She won't get away with it."

Jack pushed the door open and strode inside. "What's wrong? Who's hurt?"

She shook her head at him and pointed to the computer screen. "Rhonda found this picture of Ms. Blackwell and her fiancé this morning."

Anger had his entire body going rigid. "What the hell happened to my dog?"

Cait knew exactly how he felt.

Rhonda switched screens and he blew out a breath. "I didn't know you took that picture."

Heart in her eyes, Caitlin laid a hand on his arm. "I wanted to wait another few days to show you. I didn't want to make it harder since you already missed him so much."

He hugged Cait tight to his side. "Thanks for finding this, Rhonda."

Cait looked at her friends and said, "Can you rerun that story you did a few months ago about the Newark Animal Shelter?"

Her friend nodded. "The fundraiser?"

Cait nodded. "Can you update it with a short piece about Jack and me finding Jamie and then returning him to his owner with that picture of Jack and Jamie?"

"I love the way your mind works!" Rhonda said, making a shooing motion with her hands. "Get lost, people. I have a story to write."

But Jack wasn't listening; he was on the phone with Mitch. "Rhonda's working on a story right now. The picture's all the proof I need." His gaze met hers as he said, "I'm gonna spring Jamie."

"When?" Cait asked when he disconnected.

"I've got patients all day, but as soon as I'm finished, I'm paying her a visit." He brushed a hand over her cheek. "You want in on it?"

"I do," she rasped. "I knew there was something about that woman I didn't like."

"What if it was an accident?" Rhonda asked.

"Then she's careless and hasn't fulfilled the promise she signed off on when she adopted Jamie."

"What if she calls in the big guns—her political connections?" Peggy asked.

"We've got both pictures taken hours apart," Jack said. "A picture's worth a thousand words."

Rhonda agreed. "I'll have the story up and viral in a half hour."

Jack stared at Rhonda for a moment before saying, "It might help our cause if we have a reporter there, ready to do the follow-up story of the dog we rescued."

Rhonda slowly smiled. "I can clear my calendar for the evening. Now get going so I can write!"

Jack tugged on Cait's hand, pulling her out the door behind him. "Cait, I don't know what to say."

"Don't say anything until we've got him back."

"What if she refuses?" Peggy asked. "What if she calls her lawyer?"

Cait thought about it for a few moments, and then said, "I think image is everything to Ms. Blackwell. She won't want the bad press this will generate. Once

Rhonda makes a promise that something's going viral, she means it."

Jack agreed. "Our story and that photo will be everywhere. She'll have a lot of explaining to do once the ASPCA gets wind of it."

Cait's phone rang. She looked at the number and sighed. "Hey, Sis. Yeah, sorry, I'm on my way there right now." She nodded to Peggy. "That was Grace. She said you have an emergency over at the diner."

Peggy laughed. "I do…I haven't seen you in a few days and needed to catch up." With a sideways glance at Jack, Peggy said, "I hear tell that you've been keeping a certain doctor tied up at night. Would you care to elaborate on that?"

Jack chuckled as he pulled Cait in for a quick kiss. "See you later."

Cait couldn't stop sighing, watching him sprint down the street to his office.

"Come on," Peggy said, taking Cait by the hand. "You can fill me in while you check out the back burner on our stove."

"I thought you just wanted to talk to me?"

"I do, but Grace will probably make an excuse to come on over to make sure you're working."

"Right," Cait agreed. "Let me grab my tools." She followed Peggy into the diner's kitchen.

"Hey," Cait said. "What did you spill down this burner? It's a mess."

"Don't remember," Peggy said. "Things boil over, we mop up as best we can, but when it's busy in here, there's not a whole lot of time."

"Peggy, dear," Miss Trudi called out strolling into the diner. "How is your mother?"

"She's fine, standing watch over our currant berries so the darned catbirds and robins don't eat them all before they're ripe."

"Best jelly in the world," Miss Trudi agreed. "Always make mine around the Fourth of July."

"Depends on whether or not my dad wants *really* tart jelly or just tart jelly," Peggy said with a smile. "Before the Fourth, super tart, and if Mom waits another few days, just tart."

Cait wiped her hands on the clean rag she'd put in her toolbox that morning. "Will you call me when your mom is ready to make the jelly?"

Peggy's smile was filled with understanding. "Absolutely. You know she loves having you there helping—as long as you don't—"

"I know, I know," Cait interrupted. "As long as I don't touch the tops of the jelly jars as they are cooling...then she won't know which ones were really sealed and which ones I helped to seal."

"Well now, girls," Miss Trudi said, after getting their attention. "You'll both volunteer again to set up and clean up at Founder's Day, won't you?"

Peggy and Cait looked at one another and agreed, making Miss Trudi smile. Leaning over the counter so only Miss Trudi could hear, Peggy whispered, "Cait and Doc are going to rescue Jamie tonight. Rhonda's putting up a story on the Internet right now and then going along later to document the rescue as it's happening."

"Well, that's fine then," the older woman said. "By the way, Cait, I'm so glad Doc's tonic worked."

Cait sputtered and Peggy swallowed her laughter so she could ask Miss Trudi, "Don't you want a cup of tea?"

"Too busy right now, dear," the older woman said. "I've got to stop off and chat with Honey B.," she explained. "Details about the vow renewal. We want everything to be just perfect. After all, a woman wants this sort of thing to be just perfect."

Miss Trudi paused in the doorway and asked, "How's the design for the cake coming?"

Peggy sighed. "Kate's done an amazing job. Wait until you see it."

"Make sure it's extra special," Miss Trudi warned.

Peggy smiled. "It will be."

"I'll stop by later for that tea, dear."

Watching the woman retreat, taking in Miss Trudi's favorite outfit—jodhpurs, a crisp white button-down shirt, and wellies—Cait sighed. "I want to be Miss Trudi when I grow up."

"Me too," Peggy agreed, watching the older woman stride down the street before asking, "So how's the stove?"

"Good as new."

"How's Doc's stamina?"

Cait snorted and she slapped her hands over her mouth to keep from doing it again. "You are a wicked woman, Peggy McCormack, catching me off guard like that, hoping I'll spill all of my secrets."

"It's part of my charm," her friend preened, "and it used to work like one."

Cait's phone buzzed. "That'll be Gracie." She read the message. "Another repair job." Cait's gaze met her friend's and confided, "I'm keeping him, Peggy."

Peggy nodded. "If you change your mind, let me know."

Cait was laughing as she waved good-bye and got

into her car. She had a full day before they could put their plans to rescue Jamie into action.

By four thirty that afternoon she was exhausted, her face had scratches from the rotten wood she'd knocked loose while working on Miss Tisdale's chicken coop, and she was so hungry she could have gnawed off her right hand.

"Should have stopped for lunch." She knew better, but somehow with everything happening, time got away from her. So when Grace called, she was more than ready for a break.

"How are things on the home front, Gracie?"

Her sister sighed. "The usual, two more jobs for tomorrow and a cancellation. Your last stop has a stomach bug."

"Whoa," Cait said. "No need to catch something like that."

"That's what Mrs. Jenkins said."

"I'm going to stop at the diner," Cait told her sister. "I worked through lunch."

"I'll meet you over there," her sister said before hanging up.

"Now I wonder what that's all about." Cleaning up the rest of her tools, she said good-bye to Miss Tisdale and drove into town.

There weren't any spots left near the diner, so she parked behind the shop and walked up the alleyway between Mulcahys and the diner. The crowd of people gathered there caught her by surprise.

"Hey, Kate," she called out, stepping inside. "Are you giving away free pie?"

The younger McCormack sister's smile bloomed as

she waved Cait inside. "Peggy just asked me to give you a call…but it's better that you're here!"

Cait smiled at the familiar faces of some of her friends and neighbors before asking, "Where's Peggy?"

"Here." She beamed, and the crowd made room for Peggy and Rhonda, who was hot on her heels.

"This is huge," Rhonda said with a nod in Cait's direction. "Huge!"

Before she could ask what they were talking about, the door opened behind them and Jack rushed in. "What's the emergency?" His face was flushed, and he was limping, but he didn't notice—he scanned the crowd and looked at her when he asked, "What's going on?"

Cait shrugged. "I just got here after putting Miss Tisdale's chicken coop back together. Don't ask me."

His gaze swept past her and then back again. His entire demeanor changed. "You're hurt." The brush of his fingertips along the edge of her scraped cheek soothed her.

"It's just a scratch," she protested, moving to make room for the people crowding around them.

"Let me look—" he began as the door opened wide behind him.

A ripple went through the crowd as Cait rubbed her eyes in disbelief, but she wasn't seeing things. "Jamie!" Cait gave a hoot and elbowed her way to where Jack stood, staring at the puppy they'd planned to liberate in a few hours. The little dog wiggled in Mitch's arms until he chuckled and handed the dog over to the still-silent Jack.

"What happened?" Cait asked.

Mitch looked from Rhonda to Cait and said, "Got this

phone call about two hours ago," he told them. "It seems that Ms. Blackwell will be going away on an extended vacation and wouldn't be able to care for Crackers… uh…Jamie here."

Cait and Jack shared a meaning-filled look. "Do tell," Cait said, grinning at Rhonda and Peggy.

"She even brought back his bed, toys, food, and treats," Mitch said with a smile.

Jack nuzzled the top of the dog's head and Jamie gave a doggy groan of ecstasy. "Did she say what happened to him?"

The sheriff shook his head. "It was her only condition."

"What was?" Cait asked.

"She looked me dead in the eye and I'm still not certain if she was lying through her teeth," Mitch told them. "She said it was an accident, and that if you wanted full ownership of Jamie, you'd have to take her word for it."

"Like hell—" Cait interrupted before Jack tugged on her braid. Surprised by his action, she turned her head to tell him to stop and got distracted by the look on Jack's and Jamie's faces.

"She said she spoke to Rhonda over at the *Gazette*." The sheriff leveled a look at the woman, but Rhonda was pretending not to notice. "Apparently," he continued, "Ms. Beaudine promised to write a follow-up a story about Ms. Blackwell's magnanimous gesture if and when she gave the dog back to Jack…seeing as how she'd be traveling and no longer able to take care of him."

"What a crock," Peggy blurted out.

The crowd in the diner burst into laughter.

"We came as soon as we heard," her father said, holding open the diner door for Mary. "Well," he said with a smile, his gaze lingering on his daughter standing next to Jack and Jamie. "I see things are as they should be. Is there any coffee left?"

Laughter followed his question as Peggy scooted around the counter and started taking orders. By the time everyone gathered had congratulated Rhonda, Jack, and Cait on a job well done, not a crumb of the McCormack sisters' baked goods remained.

Cait had stopped counting the number of cups of coffee her friends and neighbors had consumed as she shared the better half of a ham and American on rye with Jamie. The little dog quivered with excitement as she held him, giving Jack a chance to discuss his options with the sheriff.

By the time he sat back down on the stool next to her, most of the crowd had gone and Jamie was falling asleep in her arms. "Do you think he'll be all right?" she asked.

"While you two were sharing that sandwich, I was talking to Mitch. We always knew he took his job seriously, but did you know he had Ms. Blackwell wait while the vet came and checked Jamie out?"

Cait looked over her shoulder and smiled. The sheriff was bending down to listen to something Honey B. was telling him. When Honey B. smiled, Mitch smiled. "He's one of the good guys."

Jack agreed. She laid a hand to his cheek and told him, "You are too."

"So, can you come home with us?" Jack asked, gently stroking the furry ball of black in Cait's lap.

"I need to pick up a few things at my house."

Jack slipped his arm around her and rested his chin on the top of her head. "Such as?"

Cait looked around to make sure no one was close enough to hear and whispered, "Clean shirt, underwear, toothbrush…you know, things."

Jack loved the way her body curved into his and fit just right. Caitlin Mulcahy and Jamie fit into his life like pieces to a puzzle. It felt good, knowing that she'd be going home with him and they'd have their family back together—*whoa*, he thought.

Family? Cait and Jamie?

Yeah, he realized, they were everything he wanted. When he heard Honey B.'s delighted laughter he ached, wishing he and Cait were married and starting on their own family. He wanted that with Cait, craved that with Cait. How had he fallen in love with her so completely, so quickly?

"Are you ready?" she asked, pulling him from his deep thoughts.

"Yes. Do you mind holding Jamie while I drive?"

She shook her head. "Not at all. Can we stop at my house on the way?"

"Can you ask Gracie to drop off what you need?"

"Hey, Gracie." Cait motioned to her sister. "Can I ask you a favor?"

"What's up?"

"Can you grab a couple of things for me and bring them to Jack's?"

After she told Grace what she needed, Grace looked at her sister and then down at Jamie. "No problem." She paused, then said, "He's such a lucky little dog. I wish I didn't get all choked up around dogs."

"I'm that way with cats," Jack told her as he helped Cait to her feet.

"See you later, Pop," Cait called out as Jack held the door open for her. "Bye, Mitch. Give Honey B. and little Mitch a hug for me."

Holding Cait's hand and walking beneath the big, old shade trees lining Main Street, Jack realized that he had turned an important corner in his recovery. He had balance in his life that hadn't been there since he'd been wounded in Iraq. He brought Cait's hand to his lips and pressed a kiss to her knuckles.

The desire simmering in her eyes went to his head like two fingers of whiskey. He slipped his arm around her while she cuddled the little ball of fuzz. Being with Jamie opened their eyes to one another—until they could see below the surface to the very heart of that person and they'd discovered a growing love that whispered of forever.

When he opened the door to his Jeep for her, he knew that he'd have to trust her with the whole story.

Jamie slept the whole ride home but woke up when the Jeep stopped. "We're home, boy." Jack ruffled the fur on the top of the pup's head.

After being set on his feet by Cait, Jamie waited while she got the bags out of the backseat. They both laughed, watching Jamie run around in circles, chasing his tail.

Taking their time going up the walk, they waited for Jamie to pee first and then catch up.

Reaching for one of the bags, Jack opened the door, saying, "Welcome home, Jamie."

Chapter 16

"I CAN'T BELIEVE YOUR PARENTS WILL BE HERE tonight," Cait said, giving Jamie what he wanted—a full body rub—before getting up to stand outside the bathroom door. "It's going to be weird not staying overnight," she confessed. "I've gotten used to you two." Life had changed dramatically from that afternoon at the diner when Mitch carried Jamie inside.

"You could stay over," Jack called out from the shower.

She opened the bathroom door and chuckled. "Oh, did you tell your parents about me?"

"Yes and no."

"Well, that clears everything up—Jamie, no!" she called out, chasing the dog out of the bathroom.

"What's going on?" Jack asked, peering around the curtain.

"Too late," she told him, holding up the mangled pair of boxers Jack had left on the toilet seat.

"Damn. Can you grab another pair out of my top drawer?"

They had been sleeping together for a couple of weeks, but it was the first time she'd been asked to go in his underwear drawer. She hesitated—it seemed so personal, something a wife would do for her husband.

"You sure?"

"Relax, Mulcahy, it's just boxers and socks."

"All right." Rummaging through that drawer, she

only found socks and T-shirts. "Nothing here. Should I keep looking?"

"Yeah."

She found shorts, jeans, and gray T-shirts from his days in the navy, but no boxers. She was laughing and pushing Jamie away when he tried to stick his face in Jack's bottom drawer. "Cut it out," she told the dog.

But he wasn't listening and continued to nose at the contents of the drawer until he unearthed a small black box and started to chew it. "Give me that." After a brief tug of war, she landed on her butt and the box fell open on the floor.

The glint of the medal didn't register at first. "Hey, Jack, Jamie just found a medal—"

"Caitlin, wait—" Jack stood with a towel wrapped around his hips, the ends clutched in his fist.

Their gazes met and held for a heartbeat before he bent and scooped the box and medal in one swift movement.

"Jack, I think—"

"Not now."

"But I—"

～～～

He took the box with him into the bathroom and got dressed without his boxers. By the time he emerged, he could hear Cait and Jamie downstairs.

"If I don't tell her, I'm FUBAR," he mumbled one of his favorite acronyms from his days in the military. He knew what he needed to do, but still he hesitated. When he heard the back door slam, he shot to his feet. "Caitlin!" He ran down the stairs, jerked open the door, and almost knocked her over as she and Jamie came back inside.

She frowned up at him. "I'm really trying to help you here, Jack, but you have to work with me."

"I know, Cait. I'm sorry—it's hard for me."

She kissed his cheek and told him, "I'm late for work. Can we talk later?"

A few hours later, Jack looked up as Joe Mulcahy walked into his office. "How did I miss that Joe had an appointment today?"

Mrs. Sweeney shook her head. "You didn't."

Joe nodded. "Can I talk to you for a minute?"

Jack's gut tied itself into a knot, but he said, "Come on back." He sat behind his desk and motioned to the empty chair.

Joe sat and asked, "What's got a bee in Caitlin's bonnet?"

Jack's shoulders slumped forward. "She and Jamie found my Purple Heart."

"So you talked about it?"

"No."

Joe's eyes widened. "So, that's what's at the bottom of your troubles?"

"I never said—"

"A word," Joe finished for him. "Does your dad know that you earned one?"

"Earned one?" Jack ground out. "An IED exploded as I was stitching one of the marines in the battalion I was responsible for back together. He died," he rasped, "and they gave me a freaking medal for it!"

Blinded by anger, tortured with guilt, he didn't realize the other man had wrapped his arms around him, but when the order came to, "Breathe, Corpsman," he obeyed.

"At ease," Joe commanded, stepping back.

Jack snapped back to the present as the red haze cleared. "Damn."

"Tell me what happened."

Jack hesitated and Joe said, "You can tell the doctor over at the VA, you can tell me, or you can tell your dad when he gets here in about two hours."

Where did he begin?

"What was the marine's name?" Joe's question burned in Jack's gut until he thought he'd puke.

"Corpsman?" Joe bit out.

Reacting to the tone, he answered automatically, "Yes, sir?"

"I asked you a question."

Jack didn't look up when he rasped, "John Napolitano."

"Where was he from?"

"Nebraska."

"What happened?"

"He was already badly injured, and I had been stitching him up but didn't realize he'd been hit again until I saw the pool of blood seeping out from beneath his flak jacket."

"He was their leader?"

Jack nodded. "He insisted that I help the others first. One of the marines was probably going to lose a leg, but I did the best I could, applying the tourniquet. I don't know what ever happened to him."

"You worked hard to save them."

Joe's statement eased the tight knot forming in Jack's throat. He swallowed and answered, "Yes."

"Then what?"

"I was stitching our squad leader back together when I heard someone shout, 'Incoming.'"

"And?"

"I reacted."

Joe placed a hand on Jack's shoulder. "What did you do?"

"I threw myself over two of the guys."

While Jack stared off into space reliving that horrible instant in time, Joe nodded. "You saved their lives."

Jack shook his head sadly. "Our squad leader died."

"What about the others?"

"They survived."

"And you?"

"Three operations and my leg's almost straight again. Removing most of the shrapnel was hell."

Joe nodded. "Caught some myself years back. Still think there's a piece floating around in my side. So the powers that be gave you a Purple Heart for being wounded in action."

Jack nodded. "Didn't seem right, what with Nappy dead."

"Nappy?"

"Napolitano."

"When are you going to tell Cait?"

"Tell her what, that I'm a failure?"

"How did you fail?"

"I didn't work fast enough. I should have saved him."

"With all of your years in the navy, he couldn't have been the first or only one you weren't able to save."

Jack's shoulders slumped again. "Nappy was my friend."

"As a doctor, you know you can't save everyone— that's up to a much higher power than yours. That IED didn't have Napolitano's name, or yours, on it. Did it?"

"No, but—"

"Don't let it be personal, Jack…it was war."

"War is hell."

"I know." Joe leaned forward. "Talk to Cait."

"I will. Thanks, Joe."

"Glad to help."

"You're pretty sharp, Joe."

"Had to be," Joe said. "I had to raise three daughters through their toughest years with only one oar, and without a rudder…my Maureen."

"Salty talk," Jack chuckled. "That's what my mom always said when Dad and I started to talk like sailors."

"Hell, you were both in the navy."

"And you were in the coast guard."

Joe grinned. "Best time of my life…aside from meeting Maureen and having three beautiful daughters."

Jack watched his eyes and noticed they weren't quite as sad as they'd been a year or so ago. "How did you cope when…" Jack couldn't finish the question, remembering how horrible that time had been in Meg's family's life.

"At first, one breath at a time," he told Jack. "And then it was one step at a time, and finally, with your dad's help, one day at a time."

"Smart man, my dad," Jack said.

"Talk to him," Joe urged, "then talk to my girl. Life's too short to throw away what you two have because of your misplaced sense of pride."

"It's not pride," Jack told him.

"What is it then?"

He hesitated. "Guilt."

Joe added, "Ah, your mother raised you to be a good Irish son, then?"

Jack's lips twitched at Joe's exaggerated brogue.
He nodded.

"So, you were raised with Irish Catholic guilt?" Jack
shrugged, and Joe said, "The worst kind."

Jack felt his lips twitching again, this time he gave in
and smiled. "Thanks, Joe."

"No problem," Joe said, turning to go.

"I thought you needed to see me about something."

Joe stopped in the doorway and grinned. "I did."

Jack watched him leave, surprised to discover he
was still smiling when he got the text from his mom
that they'd made it home and were being lavished with
puppy kisses.

He told them he had a stop to make on the way home,
packed up, and drove to the Mulcahys' place.

When he showed up at the back door, it was Grace
and not Cait who stood there smiling. "She's upstairs,
go on up."

Jack took the stairs two at a time and walked down
the hallway. It felt good, he realized. He had a mission
in life; he had a purpose—unburden the whole of his
demons to Cait and move forward with their relationship
from there. He was keeping her.

He was smiling when he pounded on her bedroom door.

"Be down in a minute, Grace."

"It's not Grace."

When she didn't immediately open the door, he
knocked again, "Open up, Cait. I need to talk to you."

"I'm half-dressed and my dad and sister are downstairs, which is where you should be. I'll be right down."

"But you've been after me to talk to you for days."

"I changed my mind. Maybe I'm not as ready as I

thought if it's taken you this long to open up. I don't want to scare you away if I don't react the way you expect me to. I can't take the chance of letting you down. Please, just go downstairs."

"I can't. I need to talk to you now, and I need to see your face when I tell you what happened."

"Can't you come back in an hour?"

"No! I've waited long enough. Open the door."

"Not yet—"

"I have your father's permission to break it down," he lied, because if he didn't spill his guts right now, he might not be able to for months!

There was a moment of silence before she told him, "Go ahead."

God, why was she hiding from him? Was she really that scared? He felt like the Big Bad Wolf, but if that was the way she wanted to play it, so be it. He took a few steps back and shouted, "Stand back, you ornery Irishwoman!"

He got a running start and was about to bash into the door with his shoulder when it opened up. At the last second, he twisted his body and rammed his shoulder—instead of his head—into the plaster wall, cracking it.

Gasping for breath, certain that he'd dislocated his shoulder, he groaned as she demanded, "What did you call me?"

"Ornery," he rasped, holding on to his aching shoulder while he struggled to stand. "What the hell is wrong with you?" he asked, digging deep to get past the pain. "You badger me for days and tell me to talk to you… and now that I am—"

Her face paled. "Please just give me a little more time. This is too important to you—to us—for me to hear what you have to say and react instinctively—and take a chance of losing you forever. I love you too much to risk it."

How could he refuse? He let her pass. "I love you, Caitlin." He reached for her. She looked up at him with fear and tears in her eyes. The emotions tumbling through her humbled him. "I love you, Cait, and I'll wait. Come over when you're ready to listen—oh and one more thing." He locked gazes with her. "I'll come looking for you if you don't."

She squeezed his hand and nodded. "I'll be there, I just need time to clear my head."

Watching her walk away, knowing what he had to do, preferring to do it himself, he slammed his shoulder into the doorway and felt it shift back into place in the socket.

"God that hurts." When he walked into the kitchen, Grace handed him a glass of water and two aspirins. "She's probably going to talk to Peggy."

He nodded, took them, and handed her the glass. "Thanks, Gracie."

"She's crazy about you, Doc."

He slowly smiled. "I'm crazy right back."

"I think you're both certifiable," Grace told him.

He drove home with a dull ache in his shoulder and a much sharper one in his leg. After all of his worry, damned if her car wasn't parked next to his folks. "Guess she sorted it out quicker than I thought she would."

The door opened, but instead of the woman he wanted to talk to, Jamie ran out and jumped on his bad leg. Jack went down hard, landing on the shoulder he had just put back into place. He saw stars and then he saw Caitlin—two of her—standing over him, begging him to speak to her.

"Speak to you?" he grumbled. "I've been trying to do that since you opened that damn door and I dislocated my damn shoulder."

"Hmmm," his mother said from where she stood behind Caitlin. "That's two damns in one sentence. Our darling boy is upset about something." Instead of offering Jack any sympathy, she put her arm through Cait's. "Why don't I make us a nice cup of tea?"

"John, dear," his mother called out as she walked into the house. "Jack might need your help getting up."

Jamie couldn't understand why Jack wasn't moving, so he jumped on Jack's chest with his two front paws and started to lick Jack's face. "At least you aren't leaving me."

"What's all this about, Cora—Son!" His father knelt down by Jack's side. "What happened to you?"

Jack cleared his throat, and told him, "It all started with this little dog."

His father helped him to his feet and checked his eyes and the back of his head for lumps and bumps. "Where does it hurt the most?"

Jack grimaced. "My shoulder. Dislocated it when I hit the wall in Cait's bedroom."

His father's eyes widened, then he said, "I'm having trouble wrapping my thoughts around that one, Jack. What exactly were you doing at the Mulcahys' house?"

Jack sighed; he'd have to fess up sooner or later. Joe might stop by and it would be better if his father knew the truth before he had to bury his son. "Breaking her door down."

"Then how did you hit the wall?" his dad asked, helping Jack to stand.

"She opened the door."

"But I thought you said—"

"I told her to stand back because I didn't want her to get hurt, but does the stubborn woman listen to me?"

"I was afraid, Jack," Cait said from where she stood on the other side of the screen door.

"I know," he said. "Are you ready yet?"

Her eyes filled and she walked outside to stand in front of him. "I'm listening."

"I'm sorry about this morning, Cait. I shouldn't have shut you out."

His father handed him the ice bag first and then held the bottle of pain relievers and water.

"Grace already gave me some aspirin."

"All right. Here," his dad said, urging him toward a deck chair. "Sit down, son. I can tell your leg pains you."

Looking at Cait and only Cait, Jack said, "I've been to the VA but wasn't due for more therapy for a few weeks. There are times when I'm there again—in Iraq and it's happening all over again." He closed his eyes, breathing deeply to calm his racing heart. When he opened his eyes, Cait squeezed his hand. "Sometimes," he whispered, "it seems like a dream."

His father and mother stood off to the side, but he motioned for them to come over. When they all sat down, Cait pulled her deck chair closer to Jack's, so she could keep holding his hand.

"I need to tell you," he said to Cait, "and my parents need to hear this too."

His mother was sitting on the edge of her seat until

his dad took her hand and patted the back of it. His mom scooted back in the chair but didn't let go of his dad. Jamie laid down on Jack's feet and looked up at him. The warmth and unconditional love surrounding him and shining in Jamie's dark brown eyes gave Jack the courage to start.

"I was caring for the wounded in our battalion when an IED struck."

"We know you were, Son," his father said. "That's why they gave you that medal."

Cait looked over at his father and then back at Jack. "Yeah," he said to Cait, "the one you found this morning."

Drawing in a calming breath, he rasped, "Cait's dad got me started talking today. It's better if I just get it all out at once, and then I won't have to talk about it again."

"There's where you'd be wrong," Cait told him. "You need to acknowledge it and not bury it, so it won't sneak up on you again."

He shook his head. "I'm OK now and have my focus back. For a while, little things used to set me off—but therapy's helped and the imagery the doctor suggested has been working.

"We weren't even supposed to be there…wrong place, wrong time. Napolitano was my friend—the squad leader. I was stitching him back together, but once the IED hit, he insisted that I take care of his men first. I didn't know he'd been hit again…if only I had just worked faster."

He locked gazes with Cait and didn't look away while he told the story. When he was finished, he grabbed both of her hands in his. "Can you understand why I felt so guilty?"

268 C.H. ADMIRAND

Tears filled her eyes, but she didn't seem to notice. "Honestly? No."

"Dad? Mom?" he asked, knowing his parents had heard every detail.

When they looked at him as if he were crazy, Cait pulled him to his feet and into her arms. "Face it, Gannon, you're a hero."

He wanted to say something, but the warmth of her embrace filled the empty spots he'd exposed in his soul. Her love seeped in, binding the wounds, healing the hurt. Humbled, he buried his face in her hair and said a silent prayer of thanks that she hadn't walked away from him.

"Why don't you and I start supper?" his mother said, tugging on her husband's arm to get him moving.

"Cora, wait," he said, but she shook her head.

"They need more time to sort this out, John. You come on inside." Reluctantly, he went.

"I've really missed them," Jack said, listening to the snippets of conversation and his father's grumbling as it drifted out through the screen door.

"They love you."

He looked into Cait's eyes, encouraged by the love reflected back at him. "Cait, I know I've made a mess of what we'd started, but can you find it in your heart to give me another chance?"

"You don't need one."

"Don't I?"

"You haven't used up the first one yet." She waited a moment before adding, "Thank you for giving me a chance to gather my wits and courage to hear the rest of your story."

"So you still love me?"

She rolled her eyes. "Duh."

"How can you make light of this, Caitlin?"

"Because I want you to understand that while it is huge for you, I don't see it the same way." She cupped his face in her hands and brushed her lips against his. "I remember the look on your face at graduation, when they announced you were headed to the Great Lakes A School and that you were going to be a navy corpsman."

She let her hands glide down his neck to his chest and then around his back. "You were so handsome, standing there so straight and so tall. I never thought you'd look twice at me. You were Meg's age…I was just a kid."

"I still think you don't understand."

"Then I saw the distant look in your eyes when you came home on leave. You weren't the same. I couldn't imagine the things you'd seen and done for our country, but my dad could. He reminded us that war is hell and that some men are scarred by it physically, some mentally, and then there are some who quietly do their duty, never asking to be recognized, just wanting to do what they'd been trained to do—some of them patching the wounded back together—like you.

"And I see you as the auburn-haired doctor who came home to fill his father's shoes and take over his practice when your dad retired and your parents announced they were moving to Florida."

She watched his eyes as she added, "You didn't have to do that, but otherwise everyone in Apple Grove would have had to drive nearly an hour to get to the next closest doctor in Newark. Do you realize how important you are to this community? Mr. Weatherbee, Mrs.

Winter, all of our older residents who can't always drive into town when they're sick? You continue your dad's practice of making house calls. Who the heck does that these days?"

He shook his head. Far be it from him to interrupt Caitlin Mulcahy when she was on a roll.

She laid her head on his chest and whispered, "You didn't have to throw yourself on top of those marines. But you did. You didn't even think twice. You just did."

Easing back, she let her gaze meet his. "If I could take away the horrors that you've seen, the pain you've suffered, I would," she told him. "But it's all part of who and what you are…the man I fell in love with."

She kissed him, pouring all of the love inside of her into him, to help him heal. "So yeah, I'm not seeing things from your perspective, but I think I get it."

Everything inside of Jack felt too big to put into words, but he had to let her know what her words meant to him. So he ignored the pain shooting through his shoulder and wrapped his arms around her, lifting her off her feet and kissing her while he spun them around in a circle.

"You're making me dizzy!" she squealed until he stopped spinning. With a hand to her head, she motioned toward the back door. "Should we tell them about us?" He eased Cait out of his arms, but he kept a hold of her hand.

Walking inside, he said, "Mom, Dad." He paused until they were both looking at him, "Cait and I are seeing each other." He brought Cait's hand to his lips and brushed the back of it with a kiss. "We're in love."

His father looked at his mother and shook his head. "We're not blind, Son."

Jack grinned. "She's been staying here with me, helping me take care of Jamie."

His father seemed to be fighting the urge to smile. "You don't say."

"Now, John." His mother gave him a look. "Don't tease. These two have been through enough today."

"Do you want us to stay with friends, so you can have the house to yourselves?"

"No!" Jack shook his head. "This is your home."

His dad drew his mom to his side and shook his head. "It used to be. You bought it when we retired, remember?"

"Why don't you and Caitlin tell us how you two started dating?" his mother said, tugging on his elbow. "After all," she continued, "you two have known each other all your lives."

Jack looked at Cait, relieved to see her soft smile. He held the back door open and called Jamie. When the little dog scampered inside, he said, "It all started when a little black ball of fuzz ran out in front of me on Eden Church Road."

———

"Your parents are great, Jack," Cait said as she snuggled against him. Unable to keep her hands to herself, she trailed the tip of her finger from his breastbone to his navel, dipping it in and then drawing circles across his abs.

He grabbed a hold of her hand to hold it still. "I think so too."

When he let go, she slid her hand over his hip around to his backside and squeezed.

"Woman, you wore me out," he groaned.

"Really?" she asked, slowly working her hands up from his backside to his waist and then back down to grab hold of his cheeks while she pressed a kiss over his heart. "Well, I guess if you're too tired…"

She found herself on her back, looking up into his dark and desperate sapphire eyes. "I can see I'll have to try harder tiring you out." He slid his hands to her wrists and pulled her hands over her head. With a wicked smile, he dipped his head and traced a path from the hollow of her throat down to her navel.

"Jack," she sighed, quivering from his touch.

"Mmm…not now," he grumbled, "I'm busy." He dipped the tip of his tongue into her navel and then drew a circle around it before continuing along the path that would lead him to wild honey—and a taste of heaven. He looked up and locked gazes with her. "I forgot to have dessert."

Caitlin bucked beneath the ministrations of his talented tongue and wicked lips. Just when she was certain she'd reached her limit, she lifted her hips up off the bed, driving his tongue deeper, and herself over the edge, free falling into madness.

She could hear his soft chuckle and felt the bed shift, but she couldn't move; her bones had liquefied. When his hands released her, he stroked his hand across her shoulders and down her arms to link hands with her.

"And now for the good part," he rasped, plunging into her life-giving warmth. "Open your eyes, love," he urged. "I want to watch the way they glaze over when I take us over the edge."

She slowly opened her eyes and let them focus on the face of the man she loved to distraction. "I don't think I have anything left to give."

His hips shifted from side to side, undulating before pinning her to the mattress, wringing the last ounce of pleasure from her, sipping from her lips to muffle her cries of ecstasy.

He wrapped his arms around her and rolled until she was on top. Sliding one hand down to cup her curvy backside, he kept the other one around her back, pressing her against his heart.

As she drifted off to sleep, she murmured, "I love you, Jack."

The last of the knots in his gut loosened, and he told her what was in his heart. "I love you back, Cait."

Chapter 17

CAIT AND JACK WERE UP EARLY THE NEXT DAY, ENERGIZED from a good night's sleep. Cait was patting Jamie on the head and telling him to be a good boy when Jack's mom came downstairs.

"Good morning, early birds." Jack's mother smile reminded Cait of an extremely satisfied feline.

"Morning, Mom."

"Morning, Mrs. Gannon."

"Please, call me Cora," she told Cait. "Mrs. Gannon was my mother-in-law."

Cait looked at Jack first, and when he shrugged, she agreed. "I have a long day of repairs ahead of me," she told Jack's mother. "I'd better get started."

"Breakfast is the most important meal of the day, dear," Cora called after. "Be sure you get some."

Caitlin didn't laugh until she got outside; she didn't want Cora to think she was laughing at her. She was laughing because it felt good to have Jack's mom worrying about her.

"Hey, gorgeous," Jack called out. "Wait up!"

She paused beside her truck and waited for him. "Hey, handsome." And wasn't he just, standing there clean-shaven, eyes bright, and lips curved upward in a smile that hinted he had a secret that he might be willing to share?

"If I don't have the chance to tell you before

tonight, I'm so damned grateful to have you in my life, Caitlin Mulcahy."

Unease skittered up her spine. "Grateful?"

He pulled her into his arms and she felt his heart pounding, as if he had been running. Looking up into his eyes, she waited a moment before asking, "Does this have anything to do with bugging you until you spilled your guts about what happened in Iraq?"

He didn't say anything but slid his hands up to cup the sides of her face. "Part of it does, but the rest of it has to do with loving you, Cait." His voice deepened as he added, "And I do."

Cait's heart fluttered before matching Jack's beat for beat. Sliding her hands over his, she lifted to her toes and pressed her mouth against his—soft, warm, giving. All of the above fit what she wanted to share with Jack...and what she received in return when he kissed her back.

"I'm crazy in love you with, Doc Gannon."

He was smiling as he bent to kiss her again. "Better 'n just crazy, Mulcahy."

She was laughing as she got in her truck and rolled down the window. "Say bye to your dad for me."

"Will do," he promised with a wave. She was about to back up when she thought of something. Rolling down her window, she called out, "Hey, Jack?"

"What?"

"Just how long are your parents staying?"

"Why?"

Her smile was just this side of wicked when she said, "We haven't tried out the kitchen table yet."

His laughter had her smiling on the inside all the way

to town. Turning right onto Main Street, she parked behind Mulcahys surprised but pleased to see her father sorting through tools and supplies in their shop. "Hey, Pop! What brings you here?"

He looked down at her and waited a heartbeat before answering, "You."

"Me? What did I do?"

He snorted. "I have it on good authority that you weren't listening and Jack dislocated his shoulder trying to break down your bedroom door."

Cait sighed. "There was a lot more to it than that, Pop."

"Well, what happened?"

Cait drew in another steadying breath. "Jack and I talked about Iraq, Pop." She turned back to face him. "He's so much braver than I thought…and that's a lot."

Her dad nodded. "So, you and Jack are good?"

"Yeah," she said. "We are, but I still think there must be some way for me to help him see what he means to this town and to those men he helped to save."

Her father agreed. "I think I might know of a way. Let me talk to Jack's dad and see if we can track down a few of those marines."

"To have them write a letter to Jack?"

Her father's face was solemn when his gaze met hers. "I'm thinking of something a little more proactive."

"Such as?" Cait prompted.

"Visiting Apple Grove."

Cait nodded. "Since he's opened up about what happened, he might be ready for a visit in a few months."

Her dad smiled. "I was thinking about a few weeks from now…say June fifteenth?"

"Founder's Day?" she asked. "Just what are you up to?"

"I'll have to ask Miss Trudi to leave about a half hour to forty-five minutes after her annual speech."

"Pop—"

He had his hand on the office door and was about to walk through. "Trust me, string bean."

She sighed at the nickname. "If I have to."

"You do."

Cait didn't have time to wonder what he was up to; she had a list of jobs that would keep her busy straight until five o'clock. *Time to get moving.*

Joe didn't waste any time tracking down John Gannon. Before he could even ask her to give them a chance to talk privately, Cora Gannon told him, "I think I'll head into town and see if I can catch up on the latest down at the diner."

She was smiling when she bent to pat Jamie on the head on her way out the door.

"Smart woman," Joe said.

Jack's dad was grinning when he motioned for Joe to have a seat at the kitchen table. "Married me, didn't she?"

Joe had to agree. Sitting across from Jack's dad, they discussed what John knew about Jack's injuries and the events surrounding them and Joe's idea to help Jack have closure. When he found out about the Christmas cards Cora continued to send, Joe knew what he wanted to do.

"So, we each take three of the starred names from Cora's Christmas card list," he suggested. "I still can't believe she sends cards to everyone of the men who served in Jack's battalion."

"That's my Cora," John said with a soft smile.

"So," Joe said, "we see if any of the men who were wounded that day are willing to come to Apple Grove."

John's eyes met Joe's. "It's a good plan. I think it'll work."

"It wouldn't be this easy if your lovely bride hadn't been so dedicated to sending Christmas cards to our service men and women."

"She started that first Christmas Jack was in Iraq, wondering if there were marines or sailors who didn't have family to send them cards. It snowballed from there."

"Why did she make a note of the marines who'd been injured that day?" Joe wanted to know.

"Cora activated the prayer chain as soon as we heard about it but wanted to make sure every person on the chain knew the names of the marines who'd been injured when Jack was."

Joe shook his head. "You've got a gem there, John."

Jack's dad grinned. "Don't I know it!"

Fingers crossed, Joe Mulcahy and John Gannon began their quest.

Cait was so tired she wanted to crawl onto Jack's bed and close her eyes—just for a little while. But she knew if she did, she'd sleep through the night. She was torn between being grateful that Mulcahys had so much work and wishing they didn't have quite so many jobs.

As she walked up to the house, Jamie barked and the back door opened. "Hey there, sweetie," she said, dropping to her knees and wrapping her arms around the little dog.

He lavished her with kisses while she giggled. "Jack is so lucky to have you," she said, burying her face in Jamie's neck fur.

"He's lucky to have you too, dear."

"Hi, Mrs. Gannon. I didn't see you there."

Jack's mother sighed out loud. "Cora, remember?"

Cait nodded. "Um…right, sorry, Cora."

"That's better. As far as why you didn't see me, you were too busy with this little rapscallion."

Cait grinned. "He is, isn't he?"

Cora smiled. "Reminds me of our old dog Jake."

"Jack said the same thing. He really misses that dog."

"He was family—even if he was furry and used to get mud all over my clean floors whenever it rained. It was so quiet once he was gone."

"I know. Jack was devastated when Jamie's owner finally showed up to claim him."

Jack's mom smiled. "I heard the whole tale down at the diner earlier today. Those McCormack girls are doing a wonderful job keeping that place running. Hard workers, those girls, but long hours. How do they do it?"

Cait eased Jamie off her lap and stood. "I'm not sure. One thing I do know: they've always been hard workers." She looked up and met Cora's gaze. "Mrs. McCormack was like a second mother to me. Meg was too, but it was different, being that she was my big sister."

Cora nodded as she held the back door open. "I understand. Now, why don't you come on inside? I've got some nice solar tea brewed. You can take a glass upstairs with you while you get cleaned up before dinner."

"Oh, but I have to—"

"Take a break. You can come back down and help me get dinner going if you want."

"I do."

Jack's mom made a shooing motion with her hands. "Then get a move on, Caitlin."

She grinned as she took the frosty glass and drank it down in one gulp. "Thanks, Cora!"

Jack's mom was laughing as Cait dashed out of the room.

"That girl," she said to Jamie, "is the best thing that could have happened to our boy."

Jamie tilted his head to one side and thumped his tail on the floor.

"And so are you," she said, giving the dog a treat. "Now, how do you feel about steaks on the grill?"

Cait rushed through her shower, oddly energized by the conversation and cold tea. When she walked into the kitchen, Jack's mom was mixing something in a large bowl. "What have you got there?"

"Just some blueberry pandowdy for our meeting."

"What meeting?"

Jack's mom smiled. "Founder's Day. We used to hold the meetings here before John and I retired."

"Can I help?"

"You and Peggy are already down as volunteers to set up and clean up."

"Is there anything else?"

Mrs. Gannon patted her cheek and shook her head. "You work awfully hard during the day, Cait. Your sisters do too. How is Meg?"

Cait grinned. "She's great! She and Dan are so happy, and those darling boys, Danny and Joey, are just so precious…even when they're getting into trouble. Meg's not nervous at all about having another baby in a few months. She's amazing."

They talked about babies and families while Cora had Cait setting the table and slicing cold potatoes for the potato salad.

"I'm not that great in the kitchen," Cait confessed. "Jack's a better cook than I am."

"Well, it's a good thing one of you can cook," Cora laughed.

Cait smiled. "He seems OK, doesn't he?" She paused, adding, "After talking to us about everything, I mean."

"More than." Cora patted her hand as she moved past her to the counter. "I worried as any mother would when we'd found out he'd been injured." She speared the London broil and turned it over, spooning marinade over it a few times before she was satisfied. "When we could finally see him, I knew from the devastation I glimpsed in his eyes that there was something horrific he wasn't telling us."

"Did he tell John right away?"

Cora shook her head. "That's when we started worrying, because if he couldn't tell his father…it was beyond what Jack could handle emotionally."

"What did you do?"

"Prayed harder as John pulled strings so that Jack would start seeing one of the doctors at the VA for PTSD right away, and another doctor from the private sector."

She was washing her hands when a deep voice called out, "Anybody home?"

Cora laughed and tilted her face for her husband to kiss her cheek as he walked into the kitchen. Cait loved the way they looked at one another. Her heart tumbled over when Jack walked in a few minutes later with a clutch of daisies in his hand. When he held them out to her, she hesitated. "Hasn't anyone ever brought you flowers?" he asked.

How could she say that without sounding foolish? Instead of answering, she shook her head.

"Then it's about time someone did," he told her, kissing her cheek as he rummaged in the cabinets for something to put the flowers in.

"They'll look so pretty in the middle of the table," his mom said. "Caitlin, be a dear and hold the door for me while I put the steak on."

"Now just hold on there, Cora," John said, standing in between his wife and the back door. "Grilling is man's work."

"Not until you wash up, dear." She winked at Cait when her husband and Jack took turns washing their hands in the sink.

Once they'd gone outside, she smiled, and said, "That'll keep them busy while you and I put the finishing touches on the dining room."

"Hey, Mom," Jack called, "we eating outside?"

"That's right. Caitlin and I are setting up for the meeting in the dining room."

An hour later, the house trilled with feminine laughter as the ladies arrived, bearing sweets and passing out hugs.

"It's so wonderful to see you," Mrs. Winter said, handing Cait a cherry pie. She was tempted to take a picture and send it off to Meg, because for as long as Cait has been working in the family business, Mrs. Winter had only given Meg cherry pies.

Miss Trudi arrived with Mary Murphy at the same time as Mrs. McCormack and Peggy. Cait pulled her friend aside while the others went into the dining room. "I didn't know you were coming over tonight."

Peggy shrugged. "Things got busy at the diner after school let out or I would have texted you."

Cait noticed what she hadn't the last few weeks—exhaustion pulling down the corners of Peggy's mouth and darkening rings beneath her friend's eyes.

"Kate and I have been talking about hiring outside the family to give us more time in the kitchen—me for the pastries and baked goods and Kate for the rest." Peggy paused. "It's hard to think of someone besides a McCormack manning the counter and serving our customers."

Cait laid a hand on Peggy's arm. "I know exactly what you mean. Most days I feel like a dog chasing after my own tail, trying to keep up with the work orders for repair jobs, hoping I'll have enough energy to work for a few hours at night on the furniture I'm building."

"Are you thinking of hiring outside the family?" Peggy asked. "Is your dad OK with that?"

Cait shrugged. "I don't know. Grace and I have been trying to think of a way to broach the subject. He can't come back to work full time, even if he swears the heart attack scare was just that." Cait felt moisture fill her eyes and blinked. "We can't lose him too."

Peggy wrapped her arm around Cait and let her head rest against Cait's. The bond of friendship forged so long ago eased the worst of Cait's fear. She sighed and confessed, "We want to ask him in such a way that he'll have to say yes."

"Hedging your bets," Peggy said what Cait was thinking.

"Exactly."

"Peggy, Cait?" Mrs. McCormack called out. "We're ready to get started."

Cait sighed. "If you come up with the perfect way to tell your mom, let me know."

"Same goes." Peggy paused in the doorway. "Maybe we should have a meeting down at the diner, your dad, my mom—"

"Things'll be crazy until after Mitch and Honey B.'s vow renewal. How 'bout if we plan to get together then?"

"Good idea."

Mary Murphy was looking over her shoulder at them when Cait and Peggy walked into the room. "Now then, let's have everyone give an update, so we know where we stand and what we still need to address. We want Founder's Day to run as smoothly as ever."

The ladies took turns catching Cora up while at the same time including her in the plans. Cait could feel the strength of the friendship these women had developed over the years; it filled the room and felt like a hug from her mom.

It was the same as always—well, at least as far back as Cait could recall—Miss Trudi organizing the floral arrangements for the tables and around the gazebo in the town square, the McCormacks and Mrs. Winter handling the food, and finally Mary handling the advertising, decorating, and setup.

"Now," Miss Trudi said, while Cora and Cait sliced cake and poured coffee, "I want Honey B. and Mitch's day to go off without a hitch. Agreed?"

Everyone did. "Fine then," Miss Trudi said. "If someone will take on the duty of organizing clean up from the picnic, then, weather providing, I've got my grandnephew, Dan, and his soccer team to lend a hand rearranging all the tables and chairs—those boys will do anything for him."

"It's a great idea to have their vow renewal the day after Founder's Day, don't you think?"

Everyone started talking at once, caught up in the prospect of two of the town's favorite people, Honey B. and Mitch, publicly proclaiming their love for one another in front of their friends and neighbors.

Cait was about to speak up when Jack, Doc Gannon, and her father walked into the room. "Did I hear a call go out for manly muscle?" Jack grinned at her.

"You're such a good man, Jack," Miss Trudi said with a smile. "Now," she said, "being that Honey B.'s still not feeling up to snuff, I told her to let me take care of the food and the cake."

"But I thought—" Peggy began, only to fall silent when Miss Trudi waved her hand in Peggy's general direction.

"Everyone knows that you and your sister volunteered to bake the cake. Where else would we go for the perfect cake but the McCormack sisters?" Miss Trudi said, while Mrs. McCormack smiled.

"Can you tell us what color it's going to be?" Joe asked, letting his gaze slide over to where Mary sat with a soft smile on her face.

Peggy laughed. "Not a chance. It's a surprise."

"But—" Cait's dad fell silent when Miss Trudi glared at him. "Joseph, let the girls have their fun."

Her dad smiled and nodded.

"Do you need us to do anything else that day?" Jack asked.

Her father and Doc Gannon shared a look and Cait suspected the two were up to something that involved Jack. She'd have to pry it out of her dad later.

"I think that's it for now, dear," Miss Trudi said.

The men left, and she said, "I spoke with Norma Jenkins today. She said the dress is going to fit Honey B. like a dream."

The women happily continued chatting about their favorite residents while Cait let her mind drift. Before she realized what had happened, Jack was helping her to her feet and guiding her toward the stairs.

"But what about the meeting?" she said, stifling a yawn.

"You slept through the last bit of it." He led her up the stairs.

"What time is it?" she asked when he closed his bedroom door.

"Bedtime." He chuckled, helping her get undressed and stripping out of his clothes, slipping beneath the comforter until he had her in his arms and tucked against his heart.

"Night, Jack."

"Night, Cait."

A warm, wet tongue woke her in the middle of the night as Jamie settled himself between them. With a grunt, Jack rolled over and pulled the little dog into his arms. Cait fell back to sleep to the music of Jamie and Jack snoring.

Chapter 18

THE DAYS BEFORE FOUNDER'S DAY PASSED IN A BLUR. Somehow Cait managed to keep up with the repairs that seemed never ending at Mulcahys and a few things Miss Trudi asked her to repair for the upcoming event, but that meant she had less time to spend in her woodshop. It was a small price to pay to help make sure Founder's Day, and Honey B. and Mitch's day, went off without a hitch.

June fifteenth was sunny and warm—perfect picnic weather as far as Cait was concerned. She was a little nervous, because although her dad hadn't said as much, she found out that he and Doc Gannon had been able to get in touch with a few of the marines in Jack's battalion.

The tables and chairs had been set up the night before, and the ladies of the committee had been setting up since seven o'clock. Cait was used to early hours, but this was more stressful—she wasn't used to working with someone telling her what to do. Miss Trudi would have made a great drill sergeant.

"Am I the only one hungry?" Cait grumbled.

Peggy laughed. "Didn't you eat breakfast?"

"Yeah," Cait said, "but we've been working nonstop for the last few hours."

"Caitlin has always been cranky when she's hungry," Mrs. McCormack said, tugging on Cait's braid as she had so many times in the past, making Cait smile. "Why don't you two take a break and bring over the box of doughnuts I left on the counter in the back of the diner?"

When they started walking, she added, "Thanks, girls."

"Girls?" Peggy said when they were out of earshot. "Will she ever think of me as a woman?"

Cait shrugged. "We were complaining and it might have reminded her of when we were younger."

"Yeah," Peggy agreed. "Like twenty years ago!"

"Come on," Cait urged. "We can start setting out the food when we get back.

A half hour later, the tables were decked out in red, white, and blue, and laden with food, some of it prepared by the McCormacks, but the bulk of it donated by the ladies of Apple Grove.

Retying the ribbon holding her braid together, Cait watched as a tall, broad-shouldered, auburn-haired man strode toward her. He smiled and her heart did a little dance. *Would it always be like this?*

"Sorry I couldn't get away before now."

She soaked up the warmth of his embrace and kissed his cheek. "Apple Grove's doctor is allowed some slack."

He was playing with a curl by her temple when he said, "You look pretty, Cait."

"So do you."

"Guys don't look pretty," he told her.

"Yeah, they do," she argued. "You've got that dimple that is just too adorable."

"Jeez, Cait," he said. "A guy likes to hear that he's handsome."

"Did you know that Meg and her friends used to call you Handsome Jack?"

His cheeks turned beet red as he looked down at his feet.

"Seriously." She tugged on his arm to get him to look up at her. "Sometimes, I just look at you and can't believe we're together. What is the talented, handsome, young Dr. Gannon doing hanging around with the awkward middle Mulcahy sister?"

He wrapped his arms around her and kissed her until she had to lean against him for support. "Does that answer your question?"

"Quit dawdling," Miss Trudi called out. "We need you over here, Caitlin. We're about to get started."

She grinned at Jack, and answered, "Coming."

———

Jack let her go, awed by the fact that he'd grown to depend on her being a part of his days—and his nights. It shouldn't have surprised him that he wanted what his parents had. When Joe Mulcahy called his name, he knew he'd even settle for whatever time he and Cait were meant to have together.

"I'd like to thank you all for gathering today to help celebrate the founding of Apple Grove," Miss Trudi said. "We're a community that relies on each and every one of our neighbors, family, and friends to keep this town going. In all my years—and they are considerable—I've never wanted to live anywhere else."

When the applause died down, she cleared her throat. "Now, if Joseph Mulcahy and Dr. John Gannon the elder will kindly come up, I'll turn the microphone over to them."

Jack looked over at Cait, but she shrugged. She had

no idea what was going to happen either. Relief speared through Jack when Cait started making her way back over to where he stood.

Their fathers were smiling as they approached the gazebo, followed by three marines in uniform. Jack recognized them at once. He wanted to turn around and leave, but then he felt Caitlin's hand on his back.

"Did you know about this?"

"I knew they were hoping to track down one or two of the marines you served with…but not this," she told him.

He nodded as his father stepped up to the microphone. "As you all know, my son, Jack, is a former navy corpsman." Doc Gannon paused and nodded to Jack. "He served two tours in Iraq attached to a marine battalion. Some of you may know that he was injured, but he never talks about it."

"Joe and I would like you to meet three of the marines he served with: Private First Class James Weinstein, Lance Corporal Alec Stark, and Corporal Tom Biederman."

The crowd around them applauded.

"Corporal Biederman, would you like to say a few words?"

He nodded and walked over to the mic. "Navy Corpsman Jack Gannon saved my life and lives of PFC Weinstein and Lance Cpl. Stark on the same day…but in the seven years he was attached to our battalion, he patched up more marines and kept them going than I can count."

Cait's hand squeezed his, and he pulled her against his side, feeding off of her strength, knowing that whatever Corporal Biederman had traveled all the way to Apple Grove to say, Jack would listen to.

"I nearly lost my leg in Iraq and would have lost my life had it not been for Corpsman Gannon's quick actions and level head applying a tourniquet to keep me from bleeding out."

Cait's arms slipped around his waist, anchoring him to the present.

Biederman motioned for Weinstein and Stark to step up to the mic. "He was trying to save the life of Gunnery Sergeant Napolitano when the IED hit."

Jack listened to the words, but for once wasn't propelled back into the horror of that day; he'd purged part of the hurt, baring his soul to Cait and his parents. Now with Caitlin standing by his side, leaning into him, he realized they had been right to force his hand. The breeze picked up, blowing through the maple trees, clearing his mind enough to know he'd be thanking his family and the amazing woman at his side later.

Glancing at the crowd gathered, he saw Miss Trudi Philo standing proud and tall in her best khaki jodhpurs and white button-down shirt listening to Biederman speak. Joe Mulcahy stood beside Jack's dad, shoulders back and chest out—proud former military men.

The McCormack sisters, Honey B. and the sheriff, Meg and Dan Eagan—every last one of them bearing witness to what Jack had held inside of him since that day.

Standing amidst the people he'd known all his life, in the town he'd come back to, with the woman he loved standing proud by his side, he realized that it was past time to face that day. With the help of three marines he'd served with and two meddling men—Cait's dad, a former coast guard ASTC, Aviation Survival Technician Chief (rescue swimmer), and his own father, a former navy doctor—he accepted his past so that he could claim his future.

The loud applause had him blinking and looking around. All eyes were turned toward him. Cait was trying to hold back her tears as the marines started walking toward him.

"Jack," Biederman said, clapping a hand to Jack's sore shoulder. "I'm glad your dad got in touch with me. I've always wanted to say thank you but haven't been back in the States long enough to look you up."

Weinstein reached for Jack's free hand to shake it. "I'm not long on words," the man said, "and thank you doesn't seem to be enough, when you saved our lives."

Stark waited his turn to shake Jack's hand. "We owe you everything."

—⁂—

Cait tried to let go of Jack's hand so that he could talk to the men who'd come all this way just to say thank you, but he held on and wouldn't let go.

She pinched Jack in the side and Corporal Biederman laughed. "I think someone's trying to get your attention, Gannon."

Cait shook her head. "I'm sorry. I just wanted to give you a chance to talk to Jack alone," she explained.

"Gannon's a man of few words." Biederman grinned. "Unless he has a few whiskeys in him to loosen his tongue."

Jack was shaking his head when he turned to explain what Biederman meant. "That was during R and R—and only during R and R. Marines, I'd like you to meet Cait Mulcahy."

"Caitlin?" Miss Trudi called her.

"Oh, sorry, gentlemen," she said. "It must be time to start slicing up the pie."

"Lead the way," Biederman said with a grin.

Dan Eagan was one of the first to come over and congratulate Jack, while PFC Weinstein finagled a third piece of pie out of Cait. Jack was still smiling when Biederman announced that they had a plane to catch.

"Thank you for coming," he said, knowing the words couldn't convey even half of what he was feeling at the moment.

"Thanks for saving our lives," Biederman said.

Jack shook hands and waved as the three left with his father and Joe Mulcahy.

Was it really that simple? Jack wondered a few hours later, as he helped rearrange chairs and tables for tomorrow's vow renewal. Maybe he could start to let go of the guilt over Napolitano's death and acknowledge that he was an instrument of healing—not the one who decides who survives and who doesn't.

"I'm proud of you, Jack." Cait was dragging a garbage bag in each hand.

"Let me take that for you."

She gave him one and kept the other as they made their way over to the dumpster behind the drugstore.

"I have a confession to make," Jack said, walking back to the gazebo. "When I recognized those marines, I was ready to walk. I didn't want to talk about it, especially in front of everyone."

"I'm glad you stayed," Cait told him. He pulled her into his arms and gazed into her eyes. "You're one hell of a woman, Caitlin Mulcahy."

"Took you long enough to realize that fact, Doc Gannon."

He let his lips convince her how much he treasured her. When he could finally bring himself to break this kiss, he asked, "Do you have a date for Honey B. and Mitch's shindig tomorrow?"

Her laughter was music to his ears. "I was hoping that you'd ask me."

"It's a date then," he said, tugging on her hand to get her moving toward his Jeep. "Oh, and Cait?"

"What?"

"Try not to outdo Honey B. Remember it's her day to shine."

"Yeah, yeah," she said, smacking him on the arm. "Let's go. I'm beat."

"Your wish is my command."

"Really?" she said as he held the door open for her.

Unable to interpret the look she sent his way, he asked, "What did you have in mind?"

"I'd love a root beer float…but can wait."

"That's one thing that I love about you—your mind. I'm never sure what you'll say next. Keeps me on my toes."

"Then we're even because there are times when I can't figure you out, but chalk it up to what Meg told me is part of the male mystique."

As they drove back to his house, he slowed down as they approached the McCormacks' farm. "We have a lot in common, Cait."

She looked at him and smiled. "The smell of fresh-turned dirt."

He nodded. "We love animals."

She laughed. "The rascally the better."

Driving past the farm, he smiled at the image of

McCormacks' ship's mast. "God, I love this town…and everyone in it." He reached for her hand and then turned his palm up so he could feel the calluses that reminded him of who she was and what she did. Lifting her hand to his lips, he kissed her knuckles.

"I couldn't imagine living anywhere else." There was a short pause and then she said, "It is wonderful to see your parents again. I know you'll miss them when they leave, but they'll come back for visits." She drew in a shaky breath and said, "When Gracie leaves…I don't know if she'll come back."

She leaned her head against his shoulder and he put his arm around her, sliding his hand to her hip. "Grace has strong family ties," he told her, "but you shouldn't begrudge her the chance to spread her wings if Apple Grove isn't what she wants."

"You're right," she agreed. "But that leaves one more hole in my life. There have been so many lately."

"You can always count on me, Cait."

She sighed. "I do and I will. Thanks, Jack."

Pulling into his driveway, he realized that he needed to ask Cait…soon. He didn't want to wait.

Chapter 19

HONEY B. AND MITCH RENEWED THEIR PLEDGE TO ONE another beneath the gazebo in the town square. Wild roses, morning glories, and honeysuckle spilled out of flower pots, surrounding the couple with color and scent. While family, friends, and neighbors watched, Honey B. smiled radiantly at Mitch as if the rest of those gathered were invisible. The couple only had eyes for one another, until little Mitch escaped from his grandmother's grasp and ran up the steps to the gazebo. His dad lifted him up and held him close.

Caitlin watched the couple and their young son, and knew that was what she wanted with Jack—the love, the family. She had never thought about having a wedding—eloping had always been her plan—but sitting beside Jack, she realized she wanted to stand before family and friends like this, wanted to celebrate the love she had for Jack, wanted everyone to know. He had become her best friend, her lover, everything.

But how could she hint that she was ready to move in that direction when they hadn't even talked about where their relationship was headed? He'd told his parents Cait was all but living with him but hadn't spoken about more than that.

When she shifted, Jack's arm went around her, steadying her. "Are you all right?"

The concern in his voice eased through some of the worry in her heart. "Mmm," she murmured.

"You may now kiss Honey B.," Reverend Smith was saying, calling Cait's attention back to what mattered. This day had been a long time coming.

Amidst the laughter, champagne, and electric blue cake, Cait wondered how soon she could broach the subject with Jack. He'd been through so much the day before, she knew she'd have to wait…not to push too hard, too soon. They had plenty of time. Why rush, just because she'd figured out what she wanted out of life— Jack Gannon.

While Jack was chatting with Mitch, she confided her worry to Peggy in between mingling. "How am I going to get him to ask me?"

"Why can't you ask him?" Peggy wanted to know.

Before she could answer, Jack walked over. "Dance with me, Cait." With Jack's hand warm around her own, she let him lead her onto the wooden platform.

They danced to two slow songs and then a bunch of fast ones. Her head was spinning from the dancing and a bit too much champagne. "I need to sit down."

Jack led her to a folding chair and told her to relax.

"Could you please get me a glass of water?"

"Sure thing," he said, jogging off to find some.

"He's head over heels in love with you, Sis."

"How do you know, Meg?"

Her sister just smiled. "I've known Jack for years. Don't worry. I have a feeling he'll ask you soon."

"It's hard to be patient." Cait sighed and Meg patted her hand. "I guess if have to, I will."

"He's a good man, Cait. Give him a chance to figure out that you're the best thing that will ever happen to him and pop the question."

"How did you know what I was thinking?"

Meg laughed. "Been there, done that. Remember that he loves you when you're thinking you might want to push ahead when he's really not ready."

"Hmm," Cait said. "I should probably take your advice."

"For once in your life." Meg laughed.

"Hey, Meg." Jack handed Cait a glass of water. "Can I get you a drink?"

"No thanks," Meg said. "Dan's getting me one and then he's promised to dance with me."

"If you leave before me, Meg," Cait said, "give Dan a kiss from me."

Her sister smiled and walked over to where her husband was dancing with his aunt.

"They're so happy," Jack said.

"I wasn't sure it would work at first, but you're right—they are happy. It shows."

"Marriage is a big step," Jack was saying when his cell phone vibrated in his jacket pocket. "Excuse me." He was looking at Caitlin when he said, "I'll be right there."

"What's wrong?"

"One of the Jenkins boys fell off the ladder to the water tower."

With a glance around, Cait made a decision that would change her life. "Let me go with you. I might be able to help."

Jack nodded. "Come on. I've got my bag in my Jeep."

Mitch must have received a call too because he was frowning down at Honey B., who stood with their little one perched on her hip. "Why can't you just let Deputy Jones handle this without you?"

When her husband stood there looking down at her, Honey B. finally pushed him toward his big red pickup. "Go on. Little Mitch and I will be waiting for you."

Deputy Jones was already at the water tower with Jack and Cait by the time the sheriff arrived. Jack looked up and shook his head as Mitch approached. "Seems somebody didn't want their name on the water tower and used cooking spray on the ladder to keep this knucklehead from going up."

Mitch shook his head and knelt down next to the youngster. "I ought to run you in for breaking the law."

"Come on, Sheriff," the boy said. "It's not official. Me and my brothers checked it out over at town hall."

"Well then," Mitch said, "I guess we'll have to have ourselves a town meeting, and we'll add it to the town ordinances. No one but no one climbs that damned water tower unless they want to spend the night in jail."

When the Jenkins boy just hung his head, Mitch added, "One of these days, you're going to start using that brain…might be a good idea."

Jack chuckled as he immobilized the boy's ankle. "Help me get him to my Jeep, Mitch."

"Let me," Cait said. "Mitch has a reception to get back to."

Jack's father was waiting for them at the office to lend a hand. Cait kept Mrs. Jenkins calm while Jack took care of her son and was ready for the news that she'd have to drive to Newark for an X-ray.

When they finally left, Old Doc Gannon smiled at Cait. "You'd make the perfect doctor's wife."

Jack stared at her for a moment before he agreed. Remembering her sister's advice, Cait just smiled and said, "Do you think there's any cake left?"

Later, with Cait tucked safely against his heart, Jack tried to come up with a way to propose. He couldn't use the water tower. Mitch had had one of his deputies go back and wrap the ladder with crime scene tape to keep anyone else from getting hurt.

Dan and Mitch had chased down their women and claimed them inside of Honey B.'s Hair Salon—kind of hard to replicate. Besides, he wanted to ask Cait in a way that would be just as memorable…something they would think back on years from now when they were old and gray.

Cait sighed in her sleep and murmured something about wedding bells and ribbon and that's when an idea started to gel, but it had to be perfect. Thinking of something Miss Trudi had said about the returning GIs from the Second World War and those yellow ribbons tied in big bows around each and every maple tree lining Main Street gave him an idea.

Jack knew what he was going to do.

Slipping out of bed, he sent a text off to Dan, who had Meg send one to Peggy.

Raking a hand through his hair, he grinned. The plan was in place; all he had to do was sneak into town while his parents and Peggy kept Cait busy.

"You are a genius, Jack," Meg told him, tying the first bow in the wide, white satin ribbon.

"Thanks. Are you sure she doesn't suspect anything?"

Meg smiled. "She's working on learning patience…I told her you needed time."

Jack laughed. "OK," he said, walking slowly from where Meg tied the bow on the railing leading to Jack's office. "This is supposed to be a mega roll of ribbon." He paused to loop it around the sugar maple on the sidewalk. While he made his way toward the bank, he looped ribbon around two more trees.

"Why the heck didn't I remember how many damned trees lined Main Street?"

Dan and Meg were laughing when he ran out of ribbon outside the *Gazette*.

"Hang on," Meg told him as she sent Dan to get two more rolls of ribbon. When he returned and tossed them to Jack, Jack tied a knot in it and then continued looping ribbon around trees…climbing partway up the ones on either side of Dog Hollow Road, so that anyone driving into town wouldn't get snagged on the ribbon…all the way to Mulcahys' front door.

"Are you sure she has no idea?"

Meg smiled. "Not a clue."

He placed the turquoise bucket on the stoop and struggled to arrange the lilacs until Meg blew out a breath. "Let me do that."

When she finished, he hung two huge, white crepe paper wedding bells on the door with a sign that said, "Follow the ribbon and your heart—Marry me, Cait, Love, Doc."

Meg's eyes filled as she stood back and looked at the bucket of lilacs, wedding bells, and the sign.

"Is it OK?"

"Perfect," she reassured him.

He worried all the way back to his office. "Are you sure I shouldn't go back home and then bring her into town?"

Meg frowned at him and Dan said, "This way you'll

be waiting at your office when she gets to the shop and finds your surprise."

"OK," Jack said, taking a deep breath. "I'm ready."

"Peggy's going to text me when they leave your house," Meg told him.

Dan grinned. "We can hang out with you and help you wait."

Jack's smile was sheepish. "Am I that easy to read?"

"Clear as glass," Meg told him.

When her phone buzzed a few minutes later, Jack jolted. At Meg's nod, he knew Cait and Peggy were on their way. When Meg got the text that they were almost to town, she and Dan left, and that's when Jack started pacing.

———ᴡᴡ———

"Why don't you tell me what's really going on, Peggy?" Cait knew something wasn't right.

Peggy laughed. "You and that imagination of yours."

Peggy turned right onto Main Street, and Cait tried again, "Would you please tell me?"

Peggy parked in front of the diner. "I know nothing," she said, getting out of the car without looking back.

"Peggy McCormack!" Cait yelled. "Tell me what's going on!"

Peggy shook her head, smiled, and pointed toward Mulcahys. "Well, that's helpful," Cait grumbled, walking toward the shop—and that's when she noticed the flowers leaning against the door.

"Oh," she said. "He got me flowers...lilacs...I love lilacs."

As she grabbed a hold of the railing, she noticed the

wedding bells and the sign attached to a wide length of white satin ribbon. *Follow the ribbon and your heart— Marry me Cait, Love, Doc.*

Tears filled her eyes as she finally noticed the ribbon looped around every single shade tree lining the street, leading the way to Jack Gannon's office. She didn't realize she was crying until she'd run down Main and started pounding on his door.

"Jack, you crazy…"

His door opened, and there he was. The auburn-haired, broad-shouldered hunk of a man who'd captured her heart in the middle of Eden Church Road when he chased that fuzzy little puppy right into her arms.

"…wonderful, adorable man."

His blue eyes deepened to sapphire as he rasped, "So, does that mean, yes?"

Joy filled her. She wrapped her arms around his neck, kissing him until they were both weak from lack of air.

"Yes!"

He was grinning as he lowered his mouth to hers.

Blueberry Pandowdy

My mom used to bake this when blueberries were in season. There is nothing like the taste of blueberry pandowdy fresh out of the oven with a cup of coffee or tea for breakfast. ~ C.H.

Note: I've only made this recipe with fresh berries, but you can substitute frozen or canned blueberries—though I can't guarantee that it will be as delicious as it is with fresh berries.

> *2 cups washed fresh (or drained, thawed frozen or canned) blueberries*
> *⅓ cup sugar*
> *Juice of ½ lemon (or about 1 tablespoon of lemon juice)*
> *Cake batter*
> *Cream or hard sauce*

Combine berries, sugar, and juice in a saucepan and cook uncovered, stirring occasionally for about five minutes. Pour into a greased (I used margarine) baking dish (9 x 9 x 2) if you have it, or if not, I've used a casserole dish.

Spread with cake batter (recipe follows) and bake in a preheated oven at 375 degrees F for about twenty

minutes. Spoon out servings hot or cold and serve with
cream (whipped if preferred).

Makes 6 servings.

Pandowdy Cake Batter

½ cup butter (or margarine)
½ cup sugar
1 egg
1½ cup sifted flour (I only used Heckers Unbleached)
2 teaspoons baking powder
½ teaspoon salt
½ cup milk

Cream butter until light and fluffy. Gradually beat
in sugar. Stir in egg. Sift dry ingredients and add alter-
nately with milk, beating until smooth. Spread over hot
berries (see above).

Acknowledgments

When Deb asked if I would be interested in writing a small-town USA series, I jumped at the opportunity to spread my writing wings. I missed writing about the small towns in my Irish Western series and welcomed the chance to recreate a part of my past and who I am in a contemporary setting.

Growing up on Cedar Hill—a tiny corner of Wayne, New Jersey—our neighborhood was like living in a small town. There were twenty-five homes in our little hamlet of dead-end streets. Unless you lived off Circle Drive, there wasn't any reason to go to Cedar Hill. Tucked away from the rest of the world, we lived in idyllic surroundings. We could run or ride our bikes to our friend's house and still hear when mom rang the dinner bell, a cowbell my dad found when he was a kid living in Colorado, not to be mistaken from the ship's bell suspended between two trees that called our neighbor home—his dad had been in the navy.

My great-aunt and uncle lived right next door and my great-aunt always kept molasses windmill-shaped cookies with the almonds on top in the cookie jar on the end of the counter, right inside the back door. It was always full. She read pirate stories and poems to us on their screened-in porch on summer nights. I remember waking up to the sound of my great-uncle whistling—he had this six-note call that I'd hear in my sleep. I'd climb out of bed and get dressed but was young enough that I couldn't tie my red plaid sneakers, but I'd put them on, careful not to trip on the stairs, knowing that he'd be waiting to tie them for me.

My grandparents were two houses away, which made it seem like we had three homes instead of just one. My grandmother was a *cheese and crackers* grandma, not the typical *milk and cookies* kind. I'd run up to her house after my homework was done and set their dinner table, nibble on crackers and cheese, watching Merv Griffin or Mike Douglas and the four-thirty movie before it was time to go home, set our table, and help get dinner ready.

For the last thirty years, we've lived in a small lake community. My husband grew up in one and from the stories of his childhood, I knew that was the atmosphere we wanted for our kids. It was a mixed community with residents who'd lived there for forty years and those of us who'd just moved in. Five of us were pregnant at the same time and forged a bond that carried over to our kids. They played together, attended preschool together, and graduated from high school together.

One element of both neighborhoods was the core group of women responsible for keeping tabs on every-one and making sure to spread the word, both good and bad; it was like having a town crier.

On Cedar Hill, it was my grandmother, my great-aunt, and both Mrs. Johnsons who kept everyone abreast of the neighborhood goings-on. In Lindy's Lake, it was Honey Baker, Marty Walsh, Ann Ahrens, and Millie Salisbury.

In the fictionalized town of Apple Grove, Ohio, it is Mrs. Winter, Miss Philo, and Honey B. Harrington who are the glue that keeps the town together and in the know.

So brew a cup of tea or grab a cup of coffee, put your feet up and relax, and spend some time getting to know the good people of Apple Grove.

About the Author

C.H. Admirand is an award-winning, multipublished author with novels in mass-market paperback, hardcover, trade paperback, magazine, ebook, and coming soon, digital comic book format.

Fate, destiny, and love at first sight will always play a large part in C.H.'s stories because they played a major role in her life. When she saw her husband for the first time, she knew he was the man she was going to spend the rest of her life with. Each and every hero C.H. writes about has a few of Dave's best qualities: his honesty, his integrity, his compassion for those in need, and his killer broad shoulders. She lives with her husband and two of their grown children in the wilds of northern New Jersey and recently welcomed their first grandbaby into the family.

C.H. always uses family names in her books, but this time something truly karmic occurred while she was writing the first book in this series; while tracing her Irish ancestors, she uncovered something wonderful— her great-grandfather was already listed on Ancestry .com with the same picture that sits on her mantelpiece. She had discovered a link to the Mulcahy side of the family; her grandfather's younger sister married a Mulcahy. After sending an email, she was delighted when she received a reply, and even more so when she learned that her connection and her sisters were delighted to be heroines in C.H.'s new series.

She loves to hear from readers! Stop by her website at www.chadmirand.com to catch up on the latest news, excerpts, reviews, blog posts, and links to Facebook and Twitter.